...ly Glass Heart

Karen Gillece was born in Dublin in 1974. She studied Law at University College Dublin and worked for several years in the telecommunications industry before turning to writing full time. She was shortlisted for the Hennessy New Irish Writing Award in 2001 and her short stories have been widely pubished in literary journals and magazines.

Also by the author
Seven Nights in Zaragoza
Longshore Drift

KAREN GILLECE

My Glass Heart

HODDER
HEADLINE
IRELAND

Copyright © 2007 Karen Gillece

First published in 2007 by Hodder Headline Ireland
First published in paperback in 2007 by Hodder Headline Ireland

The right of Karen Gillece to be identified as the Author of the Work
has been asserted by her in accordance with the Copyright, Designs
and Patents Act 1988.

3

A CIP catalogue record for this title is available from the British
Library.

ISBN 978 0 340 92448 8

Typeset in Sabon MT by Hodder Headline Ireland
Printed and bound in Great Britain by Clays Ltd, St Ives plc

Hodder Headline Ireland's policy is to use papers that are
natural, renewable and recyclable products and made from
wood grown in sustainable forests. The logging and manufacturing
processes are expected to conform to the environmental regulations of
the country of origin.

Hodder Headline Ireland
8 Castlecourt Centre, Castleknock, Dublin 15, Ireland

A division of Hachette Livre UK Ltd.
338 Euston Road, London NW1 3BH

www.hhireland.ie

For Conor

In the event of my death, I wish it to be known that this is a novel that should never be published. Sometimes I wish it had not been written. But in the summer of 2005 I saw a dark scar running along the breastbone of a young woman and became possessed by a story I couldn't shake off. It can happen that way – the story finds the writer without them ever having to go in search of it. On that bright May day, she stepped into my life and brought with her a whole new narrative. At first I didn't want to write it. But something about her touched me deep within, something too potent to turn away from. The story drew me in, at times unwillingly, and yet I cannot deny the powerful gusts of sheer joy – of *excitement* – I felt when I was scribbling away furtively into the night, anxious to get it all down on paper, foregoing sleep lest I forgot some small detail. I say "furtively" because I wrote it in secret – although it was my firm intention to publish the book – to reclaim something of my former glory – right up until the end, when I looked at what I had done and recognised the folly of it. The shame of it.

It is a novel I should not have written. After all, it was not my story to tell. I took the facts as they were told to me and embellished them, using invention to fill in what I did not know. But it is done now, and somehow I cannot bring myself to destroy it. Just in case . . . So, I am consigning it to obscurity, packing it away in a drawer where it will gather dust, where the pages will grow yellow with time and the ink fade to grey. I have known many writers who have a novel they have completed but which they are unwilling for an audience to read . . . Mine shall be a keepsake to remind me always of how close I came to falling. And yes, I am ashamed of it, but not for the reasons you might think.

This is a novel that should never be published. But if, somehow, it has made its way into your hands, let me ask one thing of you, the reader: that you understand I was not myself when I wrote it. I was floundering. Perhaps, knowing this, you may think better of me. Perhaps you may even forgive me.

Reuben Ford
September 2006

PART ONE

1

Something in the manner of her approach makes me think of a widow, a mourner. The funereal nature of her dress, perhaps, the erect posture and striding hips, her stark white face, inexpressive and unreadable. Down the long corridor she comes and I watch her advance, hear the clipping of her heels measuring out the distance in even steps. Outside, it is raining and wet footprints have made the floor treacherous, but she doesn't look down, her gaze pinned on something ahead.

I'm here before her, of course. It's her privilege to be late on this difficult day and my role is supporter, sentinel, father figure. I can't imagine her own father will be here, and I am old enough to play the part. I smile at her as my hand reaches up to adjust my tie, then swipe at my hair. These small vanities, these nervous movements! One of the guards turns and gives me a look, as if sensing I am becoming restive.

She is wearing her long black cashmere coat and a sombre-looking silk scarf; there is a severe and unadorned elegance about her. My attire, however, is more suited to a wedding – the brightness of my tie, the crimson flourish from my breast pocket, cuff links winking beneath my sleeves. Well, with my background and reputation, I feel a touch of the theatrical will be excused – expected even. In fact, we are dressed for court.

The Director of Public Prosecutions vs. Keith Donovan. How ambiguous it sounds. The economy of words. It could be anything – a drugs charge, theft, a murder.

One of the guards nods at Helen as she reaches me and I lean in, take hold of her elbow and kiss her cheek. "All set?"

She seems to shiver. "Miserable out there," she says, giving a nod to the world outside.

"It'll clear up," I say, "don't you worry," in my new avuncular tone. If only Frankie could hear me now . . . "We have time to go and grab a coffee, to calm the nerves," I say.

"Your nerves or mine, Reuben?" A playful smile lights up her face before it clouds over with the question she wants to ask. "Is he here yet?"

I know instinctively whom she means. "No, dear. Not yet."

And I cannot tell if she is relieved or disappointed by the information. Her face gives nothing away.

"Well, then. We may as well go in."

My hand is cupped beneath her elbow as we approach the doors. A moment of shadow and then we are swallowed into the brightness of Court Twenty-Nine.

Throughout the long summer days before the trial began, and even further back – when we first met – Helen and I have discussed the case endlessly. We have spent hours together over the last sixteen months analysing it from every angle. Indeed, I believe there is not a single aspect of it that we have not picked over. I fed her questions about the events that led up to that long night, what happened in its aftermath, and she answered dutifully – no, willingly. I believe she has embroidered the events on some occasions, perhaps for my benefit. But she has no one else to tell now, no one to share it with, since William turned his back on it. It was the grubbiness of the affair that shocked him, I think – the insouciant squalor of the details. The drip, drip, drip as each one emerged. He has maintained a dignified silence ever since she told him – she had to in the end. It was either that, or let him discover the facts with the rest of us once the defence counsel began cross-examination or, worse, it emerged from Donovan's mouth, his own skewed interpretation. William is not in court, not that I expected he would be. I imagine him in his office, head down, working on his research, or standing at a podium in front of a room full of his students, flicking through presentations, his cultured voice ringing like a bell. How will he get through this day?

I have no doubt William feels that the stance he has chosen has a valiant and noble appeal – his tortured solitude – when, in fact, it is cowardice. "For better and for worse," I want to remind him, but I bite my tongue. And besides, if he had stuck around, I wouldn't be privy to all the richness of information she has provided – this unexpected story.

We have been able to maintain some semblance of friendship, William and I, for the story's sake. I have put in my time with him too, for clarity, listening to him pour out his heart. All this talk, these people desperate to tell their tale, and me there poking and prodding, asking the leading questions. But now that we are here at last, in our

places at the back of the courtroom, Helen and I find that
neither one of us has anything to say.

We watch the room fill, the barristers sorting their
books and notes, conferring with the solicitors, the
registrar and stenographer sharing a joke, the guards
milling about. On a desk behind the prosecution there is a
garda evidence bag, the name of the case written in magic
marker; I wonder what exhibits are contained within it.
The weapon, of course, the blade wiped clean; and
perhaps the dress she wore, ivory silk with a splash of red
wine and a crimson flower of blood blooming among its
delicate fibres.

There is something familiar in the atmosphere, although
this is my first time in court. There was the preliminary
hearing in the district court, a year ago – but that was
different. For a start there wasn't this elegant space – these
high windows and bright white orbs suspended from the
lofty ceiling, dark wooden benches and grey carpeting. No,
the district court was seedier in comparison, with the faint
stench of urine, vomit and sweat. And I wasn't present at
that hearing. It took place when William was still around,
before it all fell apart between them. I watch the defence
barrister fixing her wig and straightening her gown, and
that's when it strikes me that the atmosphere is the same as
it is on the opening night of a play. That same blend of
nervous excitement, the latent fear of being insufficiently
rehearsed, yet impatient to draw back the curtain and start.
And as on those opening nights, I feel, too, that I have a
stake in the proceedings, that their success or failure will
make a difference to my life. I watch the barrister as she
holds back her gown, the starched white of her collar

against tanned skin, the flourish as she sweeps round to address her colleague – she has the grand gestures and elegant bearing of an actor.

The barrister for the prosecution comes towards us – a sleekly good-looking young man with a cocky bluntness about him. I have the impression he doesn't like me. On the one occasion we met before today, he addressed me as Mr Ford, although I urged him to call me Reuben, and he didn't bother to hide his surprise or irritation that I – neither family nor anyone remotely connected to the case – should be allowed to sit in on those meetings between him and Helen.

"How are you feeling?" he asks her.

"A little nervous."

"That's natural," he answers briskly. "Once things get up and running, which will be shortly now, then you'll relax. You may even enjoy it."

"I doubt that," I say.

His eyes sweep over me and his face seems to register distaste. He seems unaffected by my celebrity – perhaps he has something against Americans. All he notices is the paunch that strains against my shirt buttons and the face whose crags and dents betray a once-Dionysian lifestyle. He looks into my eyes and sees weariness and spiritual depletion. And maybe something else. Avarice, perhaps?

"A number of procedures have to be gone through first," he says. "The jury will be picked and then sworn in, which takes time. The charges will be read out. The judge will say a few words. I will make my opening statement for the prosecution. The defence, of course, won't make an opening statement – they don't show their

hand until the cross-examination of witnesses, as I explained to you."

She sits quietly, twisting her wedding band continuously around her finger, listening to the voluble young
man in his natty pinstripe suit.

"So, do you think I'll be called this morning?"

He shrugs. "Probably not." Then, giving her the full
wattage of his toothy grin, he touches a hand to her
shoulder. "You've nothing to worry about, Helen. Just tell
the truth and you'll be fine."

That said, he gathers his gown round him and returns
to his place near the bench.

But, of course, it's not that easy. Is there really such a
thing as a simple truth? What about perception? What about
the many layers within truth? And what about all those
dark, secret things that are kept hidden – truths we are
afraid to hold up to the light? Those are the things that
Helen will be asked to surrender: the weapons that the
defence team will use against her to impugn her character.

Outside, the rain is sheeting down, bouncing off the
pavement around the feet of people scurrying to work,
struggling with their umbrellas against the wind. Morning
traffic in Dublin, exhausts belching, faces pressed with
purpose. On days like these, I wonder why I came back to
this country, of which I am not a native. My body yearns
for the heat of the southern United States, the sultry fug
of my childhood. I am too old for this city and I know I
will have to leave it soon. But not until all this is over. Not
until I have done what I can. Or taken what I can.
A rogue thought. Even now, my notebook is burning a
hole of shame in my breast pocket. Why I bothered to

bring it, I don't know. I can't imagine I'll have occasion to scribble anything. Yet I have it with me. An old habit.

"Reuben," she says, and reaches for my arm.

I follow her gaze to the doorway and there he is – the accused, Keith Donovan, taking a moment to find his bear-ings. Despite myself, I feel sudden shock at his proximity. There is nothing – no handcuffs, no police buffer – to bridge the space between him and Helen. I feel her tense. But what is more shocking is his appearance – he seems harmless. As he slopes past us, head down, eyes fixed on the ground, he appears wretched, like a school boy on his way to the headmaster's office. Surely this man cannot be capable of a crime of passion: he looks no more than a teenager, nothing like the yobs in tracksuits who stalk the corridors here. There is something clean and delicate about him, a gaucheness that is oddly touching. For the life of me, I cannot see anything sinister in him. His elderly parents accompany him, and I watch his mother – a thicket of blonde hair and too much make-up – leading his frail-looking father as the three approach the dock. Of course it's not called the dock any more. Just as Helen is not the victim – she is the injured party. Prejudicial language; admissible and inadmissible; weights and balances.

Helen crosses her arms, and I notice that she has not removed the cashmere coat or the silk scarf. She is not yet ready to relinquish that defence. Donovan has sat down and is shifting about uncomfortably. His clothes are ill-fitting: he is dwarfed by his jacket's shoulders, but his narrow wrists emerge from too-short sleeves. There is something bewildered about him – his face seems to ask:

How has this happened to me? And it occurs to me that his face is his best defence – young and frightened. I have read the letters he wrote; I have seen the scar; I have witnessed the rending apart of a marriage. And yet, somehow, that face is removed from it all, unconnected.

Helen's hand goes up to the silk scarf underneath her collar. And I wonder if she wore such expensive clothes for a reason – to make a distinction, perhaps, between herself and the polyester-clad man in the dock. We are all in costume. In a way, we are all on trial.

"How much time?" she asks, voice wavering.

"Plenty."

A difficult day for her. For me too. It's Frankie's anniversary, not that Helen is aware of this. That is my own memory, my private sadness. And this is not a story about me.

Helen looks so frail, gaunt, even with make-up. I reach across and lay my hand over hers. "We've all the time in the world."

A door opens and a voice says, "All rise," and the judge makes a sweeping entrance and every one of us is on our feet.

2

It is difficult to know where to look in a trial such as this. My eyes flit back and forth, roving over the faces of the four women and eight men of the jury, wandering occasionally to the patrician jowls of the judge, skimming over the registrar and the stenographer. Every so often they are drawn to the accused – watching the proceedings from beneath lowered eyelids – but for the most part they are on the prosecution counsel, who is asserting that on the night of 5 April 2005, the accused assaulted Mrs Helen Glass on the premises of her business – Joy Flowers – causing serious bodily harm under Section 4 of the Non-fatal Offences against the Person Act 1997. I wonder briefly at that charge and all that is tied up within it. A non-fatal offence. A few more minutes lying alone on that floor, and all the life might have poured out of her. What then? A different charge. A different court. And a longer sentence – perhaps life.

It hadn't been fatal, but it had reached the threshold,

there's no doubting that. And in his opening statement, the prosecution counsel doesn't mince his words. Listening to him outline his case, it occurs to me that a trial is rather like a story told twice – two different versions of the same tale. None of us yet knows the ending; that is for the jury to decide. But how do the lawyers determine at what point the story began? How far back do they need to go in search of a motive?

And what of my own story? I suppose I should start at the point in my life when I first met Helen sixteen months ago, perhaps a little more. It was a May afternoon in France, a day that was blue, clear and crisp. I was going through a period in my life of self-imposed isolation – of rest and recuperation and, although I didn't know it then, steadily drinking myself into an early grave. I had left Ireland that February after fifteen years there, and at the time, it was my intention never to return. I had rented a villa on the outskirts of the tiny Provençal village of Bonnieux. My landlord, Gaston, also happened to be the landlord of La Flambée – the only decent pub in the village – and that summer I spent the afternoons sitting with him in his bar gossiping over a few drinks. It was there I first met Helen and William Glass.

I had been enjoying my first drink of the day, having committed about eight hundred words to paper that morning, when they came sauntering down the hill. No: he was sauntering, but her movements were more cautious, more self-aware. "*Regardes,*" said Gaston, fixing them with a baleful eye. We watched them progress down that hill, sipping our beer and taking them in – his cool, straight figure, hands clasped loosely behind his back, while she tripped along at his side in those laced-up espadrilles, her hair arranged in a dishevelled chignon. There seemed to be something fussy about her – her skirt was a complicated series of wispy layers, her face hidden by massive square sunglasses, a long scarf round her neck. She wasn't smiling, not even when they reached our table, stopped and her husband began to speak. Her face was blank.

Gaston heaved his large frame out of the chair and extended a hand to William. He seemed to assume a mayoral role, tucking his chin into the folds of fat round his neck and nodding in a stately way in response to each new piece of information. I stayed in my chair, dragging on my cigarette, one leg crossed indolently over the other. If William thought me rude, he didn't show it.

"*Ah, Irlande!*" Gaston exclaimed, turning to me with raised eyebrows, and I felt something plummet within me. I had come to France to forget Ireland and all I had left behind. I had never been one of those Americans who embrace the auld sod, believing its people and the land to be some pure, idyllic version of the States. It's fair to say that when I moved to Ireland, it had been, for the most part, against my will.

"I used to live there," I explained. "Foul weather," I added, unable to resist. Perhaps it was my second drink of the day.

At this William's smile sagged, then he rearranged his features and made some noises of agreement. His hair was a blond cloud above intelligent blue eyes – in the sunlight he seemed leached of colour. But I watched her watching me, and I believed she read my thoughts. Although her eyes were hidden, I felt them on me.

Later, during one of our long sessions, she would say to me, "You didn't like me then, did you?" giving me her slow, teasing smile.

"It wasn't you," I told her. "It was the Irish thing. I didn't want the reminder."

But that wasn't quite true. That morning, with the sunlight hitting the pretty French square, I resented her presence, her haughtiness, the cool angles of her face, the judgement lurking behind those glasses. At that moment, I saw none of the softness in her, none of the vulnerability. Instead, I had her marked as one of those women I had known before – actresses mainly, with their vanity and heartless candour. Women who gave little of themselves, who simply observed but offered nothing in return. I had counted many as friends, but on that morning, when I was feeling too much at peace with myself, unburdened for once by the grief I had been carrying for some time, I resented her intrusion. Until that point, I had convinced myself that my reason for being there was to relax and to write. Work would save me. This place – with its blue-shuttered windows, houses crouched round a hill, leaning into the rock, my landlord with his florid cheeks and overhanging belly, his easy company on this quiet lunch-time, the square empty apart from ourselves and a lone biker repacking his panniers in the sun – had been peaceful until this woman, with her unsettling stare, had come upon us. Her shadow fell across my table and felt like a partition.

As they said their goodbyes and went on their way, I followed her with my eyes, the straightness of her back, her natural poise, and realised that she had not uttered a word.

But just before they turned the corner, she stumbled. He reached out, grabbing for her arm. Something in that movement brought out in her a vulnerability that made me pause in my estimation of her.

The urge to protect.

I had come to Bonnieux to forget all that I had done, all that I had lost. Although I didn't know it yet, so had she.

3

The first witness for the prosecution is Mrs Helen Glass. I watch as she takes the stand, holds the testament and directs her oath to the registrar, then sits and fiddles with the microphone in front of her. The cashmere coat and silk scarf have been shed, and she is wearing a black dress with a V-neck, cut low enough for us to glimpse a little of the scar. Subtle, but there's no avoiding it. I glance across at the jury, and three men are staring at it. She sits with her back to the defendant. Donovan stares at his feet.

Helen is a good-looking woman, which is not lost on the prosecution barrister. When he speaks to her it is in silky tones, a curious mix of flirtation and paternal gentleness, as he instructs her to address her answers to the jury. The flirtation draws attention to the dark, fragile beauty of her features, the gentleness to that scar, as well as to the frailty of her appearance – those big eyes and that pale skin, the evident nervousness. She is thirty, but looks younger. We celebrated her birthday some weeks ago – a supper at my house, just the two of us. I had offered to take her out for dinner, but she has not been up to going out lately. I have tried to keep her upbeat but the lead-up to the trial and all that has happened with William have taken their toll on her. So it was just the two of us, and I could tell all day that she was waiting for the phone to ring. I tried to raise her spirits with champagne and my best cooking – I even opened the Mercurey I had been saving – but as the evening progressed, I could see the hope dwindling within her. It manifested itself in the droop of her shoulders as she grew steadily drunk. William didn't call. At midnight, she gave up and went to bed, and deep into the night I heard her crying in the next room until finally I fell asleep.

"Mrs Glass, could you please explain to the court the nature of your relationship to the defendant, Mr Donovan?"

"I was his employer." Her voice cuts through the courtroom like ice cracking.

"And am I correct in saying that he is no longer in your employ?"

"He worked for me for a couple months."

"When?"

"From October until Christmas 2004."

"I see. And perhaps you could tell the court how you first came to hire Mr Donovan."

"It was this scheme that I'd heard about. A friend of mine, Antonia, from university, she's a social worker, and through her I heard about the Young Offenders' Rehabilitation Programme."

"Objection." The defence counsel is on her feet. "This implies that my client has a previous record, and is clearly prejudicial and inadmissible."

"I'll allow it," the judge says. "But tread carefully."

Helen appears a little startled by this sudden sparking,

and the barrister moves to calm her. "So, your friend informed you about the scheme," he says in his honey voice.

"Yes. I thought it would be an opportunity to give something back."

"And could you tell us a little of what the scheme involved?"

"Well, I have a florist's shop. I employ one other full-time worker besides myself, and take on extra staff to cover the busier periods – Christmas, Valentine's Day, that kind of thing. When I heard about the scheme, I saw an opportunity to take someone on for a short period – someone who hadn't enjoyed the advantages I have – provide them with a new skill, train them, perhaps give them a new start. In return, I'd get help in the shop over a busy period."

Such a scheme would appeal to Helen's sense of community as well as her instinct for crusades. It struck me early in our friendship that she was the type of woman who would always require a cause, a project on which to focus her restless energy. And that was exactly the type of scheme that would appeal to her notions of charity, her idealism.

The prosecution counsel was keen to get the point across: "It was a philanthropic gesture, then?"

"I suppose so, yes."

There are moments in our lives that change the course of events. I asked Helen once, when we were in Bonnieux, if she felt that way about the night she was stabbed. Was that the point at which her life had been framed for ever into before and after? I remember that morning, the heat in the air, a couple of tourists wandering around aimlessly, and the two of us sitting on our bench, the misty look that came over her face as she tried to conjure up that time in her mind.

"No," she replied. "It started much further back."

As it turned out, she counted the truly definitive moment in her life as the morning on which Donovan had first stepped through her door.

"That's when it began," she said. "After that, everything started to change."

It was a blustery October morning, she told me. The sky was a steely blue, and the sun was breaking through the trees to catch a trail of silvery drips on the floor of the shop. The delivery had arrived late, and there was a wedding to prepare for – five bouquets as well as the buttonholes. They were both stressed, Helen said, and Iris was in one of her moods. The radio was on in the back-ground, and the other woman had kept up a succession of tuts and snorts at the opinions being expressed while Helen willed herself not to lose her temper. Iris is a small, stout woman in her late sixties with neat grey hair like a Brillopad. If it weren't for the coldness of her nature and the pinched meanness of her mouth, you might imagine she was someone's grandmother. I think Helen would have been glad to see the back of her, but she was a relic from the days when the shop had belonged to Helen's mother, Regina, who had died a year before. It seemed to Helen that Iris had taken it upon herself to ensure that Regina's memory was preserved. She resisted any changes that Helen suggested they make to the shop – any hint of modernisation, anything that might eradicate traces of Regina. Helen was tiring of her battles with the older woman, the constant bristling, the fussiness, and the unspoken perception that Helen wasn't a patch on her mother.

It was because of the undeclared feud between them that Helen had failed to mention Donovan or the scheme to Iris. No doubt she didn't tell her because she knew the snobbery and cynicism it would prompt – the derisive comments about trying to make a difference, the snide remarks about the foolishness of trying to conquer crime with tolerance and charity. It was not the first time that Helen had advanced the cause of waifs and strays.

Weddings can be especially difficult, I'm led to believe, when you're in the flower business. Not that I've ever helped in the organisation of such a ceremony, but I can imagine the pressure involved in striving for perfection – the girl dreaming of her big day, throwing tantrums, her officious mother standing by like a Rottweiler. On that particular morning, Helen was struggling with a bunch of freesias that refused to bend to her will, and Iris, who had been entrusted with the bridesmaids' posies, had ignored her design in favour of a more traditional one. That and the carping about the radio interview had built to a crescendo that she could no longer stand.

"Oh, for God's sake, Iris!" she had exclaimed. "Just give it a rest, will you?"

I can imagine the stunned silence that followed, the affronted look, the small mouth dropping open.

And then Helen with the hasty capitulation, the pointless apology.

"Look, I'm sorry. I didn't mean to . . ." Iris, lips bunched in an expression of fury, undoing the posies, cardigan stretched taut across her back, making a palaver of redoing them, all of it sending out the message in waves – that she would never have been spoken to like that by Helen's mother.

It was into this atmosphere that Keith Donovan stepped. The door opened and Helen looked up to see a tall, gangling young man standing there. She told me that what she remembers most about their first encounter was how poorly he was dressed for the weather. It was a blustery day, despite the sunshine, and he wore dark trousers, a worn white shirt, a tie and a flimsy sports jacket. There was something of the Bible salesman about him, yet when she saw him, she mistook him for a member of the wedding party, arriving early to pick up the flowers, and was assailed by a sense of rising panic. "You're too early!" she wailed. "Miles too early!"

His response was muffled – he was plainly nervous, she told me.

"I can't hear you," she said, not bothering to hide her irritation.

"I was told to come at nine."

"No, no, no! Half ten was what I agreed with Caroline. Wedding at two, flowers to be picked up at half ten. You'll have to go away and come back."

I can imagine him there, Donovan, shifting his weight from one foot to the other, tugging at his cuffs, adrift in the unfamiliar environment, being bawled at by the woman he was supposed to work for, and aware all the time of Iris's stare.

"You don't understand," he began, as the door opened and a gust of wind heralded two new customers, swallowing up his words.

"Say again? I can't hear you," Helen told him.

The little shop was crowded now, five of them shuffling around in it.

"I'm from the scheme."

"What's that?"

"The Young Offenders' Rehabilitation Programme."

The whole shop fell silent. Iris dropped her bouquet, momentarily forgetting her anger. The customers gawked at him. Helen couldn't help feeling guilty for having forced him to announce himself like that. How belittling it must have been – how demeaning, she thought. She found it hard to forgive herself for it. And thinking of him standing there, all those eyes upon him, the hastily rearranged faces, even I can muster a little sympathy for him.

"Oh, my God, of course. I'm so sorry," Helen said and moved to usher him to the back of the shop.

What a way to start! His feelings of inadequacy and her need to overcompensate for them.

"I'd been expecting them to send a woman," she explained to me later. "I suppose I couldn't imagine a male prisoner being interested in a florist's. That's baseless prejudice, I'm sure, but it's what I thought."

She had been expecting some hard-faced virago, gold hoops in her ears, rings on every finger, a dark scowl on a craggy face. Not what she actually told me, of course, but I retain the right to embellish.

And what did she get? This tall, skinny boy with pale skin and short light brown hair. He had a delicate chin and a soft mouth, and she noticed that he ducked his head to avoid her eyes. She reckoned he was no more than nineteen – twenty at most. In his favour he had a spare, open countenance.

Looking at him in court on those rare moments when he drags his gaze away from the floor, I can see that his face seems almost flat, lacking angles, and seems to hide nothing yet conceals all the miseries its owner suffered.

"He had the most sombre expression I'd ever seen on a young man," she told me.

It says a lot about Helen – her dreaminess bordering on irresponsibility – that she hadn't asked for details about the convicted criminal who would be helping her over those weeks. Not only did she not know his name or that he was male, she hadn't bothered to find out the nature of his crime. Theft, as it turned out. Breaking and entering. A gang of them, burgling houses in broad daylight. All of this she would discover later. But on that October morning, she was too concerned with other things – the wedding bouquets, Iris, how to recover from her gaffe. She made strenuous efforts to redeem the situation.

"I didn't know what you'd be like," he told her, much later when they knew each other better, when they had slipped into friendship. "I thought you might be awful."

"How come?"

"Oh, you know." He shrugged. "Do-gooders."

She decided to get him started straight away, so she found him an apron and peppered him with questions about himself. What was his name? How far had he travelled to get there that morning? Had he ever worked in a florist's before? She was surprised to learn that he had taken flower-arranging classes in prison, and couldn't help thinking how vulnerable that would have made him to bullying and worse.

He answered her questions politely. She noticed that he

talked with his head on one side, his eyes on the floor or on something beyond her head. Initially, when she had met with one of the scheme's organisers, they had discussed what role the candidate would play in the shop. Helen had imagined it would not extend much further than sweeping up cuttings and organising deliveries, yet when she asked Donovan to put together a bouquet, he moved quickly, with sureness in his hands, sucking in his lower lip in concentration.

"He had the quickest hands I'd ever seen," she told me, "yet the most delicate touch. And a great eye – a real flair for colour."

I felt she was making him out to be more than he was because of her compassion, her generosity of spirit to the less well-off, and also to go some way to explain away some of what had happened afterwards. Her account of that time is not altogether reliable, and she has a tendency to embellish situations, almost to romanticise them.

"There was something about him that was, I don't know, gentle. Meek. He was the quietest, most serious young man I had ever met."

I think of him, fixing his eyes on the floor by her feet, his troubled remoteness and her need to care, to reform. How easily these things begin. A seed is planted. He needed her help. A damaged soul just waiting to be nurtured. And she didn't even know it then. Had no idea. Nothing, only the faint awareness of a raised heartbeat drumming away inside her chest.

4

Two years since Frankie died. After the rigmarole and pageantry of his death and funeral, I fled Ireland for the south of France and set myself up in a near-reclusive lifestyle. I hid myself away from the world in the villa a mile outside Bonnieux. It had a small pool at the back in which I could swim, and a pleasant patio where I could sip wine and immerse myself in work. I no longer read the newspapers or trawled the internet. I sank deep within the shadow of my feelings and tried to locate in them some kernel of wisdom, of art, that could be transformed or translated into something meaningful.

I was running away – that much I knew. And still I was plagued by memory. Shortly after Frankie's death, I was invited to a celebration of American drama at the Gate Theatre, Dublin. It was only right that I should attend, as the greatest American playwright then living in Ireland. How many others present could boast that they had won a Tony Award and the New York Drama Critics Circle Award in the same year? Who else there could claim to have had their face on the cover of *Time* magazine, brag about drinking cocktails at the Plaza with the likes of Angelica

Houston, Noam Chomsky and Martin Scorsese? I swaggered into that party with the grace and aplomb of a South American dictator. I was very seriously drunk. Much of the evening is a blur. I cannot recall whom I might have insulted, or how many names I dropped, or anecdotes I trotted out – all sounding tatty and thread-bare, even to me. But there is one thing I do remember. A photographer from one of the daily broadsheets was there, snapping indiscriminately. He took a photograph of me propped up next to a hip young New York playwright, a man lauded as the next Mamet, whose plays are punctuated with expletives and almost always include a dénouement of shocking violence. So there we were together – the old and the new – grimacing and posing, when the photographer asked if I'd mind moving out of the frame so that he could capture the young stud alone. I was shocked, insulted and indignant, sounding off about the *Time* magazine cover and the Tony Award, jabbering about my glory days. The young stud turned to me, eyes as dead as a shark's, and said quietly, yet audibly: "Remember what Pompey said to Sulla? 'More men worship the rising sun than the setting sun.'" Then he turned his shark's eyes away from me and aimed them at the camera, and I was left, staggering beneath the weight of that final insulting truth. I was history. All I had left to look forward to was my obituary.

It is my belief that creative work reflects the emotional state of the artist. That said, I was aware at the time that my best work was behind me, and that the scribbling I had laboured over in recent years amounted to little more than a scrappy appendage. A mere footnote to a life gone bad.

And there, in my little French cabin, I tried to stare hard at my faults and failings. I tried to confront my guilt over what I had done in my life, the secret, pernicious betrayals that preyed on my conscience. And I tried to create something out of them. For a full year, I organised my life into careful seclusion, subduing any residual longings for the company of others. I had my dog, Pacino, and I could withstand an hour or two of meaningless chat with Gaston, once or twice a week, but it never went beyond that. I swam in my pool, I worked at my play, I shopped twice weekly in the local market; I spent long, languorous evenings in the dark listening to the lonely song of the crickets. There were no visitors to my villa, no intrusions upon my grief. I guarded my silence, insistent upon the rich, full, solitary existence in which I had immersed myself.

It never occurred to me that I might be lonely. What's gone is gone, I told myself. Instead of companionship, or love, I had silence. I built walls of it. For a while it seemed to calm me.

And then they arrived – Helen and William Glass – and the serenity I had achieved through my seclusion vanished. Helen's presence was at first unsettling, with the secrets she kept barely hidden, and yet I sensed in her a desperate need to reveal them. And I recognised something about her that was also within me: isolation – self-imposed, perhaps, but clamouring to be broken.

Sixteen months ago. The sun warm on my face and a voice behind me asking, "Who are you talking to?"

It was my habit, that year in France, to take myself each morning to the top of the hill above Bonnieux. There is a pretty little patch of grass there on which is planted a large crucifix so that Christ peers down over the village and the valley into which it veers. Yew trees are scattered about this patch of land, spreading their boughs over a couple of benches where an old boy like me could pass a pleasant half-hour looking down at the cherry blossoms and rows of gnarled vines.

That morning I felt unwell and I was unable to write, which has always disturbed me, and it seemed that everything was conspiring to upset me. A letter had arrived from Carmela, my agent in New York, and between its diplomatic phrasing and ribald jokes, I sensed growing impatience. It was years since my last work and although poor Frankie's death had, in its tragic way, bought me some time, I felt Carmela was nearing the end of her tether with me. In my villa, I was working on a new play, about a lifetime of regret after an aborted love affair. But every word on the page seemed dead and I couldn't escape the fear that, without Frankie, I had lost the ability to write. One must have one's muse. There was no peace in La Flambée that morning – Gaston and his cronies were up in arms about the Paris riots, bellowing about the rights of young workers being trampled. And so I had escaped up there to the sun. I summoned up the ghost of my lost lover and began to pour out my woes. Even after death, I was still troubling Frankie with my bitching.

That was when I heard, "Who are you talking to?"

The voice rang out like a bell.

I turned, and looked up into Helen's eyes, now uncovered but shielded from the sun with her raised hand.

I must have cast her one of my frigid stares, for she shuffled a little bit.

"I'm sorry. I didn't mean to be rude," she said.

I could have let her walk away and that might have been it. We might have spent the rest of the summer avoiding each other and I might never have become tangled in her history. But I saw the glitter in her eyes, understood the hint of desperation in them. I recognised loneliness when I saw it.

"I was talking to the dog," I said, with a shrug in his direction.

She looked at Pacino, a large black shaggy animal of questionable parentage, lying down with his paws outspread, brown eyes marred with cataracts, fixing me with a stare of purest loathing. There was a scattering of pastry all about him, flakes of croissant caught in the hair on his head, after I had tossed him bits of my breakfast. I'm not sure if my purpose was to encourage him to like me or to antagonise him.

"I'm feeding him breakfast," I explained, then made room for her on the bench.

There was an awkward pause as we stared out across the valley. I sensed her hesitancy, the bubbling up of insecurities within her, and realised I might have been wrong in my first impression of her. She plucked distractedly at the pale pink cardigan on her lap, as I crossed one leg over the other and leaned back expansively, stretching my arms along the back of the bench, not as a lover would, but protectively. Proprietarily.

"I'm sorry I was a bit off with you when we met the other day," she said quickly.

"That's all right."

"I was just . . . I was having one of my bad days, you see. It was nothing personal."

This came out in a rush, as if it had been building inside of her. I was struck by the notion that she had sought me out, and the frost inside me melted.

"I was having one of my bad days too, if it's any consolation," I said.

"Oh."

"I've been having quite a lot of them lately."

"How come?"

"Writer's block," I said with a theatrical sigh.

"What are you working on?"

"A play. It's no good, I'm afraid. I'll be amazed if I finish it."

I took the opportunity, during this little exchange, to examine Helen's face. It was small, with an Etruscan profile. Her lips were full, but the eyes enthralled me. Large, with heavy, languorous lids fringed densely with lashes. In the sunlight, they appeared as blue as corn-flowers, the pupils mere pinpricks. Close up, I could see that her shoulders and arms were wild with freckles, lending girlishness to her otherwise elegant appearance.

"I didn't realise, the other day, who you are," she continued. "I saw one of your plays a few years ago. *The Honeymoon*?" Her voice tapered up at the end, as if she was checking that I knew it. As if I wouldn't know one of my own plays. "I loved it. I really did."

"Thank you."

"No, truly." She nodded her head earnestly. "I did."

A lot of people I meet tend to go in for this sort of

obsequious posturing. It's not something I encourage. But there was something so guileless about her that I knew she was speaking the truth. It made me ashamed to have doubted her. But I'm a cynical old crocodile, and years of dried-up wasteful writing can turn a man in on himself. The scalding bitterness of one's own loss of faith. "And what about you?" I asked. "What is your profession?"

"I'm a florist," she said, reaching to capture a tendril of hair that had caught in the side of her mouth. She added as an afterthought, "I have my own shop."

"I see."

"It was my mother's before me. She's German . . . *was* German. She passed away."

A florist. I pictured her, with her gorgeous mane of hair, the diaphanous skirt, those dreamy, sensual eyes, surrounded by blossoms. A ridiculous, romantic image. Later, I would see her in that dark, cramped space wearing a puffy sleeveless jacket over an apron, a polo-neck sweater and jeans, that loose strand of hair, struggling with twine and stems.

It turned out that the husband – William – was an academic, a scientist, and lectured in one of Dublin's universities. He was writing a book which, I understood vaguely, was on pearl fishing in Ireland's waterways, a subject that then struck me as oddly quixotic.

"It's his idea we're here," she explained. "A colleague of his has a house he's lent us for the summer."

"So that William can work on his book?"

"Yes, that."

"And what about you?" She's not sure of me, I thought, watching her bite her lip.

"I'm supposed to be recovering."

I held back from blurting out, 'Recovering from what?' Instead, I sat there, making my own assumptions. Comfortably off, a little cosseted, perhaps. I waited for her to volunteer the information.

"The sun, the fresh air – we thought it would be good for me. Getting away from everything."

And for a moment I thought it might have been a breakdown. An easy ride through life, probably, until something had come along to jolt her into reality.

"There was an incident," she explained. "I interrupted a burglary in my shop and I was injured."

"Jesus," I breathed. "Were you all right?"

"I was attacked. A stab wound."

Sunlight streamed around us and she blinked. For a moment she looked a little lost. She was wearing that scarf round her neck. All the time she'd been holding the ends of it, twisting them round her fingers. I regarded it now in a new light, and surmised what it might be concealing.

"Were you badly hurt?"

She nodded quickly, glancing at me surreptitiously as if she was about to own up to something.

"I lost a lot of blood. My heart stopped beating for a couple of minutes. They had trouble getting it started again, so they had to perform an open-chest cardiac massage. Look, here." She turned so that she was facing me, whipped back the scarf and I was confronted by that bold purple scar, angry and vivid. I had a vision of a gaping chest cavity, gloved hands crowding around in there, ribs peeled back. A wave of revulsion crawled from my stomach into my throat.

"Good Lord," I murmured.

Mercifully, the scarf was replaced.

Perhaps she had seen the pallor in my complexion, or a tortured look in my eyes, which had seen enough of hospitals, surgery and death over the past year, because she said, "I shouldn't have shown you. It's too soon. William says I should let the sun get at it, help it to heal, but it's too ugly to be exposed."

"It's not ugly, it's just . . ."

Her eyes round with anticipation.

". . . unexpected."

"Shocking, you mean."

"Yes."

I waited for her to say something more, but she just sat there, rubbing her arm, two vertical concentration lines running between her dark eyebrows.

"Did they ever find the person, the burglar, who did it to you?"

The lines deepened into a frown. "Yes," she began slowly. "It wasn't difficult. I knew him . . . He was, well, he was known to me . . ."

Her voice trailed off and I had the sense not to question her further.

"Whatever is the matter with that dog?" she asked suddenly.

All this time, Pacino had been emitting a steady rumbling sound from his throat. His black lip was peeled back to reveal yellow old teeth and his eyes were fixed on my neck.

"We don't get along," I explained. "He's not really mine. I inherited him. And he hasn't forgiven me for it yet."

Pacino had been Frankie's dog, his pride and joy.

A mad animal with his obsession for chewing the legs of furniture, his fear of cats and, most disturbingly, his compulsion for singing in the night – his mad, crooning howls woke me abruptly, the hairs on the back of my neck standing upright. We had never taken to each other, but since Frankie's passing – no, since the time of my treachery – his resentment and distrust had been distilled into the purest hatred. It troubled me sometimes, the tenacity with which he was able to keep this thing between us going. That constant growl at the back of his throat couldn't be good for him. But I refused to worry about an animal so clearly disposed to loathing me. At night, I made sure to lock him up outside, unwilling to risk him coming into my room to lunge fatally at my larynx.

"Hush now, old boy," she murmured, pressing a hand to the dog's tormented brow. "Silly old thing," she murmured, and the growling stopped. Pacino's eyes closed as he gave himself up to the stroking.

I could have let her walk away, and that would have been it. I might never have learned about Donovan, about William, about all that had happened that winter. Our histories would have remained separate, kept apart by her aloofness and my saturnine mood, instead of being joined by the friendship we have now, the bond. Kinship, she calls it, a spiritual tie. But I didn't let her walk away: something in me was drawn to her. I don't know why, but I felt as though she was the only person whose company I could possibly enjoy then, awkward, isolated and elusive as she was. Perhaps I spotted a story lurking behind the dark shadows of her eyes, but I think it was because I liked her. Or perhaps it was simply because I was lonely too.

Later that evening, sitting on my terrace, looking out at the afterglow of light fading over the hills, I had the thought that human beings are so predictable. The need we have to seek out others and tell them our woes. What is it about us that we need to expose our pain, show others what we have suffered, as if we are offering up evidence that life is an endurance test? Part of me resented having seen that scar. But I was intrigued, too, by her vulnerability and the vagueness that seemed a fine veneer over a passionate heart. I wondered at first why her husband wasn't enough. But later, when she told me the whole sorry tale, I knew that he was the last person in the world she could have confided in.

And it wasn't until she told me about herself and Donovan that the comfort of my self-imposed isolation deserted me and the loneliness seeped through, and I realised what I was lonely for. It was what I had turned my back on: life, in all its messy vicissitudes. I spent a long morning with her sitting out by the crucifix under that lofty yew tree, and when she left, I continued to sit, looking down over Bonnieux, powerless to control the thoughts spinning through my head, comparing her history to my loneliness. I let it all wash over me, and slowly a story formed – the facts were hers, but the feelings were mine. That was the thing between us – the identification of feeling: her guilt and mine were the same. That was how Helen became my friend and how I emerged from seclusion to face life again, in all its colour and confusion, frustration and longing. She drew me to her story, and I listened, framing and reframing it in my head, filling in the gaps, imposing my own imaginings, mentally reconstructing every detail. It was impossible to relinquish it. I swept aside the self-indulgent scribbling that had formed the bulk of my work over the past year and set myself a new task, her story my subject.

There, in the bright sunlight washing through the valley, the sweet smell of lavender scenting the air, she told me, "I should have stopped it, Reuben. I could have. Even now, I'm not sure why I let it go so far. Why I encouraged it. But there was something about him that touched something in me – a naïve notion of goodness, I suppose. I wanted to help him. I had no idea things would become so fraught, that they would get so out of hand, the way he would misread them. I had no idea of the misery he would cause."

And that evening, in the fading light, I opened my notebook at a new page, the image of that scar scalded onto my brain, and began to write. It never occurred to me that there was anything wrong in it. I sought neither her permission nor her blessing. I never let on that I was writing about her. All I saw was the story. And that, I think, was my first mistake. She looked to me for friendship, but she brought with her a whole new narrative.

5

Before the defence counsel has the opportunity to cross-examine, the judge decides to break for lunch. We walk together, Helen and I, along the slick pavements to the pub, and I smoke a quick cigarette.

"Be a love and give me one," she says.

I almost say, 'Hasn't your heart suffered enough?' But that would be taking the avuncular thing too far. In any case, I'm hardly in a position to give lectures, what with my own dodgy ticker. I was born with a hole in my heart and was lucky to survive, they told my mother. I came into this world in London shortly after the end of the Second World War, and she was always convinced that my condition was a result of the rationing. She blamed everything on the war. Even after we had moved to the States, when I was six, she harked back to the dark days of the bombing and the hardships that followed. The hole in my heart – well, it was easy to explain. How could a baby form properly on what pittance the government allowed it to eat during those lean, difficult years? My mother thought that the war was responsible for a generation of stunted babies with porous organs.

The drinking establishment is dark and subdued. It has suffered greatly from the smoking ban, a whole host of even nastier odours now rising with the dust from the upholstery and carpeting. We find seats by the window and give our orders to the lounge boy. At the bar, three lads in yellow jackets and dirty boots are tucking into all-day breakfast rolls and tea. The woman at the next table shakes out her newspaper, then folds it sharply with a karate chop. I wonder if Helen's case will make the papers tomorrow. There was, after all, a flurry of excitement in the media when the attack happened. Well, why wouldn't there be? I've known journalists in the past and they're all the same, no matter how high-brow they think themselves. A pretty young woman taken in by a thug, the class difference, the hand of charity slapped back, the murky rumours that have persisted about the nature of their relationship and all the prurient suggestions – it's the stuff that sells news-papers. And although I wasn't here then, didn't even know Helen, I've heard enough to suspect the worst.

The builder nearest to me has hair shorn close to the skull, broad shoulders hunched inside his jacket. Helen is staring at him.

"Do you know, Reuben, when he first came to work for me, Keith would take his lunch across to the green and eat it on a bench beneath the trees. Sometimes he'd leaf through the paper. Othertimes he just stared about him."

I try to imagine it now – the incline of his head, the slope of his neck, the canopy of leaves framing his isolation. From the window of her shop, Helen watched him sitting there alone.

"He had such careful manners," she tells me. "He

didn't wolf his food down the way some men do, but ate slowly, chewing thoughtfully."

I have heard this before, of what a quiet young man she had taken him for. Not the dangerous individual he turned out to be. And I must confess to being a little bored with it. The nostalgia that infiltrates her recollections grates on me – the sepia of her memories – when I want to focus on the colour and vividness of what came afterwards.

Helen's shop is closed today. It will remain so for the duration of the trial. She could have brought in relief workers, but her heart wasn't in it. I think of all those flowers in the dark, untended, waiting, buckets packed tight. How long will it be before they perish, I wonder. I suppose she had no choice other than to close, really. Iris left some time ago: "It's been good knowing you, Helen, and I'm sorry for all you've been through, but this thing has changed you," she had said, with tight lips and flames in her hard little eyes. It had all started to unravel for Iris the minute Donovan first walked through that door. I can imagine her pulling her cardigan tightly about her stout figure, her eyes sliding dangerously over her new co-worker, taking in the lank hair, the hooded eyes that can't return her gaze, the look of neglect he was unable to shake off. Another of Helen's projects. But this one had a police record. This was not on at all.

And it can't have helped Helen's case that Iris liked to gossip. There was a quote in a newspaper from an anonymous source describing how Helen had mooned over Donovan. Iris – it could only have been Iris – clipping at stems with her secateurs, stealing glances at her employer as Helen gazed wistfully across to the green at Donovan, oblivious, eating his lunch. Iris rolling her eyes, watching the silhouette at the window, thinking, You silly little fool.

After lunch, Donovan's barrister begins her cross-examination. She is a young woman with dandelion-coloured hair yanked back in a careless arrangement at the nape of her neck. There is something defiantly attractive about her. She has a long face, youthful vigour and the cultured accent of one who has attended all the right schools – as if her teeth have been freshly brushed and her mouth is as clean as a whistle. It was a smart move on Donovan's part to choose a posh young woman to defend him against another posh young woman – it helps restore the equilibrium.

"Is it not the case that you found my client attractive?" she asks, confident.

Helen and I have debated ad nauseam just how much Donovan will reveal to his legal team. I think she has conjured in her mind – despite everything that has happened – a certain chivalry in his nature that wouldn't allow him to reveal the grubby reality of what happened, that such things are private. But from her first question, it seems clear enough that Donovan has told his barrister everything.

I can see that Helen is flustered, red spots have appeared on her cheeks. "No, that's not true."

"I see. And are you in the habit of kissing young men you are *not* attracted to?"

It's all going to come flushing out.

Right from the start of her address, Donovan's counsel

makes clear that this was a case of victimisation. The colourful language she employs and the aggression in her questioning leaves no one in any doubt of the roles being cast – Helen as an overbearing, obsessive sexual predator, abusing her position as his employer to take advantage, and Donovan as the lost, confused, impressionable, put-upon victim of her lust. She lays it on a bit thick, but she has the scar to contend with. It must be hard for Helen to sit through it. Her face remains stoic, giving nothing away, as she tries to bat away the questions, tries to maintain her composure, but at one point I notice her hands gripping the bench in front of her, as tense as claws, knuckles white. It is the only part of her that displays her emotion. She has become adept at appearing calm and unruffled.

Later, in the car on the way home, she comes unstuck. Her eyes are bright with unshed tears, and there is an indignant, hurt tone in her voice.

"It wasn't like that, Reuben," she keeps repeating, shaking her head. "It just wasn't. It wasn't like that at all."

She is lost in their description of her. I watch her, with her elbow propped against the window, her head bent forward and resting in her hands. The sight of her like this is arresting, the vulnerability in the slope of her shoulders, the despair in her pose, and I think for a moment about the pressure she is under from those people around her – the bullying defence barrister, her wronged husband, wounded and silent, her raging sister, her ailing, bewildered father, and lastly Keith Donovan, whose future is in her hands. Just for a moment, I remember my project – the novel – and feel a tick of guilt.

I believe her when she says they entered into the thing

between them in equal measure. To me, who started it or who made the first move is irrelevant. It is my experience that in matters of the heart there is little real hunting and chasing. It is largely posturing and play-acting, one person assuming the role of pursuer, the other the pursued. It adds to the drama and excitement but, inevitably, both know where it will lead. I believe this to have been the case between Helen and Donovan.

The arrangement with the Young Offenders' Rehabilitation Programme was that Donovan would come to her two days a week for three months, at the end of which she would produce written and verbal assessments and, based on his performance, make a recommendation as to what he should do next. His days were Tuesday and Thursday. She didn't know how he filled the rest of his week.

After the initial embarrassment of their meeting, she persuaded herself to put to the back of her mind the awkward feelings he brought out in her. She buried them beneath a layer of officialdom, exercising a vigorous, workman-like attitude to him in the shop. I believe she managed to rationalise with herself that her inexplicable trepidation was attributable to nerves at taking on a new employee, one with a dubious record, whom she had never met. That he was a man, not a woman, had thrown her too, so a certain fumbling insecurity was perfectly natural to experience.

At first, they said little to one another. He was not inclined to talk and spoke only to draw her attention to something with which he needed help, or to point out when she had overlooked an order. As for Helen, she was too keenly aware of his background, and the question marks that surrounded his past, to enter into conversation outside the boundaries of work. There was a neediness about him – the thinness of his body, the formality of his tie and the obtrusiveness of the enormous white runners he wore underneath his dark trousers – and he seemed shabby and lonely.

When she asked for his home details, he became twitchy. He wanted to know if it would be all right to give her a mobile number.

"Of course," she said, somewhat baffled.

"It's just that we don't have a phone at home. Mam says it's a luxury we can't afford."

She stared at him then, feeling again the embarrassment she had experienced at the beginning. She sensed a humiliation about his poverty. And then, as if trying to lighten the situation, he remarked: "She's probably just guarding against the possibility of my dad ringing 1550 numbers!"

Despite the levity, she felt the weight of reality. It was something she could not imagine, being unable to afford a phone, which she considered a necessity, not a luxury.

The one topic they could discuss without awkwardness was flowers, and they both entered into it enthusiastically. They talked about the different occasions for which flowers were required, the fashions in arrangements. There were roses for Valentine's Day, then Easter lilies. "Mother's Day is madness," she told him, "the busiest day of the year." Christmas was her favourite – the scent of pines with the lushness of holly and poinsettia. And throughout the year there were weddings and funerals, graduations and retirements, new babies and convalescents, with a steady stream of blooms passing into and out of the shop.

One day he asked her where the flowers were from, and she walked around the shop, touching blooms and telling him their source. Did he watch that hand? Did he follow with his eyes those sensuous fingers trailing over petal and stem? Did he suppress a shiver and wonder for just a second what those fingers would feel like trailing over his skin. Most of the flowers came through Holland, she told him, although some were from more exotic climes. The roses originated in Colombia, she explained, and the birds-of-paradise in Italy – "Strelitzia," she murmured, their botanical name, and he repeated it, sounding out the syllables. Tulips, unsurprisingly, were from Holland, and she stopped to tell him about her first time in Amsterdam, standing in the Bloemenmarkt, transfixed by the swooping mass of colour. Proteas were shipped in from South Africa – he peered at the furry bulbs, petals like feathers – and baby's breath from Peru.

"What about the lilies?" he asked.

"They're home-grown. A man on the northside of Dublin produces them. Seasonal, of course."

"Amazing," he said to her, in his shy way. "All the people coming in here, buying their bouquets, all these bunches of flowers sitting in vases in people's homes, or carried in people's hands as they walk down the aisle, and they have no idea the distance these flowers have travelled."

She looked at him then. It was the most he'd said to her in the two weeks he'd been there.

"Yes," she said eagerly. "That's absolutely right."

"Do you want to know the most incredible thing I ever saw?" he asked with a shy excitement.

"Tell me," she said.

"The Spanish flag made entirely from flowers. It was enormous – about ten foot wide! This blaze of flowers. It was like you just wanted to lie down in it!"

"Where was this?"

"At the Spanish embassy, a few years ago. My girl-friend, Suzanne, is half Spanish and her father works there. Every Christmas they have this big party – very posh, champagne and silver trays of food, like nothing I'd ever been to before. Everyone brought their families along, and Suzanne brought me. The only time in my life I've worn a tuxedo! Suzanne had on this red dress with her hair up – so glamorous. I had to pinch myself to believe it was real. It was the best night of my life. Whenever things get really bad, I always remember that night and instantly feel better."

"Suzanne," she said. "That's a pretty name."

"Yes." He smiled, bashful again. "But that flag in the middle of the room – I'll never forget it. And they had these lights above it so that all the flowers shone. I couldn't stop staring at it."

Emboldened by this first glimmer of opening up, she decided to press for more. "The flowers you worked with in prison," she began, feeling a frisson at enunciating the word, "where did they come from?"

"Dunno." He shrugged, and something about him seemed to close. "The woman used to bring them with her."

She felt she'd overstepped the mark, had trampled into territory that he had no wish to revisit, but then he said, "There weren't nearly as many different types of flowers as there are here. No azaleas or freesias, certainly nothing like protea or strelitzia. It was just carnations, lilies and shit like that."

He blushed then, the expletive out before he'd realised it, and suddenly she knew he had been minding his language and behaviour. It struck her now that the politeness had been a struggle for him, a battle to suppress all that language that he must have listened to and spoken all his life.

"Sure." She laughed. "Well, we have that shit here too and more often than not, it's the carnations and lilies they want."

He smiled then, grateful for her effort to put him at ease. A rare thing, his smile, and something passed between them.

She asked him why he had chosen flower arranging. She tried to keep her voice level and interested, conscious he might hear mocking where there was none.

"It was that or woodwork," he replied matter-of-factly, "and I always hated *that* shit."

His answer disappointed her. She had been hoping for something deeper. Not that she expected him to announce a lifelong devotion to flowers, or to being at one with nature, or the desire to be involved in a business that brought joy and consolation to people. Some of these she could admit to herself. She wasn't sure what she had hoped for from him – but not that brash shrugging off. She had watched him in the park eating his lunch.

He always sat in the same place, on the bench beneath the trees, looking about him with a kind of detached interest, whatever the weather. It spoke to her of silent communion with nature, and she had nursed the fantasy that, having been incarcerated for so long, kept away from green spaces and nature at work, he now wanted to reach out to it, to embrace it. That this was his reason.

But there was a side to him that was dark and shadowy. He harboured secrets that she couldn't fathom. Something about the stillness of his face in repose, his nerves in company, spoke to her of hidden pain.

"On one occasion," she told me, "he was washing his hands. It's a long white Belfast sink with three taps, and in use constantly – one or other of us is always running water into it. But on this one occasion I came across him washing his hands. He had his sleeves rolled up to the elbows and I was filling a vase with water when I caught a glimpse of his wrists. There were scars there, Reuben, white lines, a mesh of them etched into his skin. The shock of seeing them! It was like someone opened a door behind me and I caught a sudden draught."

She gave a little shiver. "I could only begin to wonder at what had happened to him. His troubled history."

"And did you ask him about it?" I nudged. She shook her head no. "I couldn't bring myself to. There was a side of him that was intensely private. He built walls around areas of his life. I can't describe it, really, just that there were these silences that gathered round certain things."

But that day, after he had told her about the flowers at the Spanish embassy, about Suzanne, about the classes in prison, when he had put on his jacket and was poised to leave the shop, he stopped and turned to her, and she knew from the expression on his face that he had been turning something over in his mind. Standing there, he told her: "What I said about the classes, what I said about choosing flowers because it was better than woodwork. I didn't mean it. I was just saying that."

She said nothing, just waited, feeling he was on the brink of an admission.

"That's just what I tell people because they slag me about it. And I don't like people making a mockery of me. But the truth is, I wanted . . . in that grey place with no colour in it . . . I just wanted a few hours a week where I could hold some colour in my hands, you know? Where I could touch some living thing that had grown in the earth. That's all. I wanted, for those few hours, to touch beauty."

Then he went out, closing the door softly behind him, leaving her alone amid the blooms, his words turning over inside her.

6

Funny the things you notice in court. I am particularly taken with the defendant's mother. Each time she enters, my eyes are drawn to her. She is a big woman, not fat, but weighty — an iron bosom, legs like supporting columns — and she wears a succession of dresses that seem to encase her form, feet in sturdy high heels. Her bulk is underlined by her bird-like husband, with his stringy neck and blank eyes. I am impressed by her defiant pose, the proud tilt of her head, her bearing, the bravery of all that make-up, and yet I cannot avoid the thought that she is relishing her role at the centre of this. Mother of the wronged son, standing valiantly by him, pitting the strength of her love against the squalid, lustful fantasies of a bored middle-class woman. I cannot help thinking that, like me, she sees the theatre in it.

There was an awkward moment yesterday when I slipped outside for a cigarette during recess and stumbled upon her smoking. She shot me a glance of intense ferocity, then took a last drag of her cigarette and blew the smoke straight up into the air with an angry tilt to her chin.

"I don't know how you can just sit in there with her,"

she said with that smoke-and-gin rasp, as though she had spoken only to herself.

But then, as she moved past me back into the building, I caught her steadying herself, and giving me a hard look, so I knew the words had been for me.

And sometimes, in those long moments in court — during the lull of repetition, the shuffling through notes — I have caught her off guard. I have seen her gazing at her son with a remote expression in her eyes as if she was trying to remember how he had come to be there. Then her gaze would travel across the courtroom, fixing in a blank, curiously absent stare on some point in the middle distance. But Donovan, of course, is oblivious to this.

"It took him some time to relax," Helen told me, "weeks, in fact. He was wound up so tightly that he was always jumpy. Forever dropping things. He wasn't good with sharp objects — they seemed to become slippery in his hands."

He would become tense at the sound of raised voices, she said. When Iris got into one of her moods and stormed around the shop like a mini tornado, Donovan's thin body and distrustful face tightened. But when it was just the two of them — Helen and Keith — he would loosen up, his face would soften and he would express thoughts and opinions without waiting to be asked. He seemed to her a curiosity — an oddity. She noticed he had a funny way of speaking. He lacked the hardened tones, the broad vowels of the Dublin accent. In fact, when he spoke, there was something clear and refined about his diction, a shy newsreader's voice. He talked without looking at her, his voice light and quick, sometimes veering towards a high, broken pitch with a kind of nervous tremor. When he revealed anything personal, it was always in a slightly shocked way.

Once, when business was at a lull and Helen was behind the counter, staring distractedly out of the window, he remarked, "Waiting, waiting, waiting. More like Penelope than Helen."

His knowledge surprised her.

"The relic of a misspent education," he confessed, in mocking self-deprecating tones. "All that college reading and not a single letter after my name to show for it."

"You went to college?" she asked.

"Yes. To UCD."

"But that's where I went!"

He had studied English with Greek and Roman Civilisation, but had dropped out after the second year.

"There was a problem with a tutor," he said, his face darkening at the memory. "We didn't get on. I felt she was picking on me, trying to make a show of me in front of the class, marking me unfairly – bullying me. So I brought a complaint against her."

"What happened?"

"They sided with her in the end. Oh, they tried to be fair, open and unbiased, but I knew all along the way it would be. It's not that I had to leave – I could have stayed on or transferred to another course, but . . ." He trailed off, his eyes examining the floor in front of his feet. "I dunno. I suppose I was disillusioned. I'd thought that college would be the making of me, a place where finally I could fit in, find my own little niche. Meet like-minded people. But after that, the whole thing was soured for me. I lost interest. It got so I didn't feel I could face going in any more, so I dropped out."

She was touched by the pathos of his situation. From the start he had struck her as marked by misfortune. Some are more vulnerable than others, more sensitive to the harsher aspects of life. Certain people will get away with anything, but others will always be fingered for the blame. Keith Donovan fell into the latter category, or so Helen surmised.

"Is that where you met Suzanne?"

"What's that?"

"Suzanne. Did you meet her in UCD?"

"Oh, yes," he said, blushing. "Sorry, I didn't know what . . . It's because I call her Suzy, you see? For a moment, I didn't know who you meant . . ."

The blushing and stammering. How it reeled her in.

Their talks were always conducted in quiet moments, when Iris was at lunch and they worked there side by side. He told her about his childhood in a small terraced house in Crumlin. The only child of elderly parents, he had come to them late in life and unexpected. He couldn't help but feel they had always looked upon him with wary surprise. His father was a teacher but suffered from ill health and had been forced to retire while Keith was still at primary school. His mother had been an actress once, a theatre star, although that had ended when he was born, and now, if she did anything, it was mainly voiceovers for ads. He did a little impression of her, affecting sharp, clipped enunciation, like china teacups brought down sharply into saucers. Helen laughed.

He liked to hear about her family, her childhood.

She told him about growing up in the house in Terenure, a four-bedroom semi-detached house on a quiet, respectable street.

"The leafy suburbs!" he quipped.

She told him about her older sister, and how Helen had felt all her life as if she lived in Ingrid's shadow. He, who had no siblings, listened while she explained what it was like to grow up with another's intellectual brilliance, the never-ending achievements, the constant ambition, striving and excelling.

"She seems to have inherited the German genes," Helen told him. "That hard-working, determined, never-letting-up slog. My mother had it too. A kind of dispassionate drive, a quiet self-belief. Whereas my father and I . . . Well, that's a different story."

"You take after him?"

"In every way. Physically as well as in personality. Ingrid is so like Mum – her coolness, blonde hair and brown eyes. But I'm like Dad. Definitely."

One day she told him about the time her father had gone away. It was a difficult memory for her. She and Donovan had been alone, putting together bridal bouquets, and she remembered the smell of gardenias and chrysanthemums, the hairy feel of the stems in her hands, and him beside her, concentrating on his work, but she could tell from the stillness of his body, the intent look on his face, that he was listening to every word she said.

"It happened when I was ten," she told him. "He went to England. There wasn't the work for him in Ireland at the time, so he took a job in London, and was gone for almost two years. It was difficult for Mum, I think, having to take care of Ingrid and me on her own, as well as keeping this place going. We used to come back here after school and sit in the room upstairs doing our homework, Mum popping up every so often to make sure we weren't fighting or daydreaming. When I'd finished, she'd let me come downstairs and sit in the back, watching her make up bouquets and listening to her explain how she did it."

"And Ingrid?"

"Oh, she never had any interest. I guess she's like Dad in that respect – prudent, hard-headed, no creative bent. Ingrid stayed upstairs to read or study. She was in her teens at that stage – and getting moody, like we all do at that age."

"It must have been strange when your dad came home."

"Yes. Yes, it was."

I imagine her face changed as she talked about it – the morning she had come down for breakfast and her mother had told her that her father was back – the myopic gaze I have come to recognise when she summons the memory of it, the inward-looking stare that says it is precious to her. And I wonder if Donovan noticed it, those slanty eyes of his taking it all in.

"My mother was sitting at the kitchen table in her dressing gown, holding a cup of coffee. I can't remember another time I ever saw her like that, she was such an early riser, always dressed before Ingrid and I had staggered out of bed. But that morning she was just sitting there, letting the minutes tick past, knowing she was going to be late but not seeming in the least anxious about it. 'Daddy's home,' she said to me, 'he's upstairs in the spare room.'

And for some reason I paused – excited he was home, yes, impatient to see him, of course, but something held me back. The time that had passed, I suppose – time that makes strangers of us. She must have seen the hesitation in my face because then she said to me, 'Helen, run upstairs and see him.'"

She paused in her work, wondering whether or not to go on. As if sensing her uncertainty, or the possibility of some guilty admission, Donovan stopped what he was doing and turned to look her full in the face.

"It was a shock," she told him. "My father seemed to have shrunk since I'd seen him. I remember there was stubble on his chin and it was flecked with grey. He had always been youthful to me but now he seemed old and tired. I crept into the room, and he took me in his arms. He smelled unwashed, I remember, and then the strangest thing happened. He began to cry. This silent shuddering sob. And do you know the shameful thing? My poor father, whom I hadn't seen in almost two years, but all I felt for him in that moment was disgust."

During those two years, strangeness had crept into their relationship. Even though her father had returned to resume his parental role, a distance remained between Helen and him, which couldn't be bridged by talking or treats, discipline or threats. His absence during those important years had left a silence and an awkwardness that caused a subtle shift of power. He no longer had the same authoritative sway over her. She had become removed from him, rebellious and wilful.

"At least he cared enough to argue with you," Keith observed.

It surprised her, the things she told him, the private thoughts she shared so casually with him. And yet despite her admissions, the awkwardness lingered between them. It bothered her, the distance he affected sometimes, the way he would suddenly close off without warning or reason. Once, driving through the village, she had caught sight of him standing at a bus stop, leaning against a shop window, and she had drawn the car alongside the kerb, rolled down the window and called across to him, "Can I give you a lift?"

He had hurried across to her, his hood up against the rain, and leaned down. She had repeated the question.

"Oh, no!" he said with a brief laugh, and then turned his back to her and returned to his place at the window and resumed his indolent pose.

She had felt rebuffed, and embarrassed. She lingered for a few seconds, aware that he was staring past her as he waited for her to leave, feeling the barrier between them. When she drove away, she could feel the blood pulsing through her veins, and began to dread the next time she would see him.

As I write this, a photograph of Donovan is pinned to the notice board in front of me. Helen took it shortly after he began to work for her. She used to keep photographs of the staff and her customers tacked to the wall above the sink in the shop. I remember waiting for her once as she was closing and looking through that collage. I saw Donovan's face – in among the girls beaming at the camera or bent over their work. And I must admit my surprise in discovering his image still displayed after every-thing that had happened. As Helen was totalling the till, I whipped that photograph into my pocket. Its absence has never been noticed.

Sometimes I pause in my work and look up to examine it. He gazes at the camera, face impassive. Perhaps it is the steadiness of the gaze that unnerves me, the confidence it seems to suggest. Sometimes it is as though he is watching me, silently asking, 'What is it you think you are doing?'

And I wonder how Helen felt when she took that picture, eyeing him through the lens, framing the shot. Such an intimate thing, the taking of a picture, the unashamed scrutiny. And later, when downloading the image on her computer, did she allow the cursor to linger over it, thinking . . . What was she thinking? Of the disquiet he caused her? That she was imagining things? Rationalising away the feeling of being troubled by that steady gaze?

From the very beginning – that first day when he walked into the midst of pandemonium – there was something unsettling about him that made her question herself. She was his employer and almost seven years his senior. More than that, she was his sponsor, his investor, his benefactor, she was putting faith and trust in him; she was responsible for ensuring that he had a better future. But in his presence she felt like a schoolgirl. Something about him led her back to her childhood – to the younger-child's fear of not being seen or, worse, being exposed.

And what was it? Would it have been his silence, the way his eyes revealed nothing to her so that she had no idea whether or not he was sizing her up? She was not unaware of her beauty – and I do believe it is beauty, of the gamine, dark-eyed, disquieting kind, which requires a second look to confirm that it is not just a collection of mismatched features, with oversized eyes and generous lips. She was aware of it all right, aware of its power. Yet with Donovan, it was as if her beauty was inconsequential, as if he saw right through it.

Of course, the court is not interested in any such details. Inadmissible evidence. Hearsay. The defence has no time for that kind of background information. They want to get straight to the kiss.

"That day," she had told me, "when he was starting and I should have been assessing him, seeing was he fit for the job, I felt like I was the one under surveillance. I was the one who had to prove myself. He would not engage me with his eyes and it felt like he was weighing up everything about me, casting judgement, surmising what my life was like. I felt exposed. Judged. It was as if he saw in me the confused teenager beneath the respectable wife, the businesswoman. All of the layers came away underneath that gaze. It was as if I was thirteen years old again."

7

And what about the husband – William? What about his take on the chain of events? There is a sort of gallantry in the way he seems to be surviving this squalid affair. He is a tall, slim, bookish man, who speaks with the plaintive manner of an academic. He has a lot of charm, William. I can see why she fell for him – all that calm compared to her stormy passions. A certain wisdom attaches itself to that kind of stillness in a person.

Yet his surface calmness makes it difficult to know what turmoil he is suffering inside. He is not given to opening up, to sharing confidences, although I have tried on several occasions to prise open the impenetrable shell of good manners in which he is encased, attempting to gain a better understanding of him, but he gives little away. For the most part, I have had to interpret his actions and thoughts in my own way, based on what others have said to me.

The one occasion when I caught a flash of insight into the machinations of his heart was the night he told me about his first meeting with Helen. It was a cool evening in France. The fog lay in a heavy blanket over the woods and when an occasional car passed we would see the swing of headlights through the trees, and hear the sound of tyres on the asphalt, but nothing else broke the stillness. There was a wonderful seriousness about him, and as I watched him in the moonlight, I had a picture of what he might have been like as a child – grave and stoic. Those around him might have thought he understood more than he should for his years.

It was starting to become clear to him then that there was more to the case than Helen was letting on. Her secrecy and withdrawal were masks to cover the inevitable, and I think he knew this. He was struggling within himself between the instinct to prise the truth out of her and the desire to nurse her back to health. It wasn't long after that night when she told him what had happened between her and Donovan – about Christmas, about the letters – and everything unravelled between them.

"A man died when Helen and I first met. Did you know that?" he asked me. "We witnessed a fatal accident. That was how we came together."

We had been on the porch for an hour, having left Helen asleep on the couch, and I had pulled a couple of bottles of beer for us out of the refrigerator. We were seated across from each other, staring out at the dark woods and the fog, and it seemed as though a sort of sadness had come over him. He drank his beer, kept his eyes on the night sky and said, "She wasn't always like this, you know. The lethargy . . ." His voice trailed off. "She used to be so different. When we first met, her vitality struck me most. She's the talkative one, not me. Naturally excitable. But since this all happened, something about her has changed."

I am a good listener. I can sit still and quiet, nodding, making little encouraging noises. I've been doing it all my life. But that night he needed no encouragement. I believe he just had to let it all out, relive the memories, as if that would rekindle some vigour in his wife, wake her from the listlessness into which she had slipped.

"I went to a café for lunch, a quirky, cheap little place called Blazing Salads. I'd been there hundreds of times before without any trace of the unusual, and out of nowhere, there was this woman – this passionate, fiery woman. It was so unexpected, so unlooked for – almost unwanted."

Was he surprised to be telling me this? Maybe, but he was too enlivened to stop. The impulse was there and something compelled him to go with it, let the force out into the night when there was no one to hear it except me.

"I had a seat at the window. A counter ran along the glass and I was on a high stool so that I could eat my lunch, look out at the street and watch the passers-by. I was finishing off a Caesar salad when I saw a motorbike speed past, and then there was an almighty screaming of brakes and a crash. I'll never forget it."

Within seconds, he had abandoned his place at the window and was out on the street.

"I left everything behind – my jacket, my wallet. A truck was stalled in the middle of the road, engine running, and the motorbike was lying on its side with one wheel still spinning, debris all over the place. All these people standing about – there must have been at least a dozen of us, if not twenty, frozen for a few seconds. The biker was lying on the road under the truck.

The lower half of his body was trapped beneath a wheel, pinned to the ground. Horrifying. In a strange way, he looked as though he was practising some feat of strength, like those Iron Man contests you see when huge men haul trucks along with ropes, but instead, he was holding one up with his chest. His head was tilted at an awkward angle – an unnatural angle, and he wasn't moving. I knew before anyone touched him that he was dead."

Such a thing to witness. One of the great dramas of the human body – the moment that life passes out of it, making waves in the lives of others.

"There was uproar. People were screaming, there was utter confusion, mobile phones being pulled out. I remember a woman dragging her child away, trying to shield him from the sight. There was conflict over what to do about the biker, whether to reverse the truck or leave him trapped under it. It seemed to take the emergency services for ever to arrive, and one man was at the biker's head, on his knees, something in his hands. It took me a moment to register what it was – rosary beads. I was rooted to the spot, unable to move, convinced of the futility of trying to help the poor man. And then I saw her. A girl in a red coat, skinny, cute-looking with dark hair and a white face, standing on the other side of the road. Like me, she was rooted to the spot, eyes fixed on that terrible scene. Her mouth was open – it was a dark hole – and I remember looking at it, then at glazed eyes, and it occurred to me that she was about to faint."

He cast a shy smile at me and shook his head. "It sounds ridiculous, doesn't it? My knight-in-shining-armour moment. And when I think of it now, me dashing across the road to her, a perfect stranger, putting my hand on her arm and saying something like, 'You've had a shock and you need to sit down,' or something equally clichéd. And it was so unlike me! I had never in my life gone up to a woman I didn't know. I was hopeless with women. It was such a shock when she let me take her arm and lead her away without a word. She just allowed herself to be led into the nearest pub, where I got us brandies."

It was the story of his life – the one moment of drama within a life that until that point had been uneventful, for the most part. The day he had witnessed a man's death and met his future wife.

"I let her drink, not saying anything. She sat there, still in that red coat, and I watched the colour return to her cheeks. After a few minutes I asked, 'Are you all right?' Her eyes gleamed and she nodded. And then – I don't know why – it all rushed out in a torrent, the accident, the moment of impact, everything spilling out between the two of us, each of us telling our own sides of it, recounting our thoughts, describing our emotions. She had seen more than I had – she'd witnessed every last hideous second of it – so perhaps she had more to tell, or maybe that was because she's the more talkative of us. And after a while, I began to relax to the sound of her voice. There was something about this girl, her face, that hair, the way she steamed through her account . . . I found myself staring at her mouth, willing her to smile . . ."

They would each tell that story many times over the coming weeks and years, and that evening, as they talked, they used phrases and words that would be repeated in their future retelling. There was comfort to be drawn from such talk.

With the brandies, it was therapeutic. And whenever the conversation drifted into silence, one would rush to fill it: "Did you see the look on the driver's face?" and they would be in the thick of the drama once more, reliving it, travelling side by side through the unfolding narrative.

She shed her coat and he ordered pints. They abandoned their plans: work, study, life beyond each other and what they had witnessed was forgotten. This was bigger than everything else. Neither wanted to leave. He let her talk. There was a sort of imperiousness about her, he thought, in the arch of her brow; the concentration lines across her forehead lent a majestic severity to an otherwise girlish face. He watched her mouth, the way it moved, the small teeth, the pink flickering tongue. When she smiled, which was rarely at first, then more often, dimples appeared, which made her seem mischievous. Freckles were sprinkled across her nose. Her eyes were large and round, a deep blue that was almost violet. He let her talk and she told him about her degree in politics and philosophy, the two subjects her father believed to be completely useless. William imagined that she had chosen them defiantly – her father was so strongly opposed to her choice that he was refusing to go to her graduation. She portrayed herself as rebellious and wilful and seemed proud of it.

"Don't get me wrong," she hastened to add, "he's not an ogre or anything. It's just that he's headstrong and opinionated. The world is black and white to him, and he cannot understand why others should see things differently. To him there's no such thing as perspective – either something is or it isn't. He's the type of man who goes to parties and gives career advice to others without being asked. I'm serious."

It occurred to him that she had inherited the quality.

"And your mother?" he asked. "What does she think?"

"She stands by, clutching a glass of sherry and backing him up. She's immaculately dressed, of course. That's the thing about my mother – appearance is everything, presentation. How many times have I heard that growing up? It's her business, I suppose. She's a florist. Every day of my life, there's been an arrangement of flowers at the centre of my mother's well-polished dining table. She is so well organised, and thrifty. A bargain hunter. She wears down shoe leather looking for bargains. Everything in her house, she knows where it came from and how much she paid for it. It's a source of satisfaction to her, getting something at a knock-down price. It seems to give her some kind of security. And everything is so well kept. The silver is polished once a week. Last thing she does before sitting down in the evening is to run a cloth over the top of the kitchen cupboards. I honestly believe she lies awake at night worrying about dust. She irons sheets and underwear. She's a perfectionist. Well, they both are. They're incredibly neat. They can't deal with mess, or untidiness. They like order in their lives and in the lives of those around them. Any deviation from the norm is treated as a crisis. And, believe me, when those two get together to sort you out, they take no prisoners."

He had a sudden picture of her as a teenager, taking up a stance she didn't believe in to test them, that ordinary, decent couple with their ordered lives. She spoke mockingly of them, with a kind of beleaguered helplessness, yet there was an unspoken tenderness too, and it was her love for them that allowed her to speak so freely about them.

How did they cope with their whirlwind of a daughter, he wondered, with her energy, her fierce intensity, her incandescence? Did they wring their hands and berate her while secretly brimming with pride for the passionate, free-thinking, independent spirit they had created and nurtured? The passion within her lent light to her features. Fire burned inside her and he could see the flames leaping behind her eyes.

All afternoon they sat there while she told him story after story about her family, their industry, their over-zealous budgeting. He couldn't pull himself away. Anecdotes poured out of her in scandalously dramatised tones. She made him laugh with tales of Sunday drives cut short and mad dashes home to double check that the immersion heater was switched off. "My mother lived in constant fear of that boiler exploding." She affected outrage at her father's conservatism – his manifesto, she called it, referring to his lists of goals, ambitions and things they should be striving for. William was captivated by her comedy and vivacity. In that empty pub, she was a dynamo, a force of nature, with her wide eyes and glorious hair. Her intellect, her knack for exaggeration, bewitched him. He was unfazed by her radical views, which he saw was posturing. The drama of her, the thumping energy that emanated from her, all of it wrapped round him, swaddling him.

"I felt reckless, Reuben," he told me. "And having abandoned work for the afternoon just to sit and talk to her – which I had never done before – I didn't want to let her go."

So, he took her home to his apartment. Seven o'clock in the evening and still daylight outside. Another new departure for him – daylight seduction. There, her words abandoned her. The firebrand he had found outside Blazing Salads melted into a vulnerable girl. They made love on his bed, the evening sun casting a parallelogram of orange light on the wall above them, catching the corner of her shoulder as she towered above him. It was new to him, this headiness. Into his safe, well-ordered existence came a bundle of contradictions – the part-girl part-seductress he had not reckoned on.

Over the next few months they spent days, weeks, in his bed. There wasn't a part of her that he didn't know, hadn't explored. Her body was something he needed to conquer. She was a naturally talkative person, but once he had her alone and unclothed, she became silent, withdrawing into herself. Everything she had to say was expressed through her movements, the shift of her hips beneath him, the pressure of her fingers on his skin. For all her vociferous opinions, there was a shy vulnerability about her in the bedroom. He was enraptured.

One small blot on his copybook. When they met, he was already seeing someone, Veronica – Roni – a colleague at the university. She was several years his senior and he was not sure what he meant to her. A tall woman with a lean figure and surprisingly voluptuous breasts, she was clever and erudite, a strong, steady woman who could be relied on. He thought she would make a good partner, a steady companion. But there was nothing about her to challenge him, nothing to excite. It hadn't occurred to him that this safe, solid relationship might leave him unfulfilled. When he met Helen, his whole life tumbled forward in a new and unexpected direction. The next morning, he went into the lab and, before he could change his mind, acting on an instinct so pure and so illuminating, he told Veronica plainly that it was over. There was a scene: tears were shed, shock was expressed. When she told him she loved him, he replied "I never loved you."

That surprised me. In the darkness of my porch, he saw my eyebrows rise at this callousness.

"It was unkind," he admitted, "but it was as if I was possessed of a new voice – a cruel, unrelenting one that needed to cut a swathe through all the falseness – the politeness – that was cluttering my life."

The power of this new love made him act out of character. It made him feel larger than himself. He felt empowered by it. For six months he lived with injured silences, hurt glances and unspoken resentments until Veronica took a position at the Virginia Institute of Marine Science and walked out of his life.

But by then, he was a hopeless case. Love: he did not say it out loud, didn't admit it to himself, didn't recognise it as the name for what he felt. And then one afternoon, walking over the cobblestones at the university, swinging his bag in one hand and watching the clouds scudding in the sky above the clock tower, it hit him like a wall of heat. He loved her.

"It can happen like that," he told me. "The person doesn't have to be by your side. You don't have to be staring into their eyes for the realisation to take hold of you."

I could see him, standing stock still, students filing past him, bicycles, noise, a busy clatter, happy commotion, sounds of traffic from the street outside. And there he stands in the middle of that ancient seat of learning, in a daze, for the oldest reason: he is in love.

When he told me this story, it was as if he thought it would be a revelation to me, as if I am too old, too alone to have experienced love in all its dimensions or to remember the experience. The arrogance of youth! I felt a little pinch of hate for him. If he only knew of the love I have given and received, or had any idea of how my heart has been eaten away with it. How willingly I have given it. It's a funny old heart. Sometimes I think it thrives on punishment. And whatever was left of it, after several bitter love affairs, I gave to Frankie. And as I listened to William I was overcome by loneliness and felt my limbs weaken. I don't think he noticed, so consumed was he in the telling of his tale.

Time passed quickly for William and Helen, and it got so that he couldn't imagine her not being in his life. He took her home to meet his parents, and he was also introduced to hers. He found them affable, agreeable, with all the flaws and foibles she had illustrated, only a more diluted version. What struck him most forcefully was the easy talk that wove between them. Their home was filled with conversation, all three opinionated, with determined views. It was all new to him: he had grown up in a household of almost stifling silence. The only child of academics, his world was of books and learning, not this free-flowing debate and constant banter. There was little abrasion in the talk at his own home: all arguments were carefully thought out and rationally put. And he noticed the love that flowed between her parents that she had not mentioned – did not even seem aware of.

"Are you going to marry this Helen?" his father asked him as they sat together over lunch in Roly's.

They met for lunch once a month, his father's way of keeping track of his son's life. But the question was startling. He looked at the man opposite, shoulders sloping in his tweed jacket, thinning hair, skull picking up the gleam of light above him, concentrating on cutting his food and delivering it to his mouth.

"I don't know," William answered after a few seconds. He had never spoken to his father before about love or marriage. He already felt lost and adrift in the conversation.

"Well, you're twenty-seven years old now," his father said, as if it was high time William found someone to love. "I married your mother when I was twenty-six."

William felt his father's eyes on him. Behind the spectacles they were bulbous and examining. A brief flicker, and they returned to the plate. A new topic of conversation was introduced.

But William understood what had happened. In his own peculiar, detached way, his father was showing approval. That look, the stilted talk told William, he liked Helen. He saw that his only son was happy, deliriously so. William felt silly with love.

A weekend in the west of Ireland, the rain never letting up, sitting in the car battered by the elements, staring out to sea. Exasperated, Helen said, "To hell with it, let's get wet."

They struggled into their rain jackets and scurried down to the beach, across the rocks on to the hard sand. They went as close to the sea as they could, the wind so strong they had to shout to be heard above it. She struggled with her hood in vain, eventually surrendering to the gale, her dark hair flapping loose, wet strands like fronds of seaweed whipping about her shoulders. He watched her, feeling his heart swell in his chest. The waves exploded like wild white horses, and he felt their echo reverberating through him.

"Marry me," he said. He had to roar it above the whine of the wind, the thrash and crash of the waves.

She had no words for him. Instead, her lips drew back in a smile as water poured in rivulets down her face. She reached up to him and when he kissed her he tasted salt on her lips. Would he ever feel happiness like this again? he wondered, his heart throbbing loudly in his chest.

Why did he tell me all that? I wondered. That night, as his wife slept away the wine and medication she had consumed, he had offered me the details that constituted his biography, the apex at which it had met and meshed with hers. Why did he want me to know?

I watched him rouse her gently, despite my protestation that she could spend the night on my couch. His manners and upbringing wouldn't allow it. There was such tenderness in the way he helped her to the car, such loving attentiveness, but I saw, too, the worry hardening in his brow, the confusion and anxiety that all of this had brought about. It was at odds with the innocence and freedom of the story he had told me.

Later that night, lying awake in my big bed, the shutters open so that I could stare out at the fog lifting and watch the stars, I thought of William and his story, and I knew why he had told it. It was to remind himself. A reminiscence born of fear. He was afraid he would forget, aware of the risk that, amid the frustrations, the things that were sweeping through his life that he couldn't understand, he was afraid that this was all he'd have left. And if he didn't work at remembering, he would lose the richness that had gone before. Telling me had been a precaution: he needed a witness to validate why he was enduring what his wife was putting him through, as if he needed to explain why exactly he had allowed it to happen. And I thought, too, of everything else I knew. The secrets she had told me, that he knew nothing about. And as I lay in bed a shiver ran through me, a guilty tremor. Long into the night, I lay awake, staring up at the night sky until dawn began to break, my conscience became drowsy and sleep came for me at last.

8

The oddest thing happened today in court. Donovan had taken the stand and his brief was taking his evidence in the manner of someone attending the bedside of a terminally ill patient – a far cry from the bitter, accusatory and sardonic tones to which she had treated Helen. She was pushing him gently towards describing the first time he and Helen had kissed.

"It was in the back of the shop," he began hesitantly, "where we prepared the big arrangements, and I was cleaning up, you know. It was getting late and all when she came in."

"And there were just the two of you present – you and Mrs Glass."

"That's right," he said, with a brief nod. "Iris had gone on a half day."

"Carry on," she urged and he looked at her with those fearful eyes, seeking reassurance.

He had taken the stand about twenty minutes beforehand, and whether he had been well trained by her or is a natural, his performance so far had been masterful, perfectly capturing the bewilderment and vulnerability of a wronged man, the pained sincerity of the underdog. There was something strained in his manner: it was almost as if he was consciously resisting a glance at Helen – yet he wanted us to be aware that he was making this conscious effort, as if her presence in the courtroom tortured him.

"So, I'm standing there when Helen walks in. She'd been gone for, like, hours, you know? And I can see she's upset about something, so I ask her what's wrong."

"She was upset, you say."

"Yeah, like she'd been crying her eyes out but was trying not to show it – you know? So I asked her what's wrong, and she said something about her father, about him not taking care of himself, about the house being a mess, and then she burst into tears."

"And what did you do?"

"Well, I didn't know what to do. I was distressed to see her like that, so I went to comfort her."

"You moved towards her?"

"Yeah, just to, you know, pat her on the back and that. Put an arm round her shoulders. And then . . ."

"Yes?"

He flashed another shot of those Bambi eyes at his brief – how well he employs them! – and we waited while he stared at his hands and shuffled in his chair as if struggling with the weight of his conscience.

"And then she turned and started kissing me." He shook his head as if in pain and, for an appalling moment, I thought he might burst into tears himself.

"How did you respond to her?"

"Well, I was shocked," he said plaintively.

"Did you kiss her back?"

"No!" he exclaimed. "I drew away from her. And there was this bucket on the side of the counter with all these carnations in it, and I remember banging against it and knocking it to the floor. It made an almighty clatter."

It was then that I became aware of a sort of muffled coughing noise and scanned the room. One of the jurors – a middle-aged man with a paunch and a bald pate – appeared to be choking. His whole face had gone purple, and his arms were crossed over his chest, one fist raised to his mouth as he coughed. I have studied each juror in turn, trying to surmise his or her profession, marital status, background – I do such things out of habit more than for my own amusement. This man had a look of minor officialdom about him – I imagined him to be a civil servant, or perhaps a geography teacher. A wife and a couple of kids, a three-bedroom semi in the sprawling suburbs, a few pints down the local on a Friday night: a pretty humdrum existence.

But now, at the central moment of drama, he had started to choke. Then I saw his shoulders shuddering, heard the suppressed hacking, the sudden wild snorts, and realised he was not choking but laughing, and making a wild attempt to disguise it with the cough. The whole court looked on in speechless fascination as he attempted to bring himself under control. The judge, whom I could tell had seen through it, fixed him with a baleful eye and asked pointedly if he would like a glass of water or a minute to compose himself. He shook his head, swiped at his eyes with the back of his fists and was silent. The defence counsel resumed her questioning.

But the laughter stayed with me. There is something

about constrained seriousness within an enclosed space: if hilarity sparks, it will ignite suddenly, ripping through the rest of those gathered there, throwing light on the ridiculousness of the scenario. And I saw in that moment what the juror must have seen: the image of Helen and Donovan together, the respectable businesswoman lunging at the youth overcome by sudden passion and then the farce of the falling bucket, the splash and clatter, flowers everywhere. Now I felt the laughter welling inside me. Oh God, I wanted to release a great bellow from the pit of my stomach! And I could see twitching in the faces of other jurors, now chewing their lips or concentrating on the ceiling. A couple of guards were leaning forward, elbows on their knees, staring at the ground, the stenographer was smirking, and I had the impression that every last one of us was struggling to contain our mirth. Only habitual politeness, the seriousness of the surroundings and the judge's eye suppressed it.

I couldn't laugh – of course not – with Helen next to me. Comedy would destroy her. Yet the humour was inescapable. It was in the costumes – Donovan in his mismatched, ill-fitting clothes playing the put-upon waif, Helen in her expensive dress, her imperious, chilly stoicism. Somehow their roles have been reversed. Donovan seems the victim now, and Helen the perpetrator of a crime.

The juror had conquered his laughter, but I know his composure will be tested again. I know what's coming down the line. I am already privy to the events of that night before Christmas – the grubbiness of the act, the seediness of the surroundings, the hilarity of the picture in all its prurient Technicolor detail.

"It's my own fault," she had said to me once, weakened by a moment of self-pity, "all of it. I could have stopped it."

And it's true: she could have nipped it in the bud. What makes a person risk all they have for a brief scuffle in a back alleyway? A few stolen kisses and all the grief that comes with them? Helen and William had pretty much everything they could want. Money in the bank, a comfortable home, good jobs, a steady relationship, youth on their side, their whole lives stretching out ahead of them with no kinks. The good life. The leafy, looked-after zone of houses, neat verges, speed bumps and manicured gardens. Why throw it away?

Listening to Donovan's barrister describing Helen, you would think she was some love-starved, dried-up old prune whose judgement was clouded by an insane desire for her young employee. But that was not how it happened. It began slowly, as these things do, creeping up on her insidiously. At first it was noticing that on Tuesday and Thursday mornings she would find herself springing out of bed, perhaps lingering a little longer than usual over her make-up, her step a little bit lighter on the way to work.

There was something about his quiet presence in the shop. He didn't engage with customers, that wasn't the arrangement. In any case he was inclined, she suspected, to take a background role, which suited them all. Iris preferred to be at the front, and Helen passed back and forth between the two. It was only when Iris took her lunch break that they were able to talk. Something in the atmosphere changed when they were alone.

"It was like relief," she said to me once. "It was like

being released from a corset and finally being able to breathe when we were alone together."

The awkwardness of that first day had dissipated. Ease had taken its place. And what did they talk about? What could they have had in common? As with most people, they discussed the daily incidents in their lives, the people who populated their worlds. They kept things light. He told her anecdotes about his parents, stories of childhood, and she recounted incidents that poked fun at her ageing parents-in-law – a guilty pleasure, and she felt mean, but what a relief it was to say how stuffy and overbearing she found them! They both made fun of Iris, who refused to talk to Donovan unless it was absolutely necessary. And perhaps this, of all else, made Helen forget temporarily that she was his boss as well as Iris's.

Some things they did not joke about, things that were never mentioned. She didn't ask him about prison, and he never volunteered any information. But she was itching with curiosity, unable to comprehend how such a gentle, polite, well-spoken young man – a university dropout – could have ended up behind bars and survived. The questions built up inside her. Why had he burgled that house? Did he regret it? How long was he imprisoned? What was it like? How had he got through it?

And there were questions that he would have liked to ask, I'm sure, about her husband, the state of their marriage, the nature of their relationship, in light of her flirtation. But at that point, even if he had asked her, it was getting so that Helen couldn't have trusted herself to answer honestly.

"It's not that there was anything necessarily wrong with

me and William," she told me, "nothing I could put my finger on. But there was something slippery that seemed to evade my grasp when I came close to identifying it."

"And nothing was said?"

She shrugged. "There was nothing to say."

She and William still talked, still laughed together, still made love with passion and real feeling. Their lives were wound together into a rope that, she felt, could not be severed, woven as it had been from the years of intimacy, secrets shared, fears spoken or not, these strands of sentiment. But she felt it nonetheless – a slow corrosion working between them.

"Perhaps," I suggested to her, "you were already experiencing pangs of guilt over your feelings for Donovan?"

"Nonsense," she replied.

That is something she has remained vague about – when she realised that her feelings for Donovan were stronger than they should have been. I think it was about the time Helen became aware that her father, who had appeared to be recovering after the loss of his wife, had seemed suddenly to be falling apart again. She noticed that sometimes during phone calls his attention wandered, his voice drifting into silence before he had finished a sentence; when she asked him something he would draw breath as if he were trying to summon the strength or enthusiasm to answer her.

On the day of the kiss, Helen had called over to her father's house on her lunch break.

"Oh Reuben, the sight of him when he came to the door," she told me. "He looked lost. Bewildered. All my life I've known him to be perpetually neat – fastidious even – but when he answered the door to me that day, he had allowed himself to sink into neglect. There was a wild look about him – his hair was greasy and plastered to his head, he was wearing the same clothes as he had been a few days previously but they had amassed a few stains. And when I hugged him, his jaw was stubbly and I caught a whiff of urine." The house also looked neglected – dispirited. She was alarmed to notice the pile of dishes in and around the sink. The smell of stale fat hung in the air. She found sour milk in the fridge, under his bed the putrefying remnants in a fruit bowl that might have been there for weeks – how he could stand the smell, she didn't know. The bathroom was a health hazard and cups lined the staircase, hardened rings of coffee cementing them to where they stood. When her mother was alive, there had always been freshly cut flowers, surfaces wiped, floors swept. She imagined Regina turning in her grave at the idea of her beautifully kept home falling into such squalor. "I screamed at him for ages, Reuben, about the state of the house, his personal hygiene. I browbeat him for caring so little about my mother's memory that he could allow himself and her house to fall into such a shambles. I was so angry, I went through it, throwing open the windows – the whole place became a wind tunnel. Then I scrubbed and scoured and swept and vacuumed and polished until that house was gleaming. I marched him upstairs and insisted he had a bath, shaved and put on clean clothes."

Afterwards she had driven back to work, giving way to an angry fit of weeping.

"Did you ring anyone?" I asked her. "Ingrid or William?"

"I thought about it, but I was just too worked up, incoherent with rage and grief and . . . Oh, I don't know."

With grief in her heart and her emotions still swirling inside her, she landed on top of Donovan, who was putting together a bouquet. He didn't appear to notice her emotional state as she flung her bag onto the counter, hung her coat on its hook and, with a sigh, looped an apron over her head and tied the strings at her back.

"I hope you don't mind," he began with a nervous smile, "but I'm doing a bouquet for my mother. It's her birthday tomorrow. I'll pay for everything of course."

"That's fine, Keith. Don't worry about it," she said wearily. "And you needn't pay," she added. "Perk of the job."

She was rewarded with his smile, which warmed her, the first delight of that day. He was in fine form, chatting away to her, and she was content to listen, to allow herself to be drawn into conversation.

"My mother's funny," he told her. "She has her own traditions. For example, when it's my birthday, she always gives me my present at exactly seven a.m., because that was the time I was born."

"My mother used to tell me I was conceived with the express purpose of being a playmate for Ingrid," Helen said, surprising herself with the recollection. "Not that I minded much. But it never occurred to Mum that I might take offence."

He laughed, and asked questions about her relationship with her sister, how she went about distinguishing herself from her sibling.

Helen was tired. The business with her father had exhausted her, still niggling at the back of her mind.

She told Donovan about her fiery temperament as a teenager – a marked contrast to Ingrid's Teutonic reserve – but as she recalled all the energy and fury she had channelled into her crusades, she wondered at how she had ever had the strength to instigate them. All that vigorous campaign-ing for animal rights and world peace – whatever cause had touched her heart, she had embraced it with tenacity and aggression, and was reminded of her first serious falling-out with her father.

"My parents were summoned to the school," she told him. "The authorities weren't happy about some posters I'd put up portraying in gory detail the harder facts about animal testing. My father went nuts."

In the wake of the meeting, arguments had raged at home about her poor marks, her headstrong commitment to her causes. Her father couldn't understand the contradictions that existed within his younger daughter – the goodness of her ideals, the aggression in her behaviour.

"At least he cared enough to argue with you," Donovan observed.

"True."

"And you got to university so you can't have done badly in school."

His attempt to cheer her was touching.

"Yes. Although he was never happy that I chose the arts. He would have preferred the hard currency of a business qualification or one of the professions, law or medicine."

But she had defied him – perhaps out of wilfulness, or because defying him was so deeply engrained by then it had become part of her nature. She chose not to tell

Donovan about the rows that had continued through her university years – all the bitter memories of her father's mottled face and raised voice, her mother in tears – over failed exams, the company she kept, her lack of ambition or purpose and her sneering disrespect.

"So what happened?" Keith asked, shaking her from her reverie. "Did you go straight from university to working for your mum? Is that it?"

"I suppose so. It all happened quite quickly. Unexpectedly. No one was more surprised than me. I met William, and shortly after that we were married and I began working with Mum. Two years ago, she was diagnosed with breast cancer, and she died six months later. My father . . ."

She broke off, shocked to find herself on the verge of tears at the memory of him now, bereft and bewildered. He had seemed so lost to her, like a child. All of it was suddenly as fresh and painful as a new wound, and she was struck in that moment by the force of Regina's absence. There in the shop – Regina's little empire, her pride and joy, the flowers she had nursed with such tenderness – Helen realised, with raging grief, how much she missed her mother.

She started to cry.

He stopped what he was doing and looked at her. Then, touching the small of her back, he said her name softly.

She froze. Through her tears she could see his face, the stubble on his chin, the lashes fringing the heavy-lidded eyes and the thin arm with veins standing out like ropes below the rolled-up sleeve of his shirt. She described it to me in detail, the pressure near the base of her spine, that soft hollow in her back, his hand resting there lightly but firmly, with intent – his body leaning towards hers, his nearness to her.

"It felt like . . . comfort," she said, fixing on the word. "That human contact, the unexpected warmth."

All that emotion, so close to the surface, released within the confines of that small space. He took her in his arms, folding her into his embrace, and she noticed a faint smell of unaired clothing, perspiration and some sweet pungent odour, like cloves or cinnamon, which she recognised as the familiar smell of Donovan. In the same way that a for-gotten scent of childhood can summon lost emotions, his scent seemed to stir up a memory within her of something youthful and passionate, the Helen she had once been.

Now, despite the laughter in court at the vision of the two of them locked in an awkward embrace, I should point out a few things. First, there are only seven or eight years between them in age and, despite his cowering appearance and her proud stature, he is in fact a couple of inches taller than her. Also, I have seen Helen in her working clothes: there is something much softer about her in them than the austere court get-up would have you believe. I would even go so far as to call her appearance girlish. I have wondered, on occasion, just how much experience Donovan had had with the opposite sex before his involvement with Helen. When I first heard the salient facts of the case, I had assumed it was little. But on that balmy evening when Helen described to me how he had kissed her, I suspected that perhaps he showed more charm and suavity with women than I had previously given him credit for.

Every part of her body was still, she told me, the nerve

endings erect, poised – no, *straining* – for the slightest sensation. A bead of sweat travelled down her chest, mapping a path between her breasts. She felt it pool in the hollow of her navel.

"And then he drew back, looked at me and kissed me."

All of this passed within a few seconds and yet, for her, the sensory awareness seemed to last an agonising few minutes. The innocence of the initial embrace was blown apart by that kiss.

She said his name then, said it as one might say 'no' – a disavowal, a warning – and drew away from him.

"But you didn't say no?"

"It was what I meant."

For days afterwards she couldn't look him in the eye.

"Did you tell William about it?" I asked her with a look of cool perspicacity.

Did she ever! She hadn't even told William that she had taken Donovan on.

"I thought about it," she said. "That night, I agonised over whether I should. And God knows how many nights since I've stayed awake until the early hours wishing I had. I didn't tell him I'd taken Keith on because he would only have worried. I didn't want him fretting about dubious characters in the shop. I was afraid he'd tell his mother and then I'd have had her banging on at me about how Keith's hoodlum friends would be hanging around the place, darkening the door with their pernicious shadows. I couldn't listen to it, Reuben. Such snobbery. All of that prejudiced claptrap his mother spews up."

I think she was being unfair to William there. As I have known him, William is not a man for bullying and

cajoling, nor easily swayed by his mother. He is – if anything – a fair and open-minded young man. If she had
pursued this line of thought in a more sensible fashion,
things might have turned out differently. But she didn't
mention Donovan to her husband because, she told
herself, he would have responded with unnecessary
anxiety. In a way, she was protecting him from himself.

And the kiss?

"William is so sensitive, Reuben. In many ways he's like
a child – that innocence. It would have devastated him if
I'd told him. Even within the context of my grief, he
would have seen it as a betrayal. I couldn't do that to him.
I couldn't hurt him like that."

But not telling him was, I believe, a grave error in
judgement.

And I think of Donovan and what that kiss meant to
him, how he construed it, how he would go on to construct
a whole future round it. Had Helen known then what she
knows now, she would have said no. She would have been
firm and clear and not left him to stew in his mixed-up
emotions, touched and surprised by a new wave of feelings.
She was being ridiculous, she told herself, tired and worried
about her father, wallowing in self-pity. Had she an inkling
of what was to come she would not have stepped away, the
tears drying on her face, leaving him to interpret every
gesture, every nuance into his own skewed vision.

9

After William and Helen had left that night, I lay awake thinking of all he had said, feeling disturbed. It seemed to me that the last vestiges of my self-imposed isolation were slowly being stripped away by these two people. I lay there, powerless to control my thinking, absorbed in the memory of his words, his story – their history. At some time during the night, I got up, fixed myself a drink and sat on the veranda, my overcoat over my pyjamas, smoking a cigar and watching the night fade into morning. Dawn came in bands of orange and gold, stained from below with grey, and then I was struck by why I was so hypnotised by what he had told me, why I couldn't help harnessing myself to his story, despite the anguish it caused me. For his was a story of beginnings. The newness and freshness of love, the potency of its discovery, the redemption and life force it brings with it. While I had been eking out life in isolation, I had been thinking of endings. It was as if I had been closing down chapters of my life. Love – slam! Sex – slam! Life – slam! And all the time, in the back of my mind, that one scene – the agony of remembering it – played over and over in my mind with the same weary regularity, the same pangs of guilt and regret.

*

That look Frankie gave me. I'm haunted by it.

"Are you going to leave without shaking hands?" I said to him. "After fourteen years together?"

I had to stay in my seat to maintain the illusion of composure, my hands clutching the armrests so he wouldn't see them trembling. But saying that to him was a last act of recklessness – after all I had done to him, the depth of my betrayal. As if I was the injured party.

It was a calm morning after the stormy scenes of the previous days and the final insult to our relationship that I had enacted the night before. But that morning no words were spoken between Frankie and me. He moved about the house in his quiet way, retrieving his possessions, mingled with mine, and packing them into two sports bags that lay open on the floor. They gaped accusingly at me as if reflecting the empty tawdriness of what I had done.

I sat there in my dressing gown, stirring my coffee. From the kitchen came sounds of industry – the blond kid I'd brought home the night before, the unwitting participant in the ending of our long, troubled relationship, was making breakfast for himself in the busy way of someone uninterested in and unaffected by the last act of the drama playing out around him. Frankie, to his credit, ignored him, acting as though no one else except the two of us was in the house. He stepped around the mess of meat loaf on the floor – the dinner he had flung at my head, narrowly missing, when I came home drunk and lecherous, trailing the skinny blond kid, all giddy and flirtatious. That was to his credit too, ignoring the detritus of our violent row. He didn't even look at it.

I didn't move. He didn't tell me to get up. We were beyond words. And in that moment I felt as if I *was* the injured party. I had buried my love for him deep inside me, stacking layers of accusation and retribution on top of it – his sullenness and moodiness made him impossible to live with, I told myself. The demands he made, spoken and unspoken, were killing off my ability to work so that if one of us didn't leave soon my talent might wither away altogether, I might never again write a single word. He had brought his illness upon himself, I asserted, and was doing nothing to improve his own situation; it was selfish and unfair of him to expect me to devote myself entirely to nursing him back to health. I had endured enough of him living off me, leeching my resources. On and on I went, stacking these things in my mind until the love between us collapsed beneath their weight.

I worked my way through one cup of coffee, then another. Outside, the day was brightening. It was getting to the end of summer, one of the last good days, and I told myself that seasonal change was apt. I wanted to blot out what had gone before. I wanted to conclude this business and focus on a new beginning.

He had finished his packing – the two sports bags, containing the evidence of his life with me, waited sadly by the door. Then everything was up to him. He was on the verge of walking out of my life. I had pushed him to his absolute limit, and yet . . . and yet . . . Some part of me hoped that he might not go. I had precipitated the end, and he was making the exit. He would be the one to storm out, slamming the door, a defiant toss of his head, a withering glance cast in my direction. But he stood there, checking his pockets to make sure he had everything, like someone who'd stayed for the weekend, having dipped only briefly into my life.

In that moment, I felt a sneaking admiration for him: his composure, the steadiness and purpose of his movements; his clear resolution not to give me any more emotion. Perhaps he had nothing left to give. And there was I, sitting, trying to disguise my trembling, hiding from him that I was falling apart.

I affected nonchalance and drank my coffee defiantly. I made myself look straight at him, my eyes boring holes into his face, but already he was becoming a stranger to me. Who was this man, getting into his jacket, shaking his arms into the sleeves and buttoning it, his depleted body shrunken within it? He was about to go, his hand reaching for the door handle, when I said it. Shaken with loss and mixed-up love and the petulant self-injurious mood I had nurtured for so long with alcohol and blame that it clung to me like a second skin, those words rumbled up from within me: "Are you going to leave without shaking hands?" I said to him. "After fourteen years together?"

He turned and looked at me. I read everything in that look: his hurt, his disappointment, the aching chasm that now divided us. His handsome dark features were haunted, perhaps even then with the lurking taint of mortality. But his warm brown eyes fixed themselves on me, and I believe that what I saw in them was pity. A rare sort of compassion.

He didn't move towards me, didn't shake my hand. Just held me with that look, then walked out of the house, the door closing softly behind him. I sat there listening to sounds of a car door opening and shutting, Pacino barking madly. A pause then, and I wondered if he was sitting in the front seat of his little VW bug, key poised in the ignition, wondering what he was doing, perhaps experiencing last-minute doubts. And then I heard the engine start, and felt myself grow cold. Having committed the single most treacherous act of my entire life, I just sat there. I had cast him out of my house, out of my heart, sent him out into the world, sick and, although I didn't know it, dying. Sitting there with my coffee cooling in front of me, not moving, but I felt the cold creep over me.

I have to let that memory go. It is a burden I drag around with me. Of all the terrible things I have done, this burns brightest in the dark hours of the night when I lie awake.

And as I sat down at my writing desk in the early hours of the morning, I set about writing their history – Helen and William's – in a concerted effort to forget my own, not realising at that moment that our histories, eventually, would prove inextricably linked.

10

She had to tell him, of course, eventually. And even after he had learned about the kiss, absorbed the shock – that his wife and her attacker had engaged in a stolen embrace – William stood by solidly, putting on a brave face, his stoicism and goodness to the fore. But it didn't end there. The lurid details were still to come. And finally, as summer in Bonnieux drew to a close, the nights becoming chilly and the trees heaving in the fresh autumnal breezes, Helen told him everything. I think she was half hoping that his love for her would be enough, that it would extend to bridge the gap that such an admission would bring. And, oddly, I think that if it had been sex – in a bed, in the privacy of a room – William might have been able to surmount it. But the squalid detail of what she had allowed that grubby youth to do to her was too much for him. That was what he told her. She described it to me through her tears, how his face seemed to shrivel round the word – "fingered" – as if it brought bitterness to his mouth just to speak it. It was too much for William's imagination – his wife, that boy, both drunk, him having at her down some alleyway, panting, his grubby paws seeking and invading.

It disgusted him, he told her, spitting the words at her. *She* disgusted him. The care and affection he had shown her since the attack evaporated beneath his accusations, his resentment, the boundless cruelty of her betrayal.

It was later that night when I stumbled into my hallway, bleary-eyed and sleep sodden, Pacino barking, and opened the door to find her there, eyes bright with tears, shadows circling her face like faded bruises, a bag at her side.

"What on earth . . ."

"Reuben," she said tremulously. "He's gone."

Helen did not stay in court this afternoon, not after she realised it was going to come out. I don't blame her. All those staring eyes, that ghoulish fascination. What is it about the lurid and the macabre that holds such appeal for us? The jurors, trying to appear unmoved, unresponsive, when inside each one must have been gleeful to win such a juicy case instead of some boring tax dodge, a driving offence or a cut-and-dried drugs bust. But I sat and listened to Donovan give his version of what had gone on that night, the drink taken, the brief tussle down an alleyway – squirming and evasive in the dock, making his barrister drag it out of him, such is his cunning – but then it was out there, the prurient image pulsing in the room. One woman on the jury crossed her legs and pursed her lips, some of the men were leaning forward, their rapt attention held by the vulgarity of the expression, but how else could he have put it? One of the guards was positively salivating. And me? Well, I'd heard it all before and, truth be told, I'd heard worse – done worse – in the glorious perversity of my youth. You only have to turn on your TV any night of the week to see teenagers in clubs in Ibiza doing such things to each other beneath the voyeuristic stare of cameras. And as I sat in court and watched the disguised shock on some of those faces, I caught a few glances darting at me as Helen's friend – her proxy this afternoon. They tickled some dark seam of hilarity inside me, and I began, unexpectedly, to enjoy myself.

How had it happened? How do these things come about?

After their kiss, the blushing and embarrassment, Helen decided to cool things between them. To do what she should have done from the start: observe a professional working relationship, set the boundaries, maintain a distance. There was no more room for jokes, no eye-rolling exchanges between them over Iris. In fact, Helen could hardly bring herself to look at him. But it was a little late in the day for such a change of behaviour, and Donovan noticed it. He was not the type to come out and discuss it with her – in that respect, they were alike. Instead, he betrayed his feelings with long, questioning stares, an affronted silence, a narrowing of his lips. One day she was all girlish laughter and skittishness, sharing conspiratorial jokes, and the next she was giving off an air of steely displeasure. She treated him to the *froideur* that I had experienced the first time I met her – the haughty nonchalance and that imperceptible stiffening. In response, he concentrated on his work, endeavouring to please her, returning to the taciturn silence from which he had escaped, closing in around himself. She saw all of this and had a powerful urge to put her hand to his neck, then snatched away that thought, a gross impropriety.

December came and brought with it the Christmas rush. Helen was glad of the distraction. Hurried along by the swathe of orders as much as by the accumulated anguish of the brief romantic encounter, they were awash with wreaths and yuletide logs, variegated holly and blue spruce, amaryllis and poinsettia bursting passionately around the shop. It was a busy period that necessitated extra labour and so, despite her misgivings, she felt there was no choice other than to arrange for Donovan to work five days a week, instead of the usual two. Claudine, a Polish girl, also came in to help out so that with the four of them and the constant bustle of customers and Christmas CDs playing on a loop, Helen hardly had a chance to draw breath the entire month. This pleased her, and she felt reprieved from the niggling worries that had crept like fine cracks over the silences she felt accruing between herself and William. Nothing to be alarmed about, but his increased workload and her regret about Donovan had allowed a strange atmosphere to creep into their home, which she was anxious to exorcise with the vibrancy and joy of Christmas.

With the bustle in the shop, the constant noise and movement, she hardly noticed the bleating of Donovan's mobile phone one day. He had left it by the sink when he went for lunch. It vibrated and buzzed. Finally she looked at the display, read, "Home calling," and decided not to answer it. Best to let it go to voicemail. It was only later, when he had returned and she watched him checking his messages, that something snagged in her memory. It was then that her thoughts returned to his first day when he had told her his parents didn't have a phone. There had been the shame of his admission, the forced levity, some joke about 1550 numbers, she remembered. And yet on the display of his phone it had said clearly: "Home". Yet why would he lie? Her thoughts were interrupted by another delivery, and she forgot the pinch of nerves she'd felt as she was caught up in her work.

It was not until the night before Christmas Eve – Donovan's last day in her employ – that something happened, something was said. She noticed it when he arrived at work that morning sporting a cut beneath his eyebrow, the area above his eyelid swollen and puffy, turning mauve.

"What happened to you?" she had exclaimed, horrified. Both Iris and Claudine looked up at the shock in her voice.

"Nothing," he said quickly, with a sullen, almost belligerent note in his voice. Then, repenting, he had murmured something about not looking where he was going and walking into a coat stand. She didn't press it.

Later, when they were closing, Iris and Claudine getting into their coats as Donovan swept up the last of the cuttings, Helen handed the ladies their envelopes with their Christmas bonuses. Soon they were on their way, leaving her and Donovan alone for the first time since their kiss – Helen had made sure a third party had been present at all times during the intervening weeks. She turned to him then, saw him pulling off his apron for the last time and folding it up neatly. Coming towards him, she held out her hand. "Here," she said, determined to be generous, convincing herself that what had happened between them was a moment of silliness that could be brushed aside, now that he was leaving. "Just a little something. Buy yourself a few Christmas drinks with it. You've earned it."

He took the envelope, not looking at her. The bruise over his eye was shocking under the bright lights. He gave the envelope a cursory glance, then stuffed it quickly into his back pocket. "Are you sure about that?" he asked.

"Yes – why? Of course yes. What do you mean?" Her voice jumping about.

"I thought you were mad at me. I thought . . . I'd done something to piss you off."

"No. Not at all."

She hesitated then, embarrassment swooping over her, blushing. He shuffled his feet. He looked so young in that moment, waiting expectantly, as if for some explanation, and although she couldn't help feeling that she should say something to allay his fears, to reassure him about his work, no words came to mind. What could she tell him? That she had developed a schoolgirl crush? That she was afraid to speak to him in case she encouraged him further? That she was plagued in her waking hours by the longing the kiss had aroused in her? That when she saw him bending over his work she was sometimes overcome with a powerful urge to rest her head between his narrow shoulders? No, of course not. She couldn't tell him the truth, and no other words sprang to mind.

"Okay, then," he said when the moment had passed. He shrugged as though he didn't believe her, but wouldn't push it.

"You've been great, an excellent worker," she continued, straining for the right mix of professionalism and warmth. "I intend to send a glowing report to the scheme. I wanted you to know that."

His lips drew into a thin line of acceptance. He seemed disappointed, as if he had been expecting more.

"I'm sure you'll have no problem getting a job. I'd be happy to recommend you to anyone."

He was getting into his jacket now – a black quilted thing he had recently acquired, "Umbro" stitched in giant white letters across the back. He reached into one of the deep pockets and brought out a small package. He handed it to her bashfully. "Happy Christmas," he said, and she felt something plummet inside her.

"Keith, you didn't have to do that."

He put his head to one side, considering, and his lips moved nervously over his teeth. "I just wanted to say thank you . . . for the opportunity. Not many people would be willing to take on someone like me, someone with no experience. Someone with all the wrong kind of experience – ha!" He gave a brief laugh that died while it still echoed round the room. "Thank you for giving me a start. It was very good of you, and I wanted to show I appreciated it."

Something in his delivery of the little speech made her think it was rehearsed. "I've nothing for you," she said.

"You've given me enough already. And I wanted to say sorry, too, for the other thing." He flushed, but he went on, as if he needed to say it, needed to get the words out. "It hasn't been the same between us since, and I can't help feeling it's my fault. You were upset and vulnerable. I shouldn't have taken advantage. Not that I was trying to . . . God!"

He raised a hand to his head and frowned with the effort of trying to make himself understood while he struggled with his innate shyness.

"I was just trying to comfort you, that's all," he said finally, sounding defeated. "I'm sorry for ruining it. I don't know why, but I always seem to ruin everything good that comes my way."

He seemed so forlorn in that moment, so baffled by his inability to make the most of his opportunities, that she felt moved to alleviate his guilt and sorrow.

"It's me who should be apologising to you, Keith. I was upset. I shouldn't have brought my emotions to work with me."

She smiled ruefully, and he gave her a cautious, lopsided answering grin. Some of the awkwardness seemed to dissipate.

"Can I open it?" she asked, raising the present in her hand.

"Later," he said hurriedly, and made a sound that sealed off the conversation.

He was at the door now, his hand on the lock, when a thought came to her. "Why don't we go for a drink?" she blurted out. "To show there's no hard feelings. Just a quick pint across in Ryan's?"

He seemed to think about that for a moment, then smiled shyly and nodded.

"Why not?"

A corner table in Ryan's, a homely, familiar pub with a pseudo-Victorian feel – dark wood and red-patterned wallpaper, Sky Sports and every seat at the counter taken by men in their coats, watching the sport or reading the paper.

She asks for a white wine. He orders a pint of Bulmers. She sips her drink slowly, watching the level in her glass. At first it is awkward. There is a faded Christmas hang-over feel about the place, last-minute shoppers collapsed on the banquettes, shopping bags piled behind their legs, garlands of gaudy tinsel swinging between the pillars. Helen feels the weight of expectation upon her – she should be more festive than she is – and resolves that a silence will not be allowed to develop. Their conversation needs a kick-start.

"What will you do for Christmas?" she asks. A standard question, a little predictable.

They are sitting by the window, coats off, cupping their drinks in their hands. He is wearing a crisp blue shirt that looks new – the creases from the packaging make indents down his chest. The sleeves are rolled up and under the dim lights the downy hairs on his arms appear golden.

"Dinner at home with the folks," he says, with forced heartiness. "Mam does a great Christmas lunch with all the trimmings. Brussels sprouts, carrots, stuffing, the works."

She has a picture of them then – Keith and his parents – sitting round a rather sad-looking table with a giant turkey in the middle, paper hats on their heads, crêpe-paper decorations festooned from the four corners of the room, with Keith at the centre, trying to keep it going with his valiant charm.

"What about Suzanne?" Then, correcting herself, "Suzy. What will she do?"

He stares down at the table in front of him. "Spend it with her family, I suppose."

"You suppose?"

There is sadness in his posture and she reads from it that his love affair is over.

"It's finished between us," he says with quiet resignation and gives an affirming nod.

"I'm sorry to hear that. She sounded like a nice girl. You seemed fond of her."

He thinks about this for a moment, then softly – almost inaudibly – he says he loved her, then reaches for his pint.

She thinks he is closing the conversation, anxious to be away from her now, knocking back his pint so that he can get out of there, beyond her questioning looks. But she is wrong.

"It ended between us a long time ago, Helen. I just never said. I didn't like to think about it. The truth is, Suzy left me shortly after I dropped out of college. It seemed she wanted a student for a boyfriend, not some tosser making sandwiches in the Spar."

"Oh, Keith. That sounds a bit mean."

But he shakes his head furiously.

"She wasn't like that. I didn't mean it like that. Just her parents put a lot of pressure on her, and I was a mess back then. I was so angry about all that had happened in UCD with the tutor, still hurt and indignant, and angry with myself for giving in and letting them defeat me. At that time, I just seemed to be falling apart. It was like I had no control over my future, that there was no point to anything. I felt so despairing, Helen. I can't tell you what it was like. And it's no fun being around someone when they're in despair, let me tell you. So I don't blame Suzy. I'd have done the exact same if it'd been me."

He picks up his glass, leaving a wet circle on the varnished surface. He takes a long swallow and sets it down again. She notices his fingers, long, pale and strong. She notices again the bruise above his eye – angry looking. He stares at the TV screen, his eyes glazing over.

Helen has always maintained that Donovan is one of those strong, moody men whose silences cover the teeming mass of emotions inside them. I can't say I agree with her. Sometimes people are silent because they've nothing to say. Rather than keeping high-minded ideals and passionate beliefs pent up inside, their minds are vast tracts of vacuity with only a few pedestrian ideas and beliefs in them. But Helen insists on Donovan's intelligence, his hidden depths. She won't be persuaded otherwise. Somehow that would be the final insult for her – to have become embroiled with a thoughtless idiot. So she clings to the belief that when he stared at the TV screen that night, his eyes following a ball flicking from one corner to the other, he was trying to suppress the deeply felt emotion that was bubbling inside. When he was silent, he was struggling against the words tumbling over themselves to get out, the heartfelt cries of a misunderstood man.

Thinking of the present he had given her, unopened in the bottom of her bag, she wonders again what it might be and takes another sip of her wine. "Is that why you did it?" she asks, feeling brave now. "Your crime? Was it because you felt despairing?"

He shrugs.

"Yeah. Maybe." A heavy sigh. Then he glances at her with a weariness that allows her to glimpse the despair he must have felt. "I did it without considering the consequences. It was stupid, I realise that now, undertaking your first crime in broad daylight when you have all the time in the world to back out. But it was as if I was parted from myself that day, inhabiting a different reality. That's the best way I can explain it. God, it was trippy, and I wasn't even taking anything at the time – I was sober, honestly."

"I believe you," she says. And she does.

"Ten months," he says then. "Ten months for a random act of foolishness." He shakes his head in self-admonishment, as if disbelieving his own actions.

They are sitting side by side, and he turns towards her, and suddenly he is telling her all about it. An older lad from the estate, someone he grew up with, Lurch they call him, it was his idea, his gig. It was a lazy bank holiday Sunday with nothing to do and it occurred to them that people would be travelling to their relatives for lunch, leaving empty houses. They had picked out a road in Clontarf, Lurch and Steo. It was supposed to be a quick in and out. Keith would go around to the front door, ring the bell, and if anyone answered he'd ask did they want their windows washed. They decided that he was best for this role with his natural charm, that boyish gaucheness. If no one answered he'd text Lurch at the back, and the two lads would force a bathroom window, squeeze through, then let him in at the front door. The idea was to cause as little fuss as possible. They weren't interested in trashing places, creating mess, all they wanted was to pinch a few bits and pieces, things that could be easily carried – iPods, laptops, camcorders, mobile phones, money, but not jewellery, no one wanted jewellery any more, and no TVs or DVD players, which were too heavy to handle. Steo had a friend who'd take the stuff off their hands for a reasonable sum, split evenly three ways.

"It was stupid," he says to her, a little worked up now at the recollection, "really stupid. But when they put it to me, it seemed like something to do – something different. You have to understand, Helen, that I'd been sitting around for months, depressed and miserable. I'd have done anything if it meant a break from the monotony of going over all the mistakes I'd made, the things I'd lost, everything I'd spoiled."

He shakes his head again, bites his lower lip and looks down at his open palms. Then squeezing his hands tight, he fixes her with a guilty stare.

"It was my fault we got caught. We'd have got away with it if it hadn't been for me. But this one house, this little old lady, she took for ever to answer the door."

It transpired that Donovan, waiting on the doorstep with no answer after three rings of the bell, texted Lurch and waited for them. The front door opened a minute later, but instead of seeing his partners, he was staring down into a wizened brown face, white hair framing it, purple cardigan buttoned up to the neck. Behind her Lurch and Steo were emerging from the downstairs toilet, Steo looking puzzled, Lurch as if he was going to faint. Within seconds they were brushing past her, knocking her aside, all three sprinting, fleeing, Keith's heart beating loud and enormous in his chest. She'd seen him though, had had a good look at him.

And it mightn't have been so bad, he says, had they not knocked the old dear aside, shoving her up against the door frame, "frightening the life out of her". The judge might have been more lenient. "First offence," he tells her and she believes him.

"But it's my own fault in another sense too. I'd never have been mixing with those lads – the likes of Lurch and Steo – if I'd stayed in UCD. That's the thing that tortured me afterwards. If I'd stayed at university, then I'd still have Suzanne, and instead of me breaking into people's houses on a Sunday afternoon, she and I could have been off doing something together. That's what I kept thinking."

The windows above them are steamed against the cold outdoors. He goes to the bar for more drinks and she looks at his coat on the empty seat, then at him standing by the bar, counting the change in his palm with an index finger.

She hasn't experienced close proximity to criminality before. He is the only criminal she has ever met, apart from a cousin of William's who was found guilty of tax evasion. "White-collar crime," he had told her defensively, as if that made it any better. But despite all her crusading in her teens and university years, all her campaigns to improve the lot of the poorer classes, she had not come up close and personal to it. Until now, it's always been at a remove – a theoretical issue rather than a living breathing person.

It's my own pet theory that it helped Donovan's case with Helen that he didn't go in for the badges and sartorial mistakes that so many of his peers indulged in. There were no gold ropes round his neck, no signet rings or bracelets – he eschewed jewellery. If he supported a football club, he kept it to himself, not choosing to adorn his torso with their strip or winding a club scarf about his neck. His shoes were obtrusive all right – those large, unwieldy runners – but his hair was cut neatly, and there was no caterpillar moustache crawling across his upper lip. The only concessions he made were the Umbro jacket and the occasional fake designer T-shirt that he had sneaked into his wardrobe. And there was his education, his respectable family background despite the poverty, and Suzanne with her diplomatic-corps connections – it all helped in drawing him far away from the yob image Helen might have expected.

So how does she explain away his criminal past? Simple. The age-old excuse – he fell into the wrong company. Quiet and impressionable as he was, going through a personal crisis, his mind in turmoil, he was an easy target for any ambitious thug to latch onto and use. To her mind, the real criminals are Lurch and Steo, taking advantage of Keith's innocence, his good nature. According to Helen then, his only real crime was naïveté.

The pub is filling now, a sharp draught heralding the arrival of more punters. He shoves up on the bench next to her to make room for them and, despite herself, a small shudder passes through her leg as it brushes his thigh. Voices build around them, forcing them to lean together to hear each other speak.

"It's something I find hard to put together," she says, "you and your crime."

"Oh, Jesus, Helen," a sudden flash of irritation, "will you let it go?"

"No, really. I'm just saying. It seems so, I don't know, at odds with your nature."

After taking a long draught of his pint, he arrives at an answer: "I know you'd like to think I did it for some noble reason, but the truth is, Helen, that I did it for the cash. I'm sorry if that disappoints you. I'm sorry if you were hoping for something more insightful, more telling, but that's the way it was."

He pauses, and she regrets having brought it up, surprised by his irascibility. She wonders if she has overstepped some invisible line. But then he seems to relent. "Look," he says, softer now, "I know it was wrong, selfish, sinful and all the rest. And, more than anything, I regret frightening that old lady – I really do. But, Helen, it's all very well for you, and people like you, to look down and point the finger, but your world is completely different from mine. I look at you with your nice little set-up – a shop you inherited from your mother, a brisk little business, nice customers and product – yeah, yeah, there are stresses, I know, but every night you still get to go home to your big house – you and your husband – a nice big house between you, full of nice things, comfortable furniture. I'd like to have that. Or, at least, something close to it. My own place, my own four walls, with art that I've picked out myself hanging on them. Nice car, nice holidays, a little money in the bank. It's not too much to ask, is it? But sometimes, when I think of all that, and then I think of where I am, it seems like too much of a gap. Too big a hill to climb and I'm never going to get up there, never even come close. There are times when it feels as if it'll be twenty years' time and I'll still be living with Ma and Da, still in that poky boxroom, and just thinking about it, not able to see any way of changing it, I sometimes feel like I'm suffocating. Drowning. I don't expect you to know what that feels like, but it makes me angry, Helen, and frustrated, to be stuck and unable to do anything about it. I know, I know," he says quickly, sensing her rebuttal, "I could have stayed in university and got a decent job. And you've no idea how many days and nights I've spent thinking the same thing. But at the time, dropping out seemed like my only option. I couldn't stay on there, not after what I'd gone through."

"Was it really that bad?"

"God! You've no idea." He stares into his pint glass.

"It was awful," he says, and then, in a quiet voice that arouses pity in her, he goes on, "This tutor – I've never known someone who could be so hateful. It started with just the odd snide comment, a put-down in response to a question I'd asked or an opinion I'd offered. I tried to shrug it off, but those kinds of things can be cutting. It got worse and worse, and suddenly I was getting bad grades when I was putting in so much work. It didn't make sense. I knew I was being treated unfairly, but I didn't know what to do about it. So I called to see her, figured the best thing to do was talk it out with her, try to see where she was coming from, reason with her. But the meeting turned into this almighty scene. She starts ranting and screaming at me, making all kinds of absurd accusations, and I'm just sitting there, staring at her, thinking: this woman is off her rocker. And the next thing I know, she's making complaints to the department, saying I'm harassing her, like I'm some kind of fucking stalker. Alleging I'd made lewd suggestions – can you believe it? 'I have a girlfriend,' I told them. 'Why the fuck would I be interested in this woman when I have my Suzy who was ten times as pretty?' The whole thing got so out of control. I felt lost in it. I felt like I was spinning through the mess of bureaucracy I didn't understand. That wasn't what I'd signed up for. All I wanted was my education, to put my head down, do the work, get my degree, you know? Make my parents proud. But all this shit was down on top of me. I couldn't take it. I couldn't face going there – even after the disciplinary committee had finished, and I was exonerated of the allegations she had made. All of it had gone sour. Because the shame of that still sticks to you. My classmates knew about it, all eyeballing me in lecture theatres, no one wanting to be in a study group with me. I felt like a leper. It was too much. So I dropped out."

They are both silenced. The rawness of the emotions he has expressed seems palpable. Helen gazes at his profile. He looks so young to her, with such a fresh innocence about him. How could anyone have made such lurid accusations about him?

In my time, I have known a lot of women who are capable of self-deception, but Helen takes the biscuit. She is constantly having to remould her opinion of Donovan. A convicted housebreaker who reads Homer and Dostoyevsky, a petty thief who arranges flowers. She is assailed on all sides by contradictions. "That's it, anyway," he says with finality. "My pathetic history."

"It's not pathetic," she says softly.

"So what about you?" he asks when she returns with more drinks. "Any crimes and misdemeanours in your past?"

The alcohol has loosened his inhibitions. Hers too, and she gives a good-natured shrug.

"No, I can't imagine there are."

"You make it sound like something shameful."

"No!" He laughs. "You and your husband seem to me to be fine, upstanding citizens."

She hears something mocking in his tone, but laughs it away. "I suppose we are."

"What does your husband . . . William, is it? What does William do?"

"He's a lecturer. Biology."

"Cool."

"I suppose so. Well, I don't really understand it, to tell the truth." She pauses, as if trying to make up her mind whether to go on, and leans towards him and speaks in a low, confidential whisper. "He's been working on a book for the past few years. Pearl fishing in Ireland. You should see the stacks of research he's done. But between you and me, I can't help but feel it's a bit frivolous."

He answers this with a grin and a nod.

"I mean, science is fine. Science is great. But it's not as if he's looking to cure cancer or discover a vaccine against Aids. Pearl fishing is so self-indulgent."

"Very into it, is he?"

"Oh, my God, you've no idea. He's so embedded in that book, obsessed with it, that sometimes . . ."

He waits.

"Well. It's like he doesn't see me, you know? Like I'm not even in the room."

He doesn't say anything to that, just sits and waits. And when she looks up into his intense gaze, does she have any idea of the thoughts that are whirring in his head? His own private yearnings and desires fed by this new information, this hint of weakness, like a chink of light through a door?

"It would be different, I suppose, if we had children."

"I suppose." He turns to her then, trying to swivel on the seat, but there isn't enough room. "How come you don't?"

She shrugs off the question, and excuses herself.

In the ladies', she stares at her reflection in the mirror. The drink has gone to her head, making her feel woozy, but she cannot escape the question he put to her. Why doesn't she have kids? The impertinence of the enquiry, put to her so casually, has struck her like a blow, his insensitivity to the possibility of myriad reasons – some uncomfortable, even unpalatable, a host of private biological facts that he seems to feel entitled to know. She cannot reveal to him that, for a year now, they have been trying to get pregnant. She cannot explain to him what it's like – the panic that nudges her, the tears in the toilet each month that greet her period, the stacking up of what-ifs in her own head, the growing pressure from the unspoken but understood expectations of her parents-in-law. Indeed, her own father has raised his eyebrows more than once at her failure to provide him with a grandchild.

Her reflection stares back, tired and drunk. She is aware of a stabbing regret – she shouldn't have told him about William and his work. That was disloyal. But all she knows is that her head is starting to hurt, the room is spinning, and the noise is building to an unbearable crescendo. She wants to be at home kicking off her shoes and falling into bed.

It is getting late when they leave, but not so late that he

has missed his bus. She is too drunk to drive, and has to get the DART instead.

He offers to walk her to the station and she protests, then staggers against him, suddenly light-headed in the cool night air.

"Whoa!" He steadies her and laughs. "I think I'd better. And besides, I'm in no hurry to get home."

She is drunk – steaming – yet still she is sensitive to this last statement. In the lamplight, his face is cast in shadows and he looks curiously melancholy.

"Keith," she says solemnly, "tell me the truth. How did you get that cut to your eye?"

He sighs, and his hand goes up to it, feeling for it. It is a gesture that seems to her completely natural yet sharply intimate. Touching his pain in front of her.

"My mother gets upset sometimes," he says quietly, staring at his feet as he walks. "Christmas is difficult. Added stress. She got drunk, we had a row, she let go with the back of her hand."

He gives a dismissive shrug, but Helen is shocked into silence.

They walk past the green, past the closed shops, along the quiet avenue lit by intermittent orange lamplight. It is a silent, strange walk. There is an emptiness about the streets – people have already deserted them for Christmas, and it is not yet closing time, the pubs still not relinquishing their hostages. She cannot stop thinking of what he is going home to – all that anger, bitterness and resentment. An unpredictable woman, drunk, grotesque and bawdy. The fear that must engender. The dread of going home.

It occurs to her then – the room above the shop – and

before she has time to change her mind she is reaching into her bag, sifting through the contents, finding her keys. She fumbles to separate them, then thrusts one into his hand.

"There," she says firmly. "It's the key to the shop. There's a room upstairs with a sofa you can sleep on. If there's trouble at home, you can stay there. No, really, I won't listen to a refusal. You know the code for the alarm? Good. Well, I'm not saying you have to stay there, but you've got the key if you need it, just for the Christmas holidays."

He looks down at it, then fixes her with that look of his. The whites of his eyes seem exceptionally clear. "You don't know what this means to me."

His intensity holds her for a moment, then they continue walking. The awkwardness is back with her. It's never far from her mind, yet for a good part of their evening together, they had managed to dispel it with alcohol and talk. But now it is back. She feels it inside her.

"So, it's been good having you working with us," she says as they walk, trying to sound coherent while seeking to reach some finality, a sense of closure. "Have you decided what you'll do next? For work, I mean."

There was something so depressed about him, she told me later, so defeated.

"Not sure. I'll see what's out there."

"If you need a reference, I'd be happy to give you one. Really, you've learned so much over the last few weeks. I'm sure anyone would be only too happy to take you on."

He gives her a look. She sees the unhappiness in it and glances away.

They approach the DART station and it suddenly feels very quiet and bright, illuminated by the white lamps of the station house. She hears the evenness of his breathing and sees the shadows running under his eyes, feels his reluctance.

"Well," she says, unfolding her hands in a gesture of mild surrender, "take care."

There is an awkward pause, both of them unsure how to effect a farewell. Then she leans forward and kisses him hastily on the cheek.

Afterwards she told me that she was not sure why she did that. Usually she does not go in for that sort of thing, and she knew instantly, from the mixture of surprise and confusion on his face, that it was about the last thing he had expected.

A new silence grows up around them and she begins to feel he is never going to walk off and leave her. He seems to be grasping for something to say, and just then a group of people walks past, whooping and screeching with laughter. He shoots them a look, then backs away from her into the shadows. At first, it seems that he is recoiling from her, but then he glances at her and she realises that he is not shrinking away but entreating her to follow.

It was stupid, she told me later, to be drawn in like that. She knew what might come next – she was aware of the risk. But she was overpowered by a greater instinct – that was how she described it – and felt unable to control it.

So she walks towards him slowly, out of the light, and he stands beneath the shadow of a high wall and watches her. There is just enough light for her to see that he is trying to gain control of his emotions. He looks at her solemnly, tears making the whites of his eyes glimmer, and she knows in that one instant exactly what will come next. She can feel the electrical current snapping between them.

"I don't want to think about not seeing you any more." His voice seems to hum with a low intensity. "That's all I think about – those days when I can come in the shop and see you."

"Keith . . ." She gives a tense little laugh.

"It's been there for weeks. I watch you there, working, oblivious to it all. All those flowers, all that scent, and yet nothing in the shop is as beautiful as you."

When she repeated that sentence to me the first time, I almost laughed at its clumsiness. Yet, she didn't see it. Not then. All she saw at that time was the romance, the purity of the sentiment. Even the gift he gave her which she would open later – a little book of sugary love poems, illustrated with photographs of different flowers – she regarded as a thoughtful token of admiration.

But when he says those words, she feels panic.

No. She shakes her head, crossing her arms defensively across her chest. It feels to her as if every muscle in her body is pulled tautly.

"I think about you all the time."

"Keith, please," she says, trying to summon authority into her voice.

Until now, his gaze had been lowered, but when he speaks again he looks at her intently. "Helen, if you only knew. Don't you remember our kiss? I know you felt it too. I think about it constantly. In some ways, it's the only thing that's kept me going. You're the only thing that's kept me going. You're the only reason I've stayed in the rehab programme. If it weren't for you, I'd have dropped out long ago."

Now that sounds to me like a nasty little ploy. Until that moment, as I listened to her story, I had been prepared to give him the benefit of the doubt, making allowance for his florid tone, his clumsy protestation of desire. But this was calculated to get to her conscience. It was a blatant attempt to win her through guilt. But Helen, in her confusion, in her despair, saw none of that.

"Please, Keith," she says again, her voice weak, repressing the sliding panic.

He gives her a look of such unhappiness as he moves towards her. She doesn't step away – the moment when she could have turned back seems to have raced past them. They stare at each other, unable to speak, sensing they are on the verge of something – the brink of a precipice – conscious that a move in any direction will be huge in its consequences. And although she is the elder, although their positions are such that she should be in control, he is dominant suddenly as he reaches for her and draws her to him, turning her so that he is pressing her against the wall. His mouth when he kisses her tastes of apples, something sugary, and for a second she draws away and they assess each other's faces in the half-light. Then he kisses her again, with a new ferocity, the sudden touch of his tongue against hers – a shocking contact – that whips something alive within her depths. A sound rises in her, a moan that makes him hungry. His body is pressing down the length of her, his hands pulling greedily at her clothes, hands that rove, seeking a way in. Their kissing becomes insatiable as their passion rises. She breaks away desperate to breathe, and he lunges at her neck, pressing his head into the nook above her shoulder and her hand rises to hold him there.

It is breathless, rushed, hasty, with a frightening intensity that leaves her speechless. All words have abandoned them – they are strangers to each other, forgetting in that moment who and where they are. There is nothing beyond that moment, nothing but each other, every need within them rising to the touch. They are clumsy, rushed by alcohol and the force of their own desire, and she feels him tugging at the belt on her jeans, releasing her to free up his other hand and pull at the buttons. Then he is pressing her against the wall, one hand firm in the small of her back, the other hand slipping inside her underwear, searching, and she gasps, feeling his fingers enter her, her spine stiffening, then juddering as they move within her, slowly, carefully, leading her with him, bringing her to a rise, and it aches within her – this new obliterating sensation. She can feel the wall at her back, his breath shivering on her neck, but the steadiness of his touch, the confident pressure, holds her somewhere else, transfixed, willing him to continue – they have come this far, there's no point in going back. It is only when he whispers something in her ear that she is pulled back to the present. It is something urgent and muffled, and she finds herself gasping, "What?"

"My belt," he says. "Open my belt," he says tersely, his breath panting round those forced syllables, and it is then – at that moment – that she stumbles over the reality of what she is engaged in. As if she steps out of her body, and becomes a bystander witnessing this act in all its coarseness and vulgarity: the two of them pressed against a wall in a dark alleyway, rubbish strewn among the weeds at their ankles. She has a vision of a used condom left behind them on the pavement.

"Jesus Christ," she says. Then realising his fingers are still inside her, she repeats it louder, "Oh, Jesus Christ," and pushes him away.

"Helen."

But she doesn't look at him, just staggers away, buttoning and belting, her heart thudding in her chest.

"Helen!" he calls after her.

"No," she cries, making it to the steps and running up them. She almost slips, but reaches the turnstile and goes through it to the platform.

It is only when the train comes and she takes a seat at the window that her hammering heart begins to calm, a normal synapse returning. Her hands continue to shake and her face looms large and pale in the darkness of the window. And all the way home, running alongside the hum of the engine, a small voice whines inside her; oh no, oh no, oh no, oh no, building slowly until it is screaming in her head.

PART TWO

11

A few evenings ago, I took it upon myself to walk the strand at Sandymount. It was a fine evening, unseasonably warm for October, a thin sliver of a moon peeking out from the blue sky burning orange with the setting sun. I was not the only one making the most of the weather, and I noticed as I walked that amid the dogs and the armies of middle-aged women in tracksuits with swinging arms and the joggers hooked up to iPods, there was a generous scattering of couples: lovers holding hands or stopping for a passionate embrace far out upon the sands, distance protecting their identity. Heat is sensual, and I couldn't help feeling a little sad, my loneliness and isolation – my singleness – marked by the presence of all that clamouring potency. Not that I have ever held hands with a lover in public – I am not one of the new 'proud' generation: fragments of a repressed childhood have clung to me throughout my adult life. But in the privacy of enclosed spaces I have known days and nights incontinent with desire, when I had no sense of how passion can wear out even a submissive partner.

Let me make it clear that it was my decision to renounce that part of my life after Frankie died. The sexual act without love is too depressing at my age. Oh, I have known many gays who persist in chasing it, cruising well into middle age and beyond, but I cannot help feeling there is a sort of desperate avarice about this that becomes graven in their faces, reflected in their wolfish eyes. I am too old now, too tired and set in my ways, to embark on a new love affair. I also cling to the outmoded, romantic notion that love must be earned, that one must be deserving to receive it, and after what I did to poor Frankie, I have lost any hope of redemption in the years I have left.

And yet it is not an easy thing to do, when still vital, still in working order, to renounce those urges. To turn your back on the contaminant of sex, holding up moral virtue as a flimsy defence against clamouring desire.

I think Helen tried to put it out of her mind, the memory of that night. It was a decision she made, to blot it out, will it away, obliterate it from her thoughts and pretend to herself that it never happened. And, for a while, I think she succeeded.

Christmas came upon her with all its fuss and fury, and then there was the move, which caused her stress and sleepless nights. It had been decided some time that year that William and Helen would take over the upper half of the three-storey red-brick terraced house while his parents moved down to the basement. A swap. Helen was not altogether sure how she felt about it. Until that point, their living arrangements had suited her, despite any initial reservations she might have had about living in such close proximity to her parents-in-law. She liked them, for all their austerity and intellectual snobbery.

They had welcomed her fully into their family, and their withdrawn manner agreed with her, allowing her freedom and space.

But this move brought about doubts that, until then, she had not experienced.

"What about the furniture?" she had asked William, lying awake in bed one night. They had turned onto their sides to face each other, blinking in the darkness, trying to read each other's expression through the shadows. So many of their serious decision-making conversations seemed to take place in the dark and quiet of night, whispering to each other, even though no one was around to hear them.

"We'll change the furniture," he said, in his affable way. "Buy new stuff, our own stuff, if that's what you want."

She loved him for his easy willingness to please her. But she knew that it wasn't as simple as that. There was history in the house, in its solid furniture – in the dark mahogany expanse of the dining table and sideboard, in the brown and green armchairs, the portraits and dark landscapes in oil set firmly in place on the walls. Good, solid furniture – a dresser crowded with china in the kitchen, solid painted units that reached up towards a ceiling stained with the vapours of generations. Bakelite fittings and painted-over wires running the length of the window frames, heavily curtained. It was a good house, a solid house, with potential. But therein lay the problem.

"But if we start tearing down wallpaper and throwing out furniture, won't your mother be offended?" she asked.

"It'll be our house, Helen. Our home. We can do as we like with it," he answered sleepily. "And anyway, it's not

like we're going to radically overhaul the place or anything. I don't think Mum and Dad are going to object to
a lick of paint and a new sofa."

"But what happens if we want to move?" she persisted.

"Why would we?" he asked, smiling. "I thought you
liked living here."

"I do. It's just that . . ."

"Helen, it's a great house in a great location, and we
would never be able to afford it for ourselves. I understand
that you're nervous, but think how lucky we are. Think
how many of our friends would kill for a gift like this.
How generous is it of Mum and Dad to do this for us?
Don't worry about it. Everything'll be fine, you'll see."

Satisfied that he had placated her, he slipped into sleep.
She lay there listening to his breathing. She was not sure
how she felt about his parents' generosity, this act of
charity. She had never been good at accepting it. The
house upstairs was quiet, and she thought of how she felt
about it when she was there, trying to locate in her mind
the exact word to describe it. Deadness. That was it. Even
when the house was full of people, deadness ran alongside
the life. And that was what troubled her.

The move happens over Christmas. In the end, it's pretty
painless, and despite her misgivings Helen even feels a
degree of excitement. The evening they move in, she and
William walk from one room to the next with a glass of
champagne each and marvel at what they now possess.
Their new home. So familiar, yet they find themselves
looking at it with fresh eyes, admiring the high ceilings,

the cornicing, the majesty of the windows and fireplaces, the elegance of the turn of the stairs.

In an act of goodwill to her mother-in-law, Helen prevails upon her to return to her kitchen on Christmas morning and take charge of the lunch – a tradition, Helen knows, that her mother-in-law savours. Miriam takes control of the proceedings, with Helen as commis-chef. Down the hallway, she can hear the men – William and his father, her own father too – their hearty tones, discussing the Christmas morning swim at the Forty Foot. She experiences a sudden trill of joy. This house, full of voices and festive cheer, is her home. All the feelings of insecurity and niggling doubts, as well as the guilt and shame that come over her in waves, like nausea, every time that night creeps into her mind, all seem to have been dispelled.

"Oh, that looks lovely," Miriam says, admiring the plate of smoked salmon that Helen has arranged. "And capers! What a good idea."

She bustles round the kitchen in a whirlwind of activity. Dressed in a shapeless Aran sweater and cord trousers with leather moccasins that are almost falling apart, Miriam has made little concession in her dress for the occasion. Her daughter-in-law has made more of an effort and has donned a loose black jersey dress with a scooped neck, her hair knotted into a loose chignon to show off the necklace William had given her that morning – a pearl pendant hanging from a gold chain. This escapes Miriam's attention. She is a diminutive woman whose pudding-bowl haircut speaks volumes about her belief in practicality rather than vanity. Swaddled in an enormous apron, she floats back and forth, fridge to counter, counter to sink.

Helen watches her set the plates on top of the stove to warm, then peer into the oven at the crisp turkey, basting it with a spoon in quick choppy movements.

"No, not those mats, dear. Use the good ones. They're in the sideboard drawer."

Her tone is brisk with industry, authoritative. This is Helen's kitchen now, but the transition has not yet become apparent to either woman.

"We didn't take to each other straight away," Helen had confided in me once. "It's to be expected, I suppose – her only son, her only child, and there I was, a virtual stranger, swooping into his life, getting all tangled up in it. Part of it had to do with the way it happened so quickly. If she'd been given more time to get used to the idea, I think she'd have been warmer at the start."

I had a picture of her then, a small woman with a beaky face, vast, staring eyes, a chilly smile on her lips as she examined, with scarcely concealed displeasure the girl – a young slip of a thing – with all the dark hair, the carefully controlled passion, and wondered what weapons she had used to ensnare her precious boy so successfully.

In my time, I've had the misfortune to meet the wives of academics. A cool, frigid lot, I'm afraid, every last one an intellectual snob. Not that they've earned the right themselves to such snobbery – a borrowed right, if that – for most of them (and I understand Miriam to be no exception) have accomplished barely anything apart from purloining an academic as a husband.

She's a housewife, William's mum, and an active

member of the community. She bakes apple pies and her own bread, pickles fruit and tends her garden. She is a voracious reader, a member of two book clubs and, at a recent Readers' Day in her local library, sat on a panel with three writers and gave her opinion on an array of books – the only non-author asked to speak! This she considers a tribute to her erudition, but none is as great as the success of her son, who had earned a PhD and now taught at the same university as his father. And into that gulf walked Helen, barely a graduate, with no academic calibre to speak of. Neither of her parents had been to university, and while they were a respectable family who earned a good living, they were lacking in Miriam's eyes, as they had no further education.

"Things changed when Mum got sick," Helen told me. "That was when Miriam came into her own. She's like that. It takes a crisis to bring out the best in her. Of all the people I would have thought I could lean on at that time, I wouldn't have dreamed it would be her, not for a second."

But that was who it was. Helen remembers coming out of the hospital barely an hour after her mother had died. It was a bright December morning, pale sunlight colouring the front of the building, a cold wind booming off her face. It was just beginning to hit her – the knowledge of it. Words pummelling her body – loss, pain, regret, sorrow – like hailstones. An ending she hadn't been fully prepared for. And there, hastening across the car park, she saw Miriam with Norman bringing up the rear at a steadier pace. Her mother-in-law, with her headscarf and voluminous waxed jacket, was coming towards her, her arms outstretched when she was still twenty metres away, her face, her eyes, her lips mouthing the words – "Sorry, I'm so so sorry," she seemed to be saying across that expanse of empty air. And then Helen remembers the impact of Miriam's body as she allowed herself to be gathered up and embraced – its light, sinewy composition, those strong hands kneading away, the strength, the sheer ferocity of her compassion – while Helen gave way to broken syllables, grief's own language.

Christmas lunch passes peacefully – happily, even. There is a moment of awkwardness as William and Helen take their places at either end of the table. Everyone is conscious then of the difference – the changing of the guard. But there is happiness in that room. They talk about the unseasonal heat, the rise in crime, rocketing property prices. Helen notices with pride that her father has scrubbed up for the occasion: his hair is neatly combed, his jaw clean-shaven, and he is sporting the new shirt William gave him. He is listening intently to Norman's advice on selling his house, buying a smaller property and investing the remainder. He smiles and nods politely, uttering affirmative, appreciative monosyllables. Helen's heart heaves a little with sudden love for him. And there is her husband, handsome, kind-hearted, pulling a chair out for his mother, giving her shoulders a quick, supportive squeeze. This day, in its own way, is hard for her, relinquishing her grip on her home, taking a step back – a step away – from them. For all her stoicism, her vulnerability peeps through in the unsteadiness of her

voice as she says, "Right, everyone, dig in." And despite
Norman's bleating, pedantic tones and Miriam's barely
concealed innuendo that maybe next Christmas there will
be a new member of the family, Helen feels genuinely
happy. The turbulence of recent weeks seems wiped away
– chased out by their combined industry and festivity. Her
doubts are drowned out by their collective voices.

Later, she is stacking dishes while her mother-in-law
idles over a box of books that has yet to be unpacked.
When Miriam says, "What's this?", Helen turns and sees
her holding a small book with a red spine and flowers
blooming on the cover. A chocolate-box book of sugary
love poems. All at once she is transported back to that
moment in the alleyway, his face illuminated briefly by the
fluorescent lights of the railway station, his breath hot and
sour on her face, fingers burrowing inside her, and that
book – his gift – burning a hole in her bag.

Her face floods with a rush of blood. Miriam's cool
gaze pins her to the spot.

"Nothing," she says after a moment. "Just some silly
little thing that I got as a present."

She turns back to her task. But her heart beneath the
new pearl pendant is thumping like that of a criminal
fleeing the scene of their crime.

12

William Glass had fallen in love with pearls or pearl fishing when he was thirteen. It was on a fishing trip near Omagh, Co. Tyrone with his father in late spring 1986. That was also the year he was taken out of boarding school and taught at home by his mother for the last few weeks of the summer term while his father applied for a place at a local day school for him. Some of these facts I have gleaned from Helen, some from William. The rest I have had to imagine.

I can picture William as a child – a quiet boy, vague, dreamy, with a rich internal world, few friends and unaware that he should be unhappy about it. A boy who does his homework, is mindful of the trust his parents place in him, aware of the responsibility he has to his education and the perils of wasting it. I can see him mooning around school-yards kicking stones and the moss that grows between the paving slabs, while the other boys run like savages, playing war games, smoking sneaky cigarettes behind walls, placing bets, jeering and teasing, poking each other in the ribs and pointing out the solemn boy wandering about alone, his lips moving, lost in silent conversation with himself. Such a boy is a target, I know. I still remember what it's like. He lacks a hard shell to protect himself, veiled only in his innocence – shifting, unreliable, a soft membrane that leaves him exposed.

William told me once, in one of his wordy diatribes, that the best pearls come from diseased shells. He imparted this piece of information with a kind of unintentional joy, and I could tell that it tickled him, the idea of beauty emerging from that which appears damaged or scarred. I like to think he sees in it an analogy with his own life – the trauma he suffered, the great love, a true passion, that grew out of it.

"He was bullied," Helen told me when I pressed her, sniffing out a reason for his sudden disappearance from school.

"There was a scene," she said vaguely, looking into the distance, so that I could tell she knew what had happened but felt unable to speak about it. A hard scene. Something humiliating. Something devastating. "William's parents were called. The boys in question were expelled, and William might have stayed on. The headmaster, the teachers, made solemn vows to look after him, to make sure that nothing like that ever happened again, but William's father wouldn't have it. He made William pack his things, and they left that day, even though there were only a few weeks of term left. It's something I admire him for – William's dad. Making that decision. Rescuing him like that."

I never went to boarding school – well, there was no need for it – so my first experience of boarding school boys came when I went to the University of Missouri. There, I had the mixed blessing of being pledged to a fraternity – the Gamma Rho chapter – and lived in the frat house with the other boys. For the most part I enjoyed it. Looking back on it now, the things we did seem curious, the customs that were formed, the strict discipline that had to be observed – our own code of honour – and the punishments we issued to each other for our transgressions, at a kangaroo court held once a week.

I never got to "paddle" anyone, although my own backside was reddened often enough. But I noticed that a certain group of brothers – we nicknamed them the Poison Paddlers – took sadistic pleasure in wielding the wooden spoon. This group had gone to boarding school together, and their little clique was glued together with a mutual contempt for anyone who had not been with them, as well as a shared pleasure in cruelty. On one occasion a boy named Tommy Lucey – a persistent offender with an egregious temper whom nobody liked – had been caught yet again stealing another brother's clean shirt. When he stood there with his pants round his ankles, his backside bared for the paddle, biting his lower lip, one of the Poison Paddlers came up with the wicked suggestion that Tommy drop his balls. A vicious idea: he should leave them to dangle, exposed to the slapping of the paddle. That was what they were like, those boarding school boys: one would make a suggestion, shocking in its sadism, and the others would jump in to support it. On another occasion, I came back to the frat house and found two Poison Paddlers conducting a fierce row with a boy called Roger Hamstead, a quiet lad from Pennsylvania who always seemed a little bewildered to have ended up in our fraternity. What they were arguing about, I don't know. I just remember one coming towards me, taking the door handle and telling me menacingly that as this had nothing to do with me I should shove off. As he went to close the door, I asked him what they were going to do to poor old Roger.

"Why, Rube, we're going to corn-hole him," he said, and slammed the door in my face.

They were perverts too, nasty little pederasts.

So when Helen had intimated that William had gone through a difficult scene that was now cloaked in a dark veil of shame and secrecy, my mind spun off in all directions.

The details emerged slowly and I have filled in the gaps myself. It is my prerogative after all – my authorly interpretation of events. I have imagined it quietly, in the dark hours of the night, thinking of the young William dawdling in the playground, his mind spiralling through his own universe. Then the force of hands gripping his arms, intruding upon his daydream, the violence of the tug and the corresponding force of his own resistance, muscles straining, heels digging in, a great lonely "No," expressed on a rising note of fear. A scuffle follows, brief and peremptory. There are three of them, and he is alone. He knows the boys, has been aware of them gathering at the penumbra of his consciousness, forming a pernicious new shadow. They are older than him, with acne crusting their chins and a sprinkling of stubble shadowing their upper lips. He has felt their small eyes on him, the dark interrogative looks they have beamed out to him across the schoolyard, in the long corridors, feeding the fretful suspicion within him as they peered menacingly at him across the distance of the dining hall.

Now they are dragging him into the bicycle shed – a long, low, windowless, concrete structure at the edge of the grounds, bicycles lined up along one wall, dank water pooling in the irregular dips of the floor and a smell of rotting fruit, old socks, the whiff of urine. Another word has emerged: "Please," he says, his voice cracking on a higher note. The shed is dark after the bright sunlight outside and his eyes struggle to adjust. In the gloom, he can make out the form of Andrew Knox, the red glow at the tip of his cigarette, eyes screwing up as he takes a drag, then raking over William's shrinking, stuttering form. Andrew Knox – that is the name I've given him. It seems appropriate somehow to name him after Betjeman's bully. Andrew Knox, with his reputation for violence, enhanced by his stealth – his discernment – for he does not engage in random acts of meanness, no petty scuffles or half-hearted bullying. He saves himself for bigger acts – he plans them. There is discipline, order and intent behind the punishment he delivers. And that is why William feels a cold thump in his heart when he looks at him. He knows that he is not going to get away with a mere kicking and a few slaps round the head. This is serious.

They have pushed him down on his knees, bones cracking against the concrete to send shooting pains up his legs. They have released their grip on him, but he can feel their presence close behind him. One stands watch at the door. There is no escape.

Andrew Knox fixes him with an intent, speculative stare. "William," he begins, his low, rasping voice scraping across the concrete and mingling with the blood roar in William's head. "Bill. Do you mind if I call you Bill? Billy?"

"Please," William says again.

"Billy," Knox continues, his voice so low it is a near-whisper, "what do you do all day, Billy, mooning about the place, hmm? Wandering around, that mouth of yours moving, moving, moving. What is it you're saying, Billy? Who are you talking to?"

"Talks to himself," one of the others pipes up, with a whipcrack of a laugh.

Knox barely acknowledges it and the reverence of silence returns.

"Only mad people talk to themselves. Are you mad, Billy?"

William shakes his head, speechless, his whole body shrinking round a brilliant point of fear.

"Then why the talking? I'm asking you a question, Billy."

"Please, I . . . I just . . ." The thumping underpulse of dread makes him stumble.

"That mouth of yours moving, moving, moving. Such a pretty mouth it is too. Like a girl's. You have a girl's mouth, Billy. Those red lips. Do you wear lipstick?"

There is sniggering behind him. He starts to cry.

"No snivelling, Billy. Only girls snivel."

But he cannot stop. Andrew Knox looks down on him with disgust, then delivers his shocking, dismissive verdict into the silence.

"You are a girl, Billy."

He must have known where it would go then. The dread within him must have shifted in a new direction under that ferocious gaze. But he cannot move, doesn't know how to defend himself. Words have abandoned him.

He has the wrong kind of intelligence. It is no match for this scheming maliciousness.

"And if you're not a girl, what are you?" Knox asks. "Maybe you're a faggot."

William is whimpering now, feeling the warning chill in the air, helpless in the face of the cold glare of Knox's unaccountable hatred.

"Are you a faggot? A poof? Do you like to suck other boys' cocks?"

There is a movement behind him. The other boys are perking up. This is about to get interesting.

"Would you like to suck mine?"

It gives me pain in my heart to think of that scene, a young boy trapped, lonely and sick with fear, on his knees, shaking, those young thugs standing rapt, witnesses to what comes next: Andrew Knox, unzipping his fly and presenting his tumescent organ to William, whose astonished fear has risen to a howl. Everything is stripped down to that one moment, which will harden in his memory, lodge deep within him and stay with him for the rest of his life, a piece of shrapnel that marks the end of his childhood.

And maybe the sight of that small face streaming with tears and snot evoked pity within the bully's heart. Or maybe it was just revulsion. But instead of penetrating that mouth, he lets go all over him, a steady stream of piss hitting the boy in the eyes, washing over his hair, yellow piss caught by the sunlight streaming through the doorway. The boy has to close his mouth to it, swallowing his howls and, for a moment, there is silence, just the dwindling susurration of urine streaming onto concrete.

They are all watching now, the three boys, eyes riveted by the drama, the act of degradation. Even the one who is keeping watch cannot tear his gaze away. And it is his negligence that is their downfall.

A teacher is patrolling for secret smokers when he passes the bicycle shed and sees the boys standing quietly, only the backs of their heads visible. When he goes to investigate, he finds a scene so repellent that for a moment he can only stare, and for that one moment he is, like them, a shocked spectator, watching with helpless fascination, gripped by the appalling act taking place in the shadows.

You may ask how I know all this. How I can be sure of the details. The answer is: I can't. I don't know, I imagine. That is all I can do. Faced with lack of evidence, I must create the details myself and, in one respect, I cannot be sure whether I am hitting the mark or merely attaching my own fanciful notions to another human being. That is the chance I take. It is the chance every writer takes – that reliance on the imagination. I lean heavily on it. It's my job, after all. It's what I do.

Within hours it is all over. It is also all over the school. By the time the wheels of Professor Norman Glass's car come spinning over the asphalt, everyone from the lowliest first-year right up to the head boy – and the entire teaching staff, of course – knows that Andrew Knox had been caught urinating over William Glass in the bicycle shed.

William has showered and changed and has been allowed to sit in the staffroom with a cup of hot chocolate, his wet hair leaving a damp mark on his collar. The window is open and from outside comes laughter, shouting and far-off music. Ordinary school sounds filtering in. Soon the gong will sound for dinner, but William knows he won't be joining the others. His father has been upstairs in the headmaster's office for almost an hour now. He tries not to think about their conversation, the scene described in detail, his father having to listen to the enormity of his son's humiliation. William tries to blot it out of his mind, focusing instead on the noises outside, the heedlessness of those voices, the easy brimming gaiety that seems at once familiar and remote. The hot chocolate cools in his hands and the time ticks past until the door opens and he sees his father. Professor Glass closes the door behind him and looks at his son without a word of greeting. He lets himself sit in a chair next to William and exhales slowly. Silence hovers between them, distinguished by the shouts and laughter outside. William is aware all at once of his father's physicality – his height and his nose, the hair bristling from his ears and nostrils, the sharp lines carved down to the corners of his mouth. He is wearing a suit and seems at that moment to have immense presence, a distinguished power.

"Are you all right, William?" he asks, his voice quiet and barely controlled.

He isn't angry, but William can't tell whether or not his father is ashamed of what has happened. But his own mortification is thumping within him and suddenly it is too much. He begins to weep. Digging his fists into his eyes, he tries to stop but can't. And then he feels a hand on his back. His father keeps it there for a moment, then gives his shoulder a squeeze and stands up. "Get your things, son," he instructs. "We're leaving."

They don't talk in the car on the way home. His father listens to an audio book while William stares miserably out of the window. They don't talk when they get home either. They are constrained by habitual politeness. His mother cries for days, battling valiantly to hide her tears. But he can see them in the pinkness round her nostrils, the discolouring of her eyes. A balled-up tissue seems to reside permanently in one of her hands or up her sleeve, and he has caught her pressing it firmly to her closed eyes. Once or twice he has seen her looking at him inscrutably – a kind of horror lurks behind her eyes and he can tell she is reliving his agony for him over and over again. He knows that she would like nothing better than to hug him, to draw him protectively to her chest, and resents her for it. He is past the age of wanting his mother's help. It becomes almost unbearable for him.

Then, finally, some relief: his father suggests a fishing trip. William suspects that the motive behind it is for them to talk about what happened, but he doesn't care. It is preferable to the agony of his mother's mournful looks and sad stare. So into the car they get, barrelling down the motorway, and his father takes him north, to Co. Tyrone – the river Lagan, which he had fished himself when he was William's age. They settle on the bank at the edge of a meadow. Behind them, buttercups grow like yellow whispers through the long grass, and the river twists and bends in a lazy meander under dipping boughs of apple blossom.

They are alone, with nothing between or around them except the stillness of the air and the sounds of nature.

"You won't go back to that school," his father begins stiffly.

"No."

"You'll have to study with your mother for now. It's too late to get you in somewhere else before the summer holidays."

"I don't mind."

"Well, if you work hard, you'll be all right," he intones gruffly. "I think perhaps you should go to a day school from now on. I'm not sure boarding school's right for you."

William says nothing. He can't help but feel that while his father is doing all this – saying all this – out of a need to protect him and paternal love for him, he is disappointed by the accident. It isn't spoken, isn't uttered out loud, but he feels it. "I suppose not," he answers tonelessly. He closes his eyes and leans back so that the sun falls full on his face.

His father is mustering up for it now: "What happened there, what those boys did to you, was a terrible thing, William. You didn't deserve it. You should never have had to go through it. I'm deeply sorry about the whole thing."

William sits forward, his eyes open now, and turns his head upstream, away from his father's monotone. A man in waders is moving slowly through the water towards them.

"Your mother and I were shocked to learn about it. We didn't know you were experiencing problems – being bullied – at school. You should have told us, William. We might have been able to do something. We might have been able to prevent it."

"I know. I'm sorry," he answers distractedly.

The man in waders lowers an instrument into the water – it looks like a long wooden box – and proceeds to peer into it. His other hand clasps a long rod.

"We haven't talked about it," his father goes on in a hapless way. He is a man with a quick temper, yet there is a sweet, shy side to him – a kind of embarrassed empathy – and it is this side that comes to the fore now. "I would hate to think of you going through this alone. That you felt you couldn't talk to me about it – couldn't confide in me."

The man moves slowly through the water, his gaze never shifting from the sights of that box. The water moves around him in scintillating ripples.

"What's that man doing?"

Professor Glass pauses in his anxious delivery to look up. "He's a pearl fisher," he says. "They're rare nowadays, but I encountered one or two when I was a boy."

"Pearls? In the river Lagan?"

"Oh, yes. There are pearls in lots of freshwater mussels. Not as valuable as those found in oysters, but they're there."

"What's he doing now?" William asks, staring at the fisherman as he stabs at the riverbed with the rod.

"The box has a glass bottom and, through it, he can examine the riverbed. He's looking for mussels. When he finds an open one, he thrusts the rod into it to pluck it from the water."

William listens, aware that he is casting back into his recent past, back to a time when his father's instructional tones opened windows to new worlds. His father had the answer to so many of his questions, but then things changed, became muddied. But now, under the warm sun, the water lapping round them, he is willing to give himself up to the memory of that time, embracing his old man's wisdom.

In so many ways that afternoon was a turning point for William. It closed a door on a painful episode in his past, and opened a new avenue of exploration and discovery. The pearl fisher – Tom was his name – sat with them on the banks, and for a while the three talked. He had been fishing the Lagan for thirty years and in that time he had found a good many pearls. One day in 1973 he had got three good ones. On another expedition in 1967 he had taken a pearl of eighteen grams which fetched forty pounds. William was awed when Tom told him he had once found a shell that contained eight small pearls.

A hip flask was produced and passed around, and on that occasion, Professor Glass allowed his son a swig. William's first taste of alcohol. Another new departure.

Tom talks and talks. He tells them that the real name for the freshwater pearl mussel is Margaritifera – William whispers it to himself, pleased with its exoticism. He learns that the best pearls are to be found in diseased shells; that the magi of ancient Ireland believed that swallowing a pearl brought eternal youth; that to restore a pearl's lustre it must be worn by a woman against her skin. He learns that pearls were once given as gifts to newborn babies, said to guarantee the infant a long life and that for some, pearls symbolise tears and are considered unlucky, especially when worn by brides.

Warmed by the alcohol and the afternoon sun, William basks in the glory of his new knowledge. Something has happened here – something important. He watches his father, silent now, deferring to another's superior knowledge. There is something brave and stoic about his features. His father's face in repose, when he is not aware that he is under surveillance, has a restful calmness about it that he finds reassuring. It returns to him now, in the manner of a long, slow remembering – an old love, an old reliability. He'd like to lean over and touch his father, but theirs has never been a physical relationship. Instead, he just sits there, happy in his proximity to the older man's stoic heart. He sits and listens, and slowly he starts to recover.

13

Helen had no further contact with Donovan until late in January. By then, she had put the incident behind her and had resolved to move on. In fact, she told me, everything in her life seemed to slip nicely into place. The shop was ticking along, she had reached an understanding with Iris – an unspoken truce – and at home they were settling into life in the big house with relatively few interruptions. There had been the odd occasion when Miriam had walked in without knocking or ringing the bell, which had unsettled Helen, but other than that, she had no complaints. So when Donovan had walked into the shop on that brisk, breezy winter morning, she had been clutched by panic, as if something from the past had reached out to grab her. It was not a pleasant feeling.

She was working at the back when she heard the familiar tinkle of the bell over the door, then heard the surprise in Iris's voice, singing through the arc of her "Hello." Helen was well accustomed to the nuances of Iris's tones and heard through the surprise, a hint of frost, a chilly welcome to whoever was present.

Donovan has one of those distinctly recognisable voices,

something faintly melodic about the depth and tone – a textured voice that resonates like an instrument – so when Helen heard his response, quiet and measured though it was, she knew immediately who it was. Her heart fluttered and she tasted bile at the back of her throat. She was aware of sudden perspiration and was struck by indecision. She told me that for a split second she considered bolting out of the back door to avoid him. But she pulled herself together, gathered her resolve, shook her head to settle her hair, then walked purpose-fully into the shop.

She glanced at him, maintaining a steady composure, and greeted him airily. "Hello there, Keith. Happy New Year to you," she said breezily. "What brings you back to Sandymount?"

He mumbled something, and she had to ask him to speak up. His eyes shot to Iris, then flickered back to her and she read in the little semaphore that he wanted to speak to her alone. She chose to ignore this, gambling that it was safer to stay within Iris's earshot if she wanted to avoid any awkward discussion of what had happened that night, and stood there, waiting for his answer. She might even have drummed her fingers on the counter, but all the while she was experiencing little waves of shock. She was struck by how awful he looked, how much he had deteriorated in the few weeks since she'd seen him. He was hunched in his jacket, his shoulders sloping forward. Dark shadows circled his eyes, which seemed smaller and more sunken, rimmed with tiredness. And she noticed the minor skin eruptions round his mouth and chin, an angry little cluster of acne crouched in the corner of his face.

"Are you working around here?" she asked brightly, and he told her that he had a job in the kitchens of the Berkeley Court Hotel. Through the gap in his jacket she could see a white T-shirt stained with a tea-coloured substance, and noticed that a faint smell of disinfectant emanated from him.

The phone rang and Iris answered it, giving him an opportunity to lean forward across the counter and whisper urgently, "I want to talk to you about something. I want to explain . . . to apologise. But not here."

She felt herself colouring, became aware of the tightness of her polo neck. "Really, there's no need."

"Please, Helen. Just meet me for ten minutes, that's all. What time's your lunch at?"

"Honestly, Keith, we have nothing to discuss. This is just silly—"

"I'll wait for you down at the strand," he said, interrupting her. "I'll wait there until half two. If you're not there by then, fine. I won't bother you again. But please, Helen, please come and meet me."

He fixed her with his intense gaze, and she found herself at a loss for what to say. But before Iris had hung up, he was gone.

Throughout the case, Donovan has been portrayed by his defence counsel as a person of below-average intelligence. That, despite his university years, he suffers from learning difficulties. It is in his interest to have the jury think of him as a simpleton. It makes it easier for them to believe that his intent was somehow negated, that his hold on his own mind was not sufficiently strong. I have always believed that Donovan is a shrewd young man who can turn his intelligence towards manipulating people. That is his great gift, I think. He sees a person's weaknesses and knows how to use them to his advantage.

That morning in the shop was a perfect example. On the one hand it would appear that he was offering Helen the power, giving her the opportunity to choose whether she would see him or not. Not that I believe he would have followed through on that – not for an instant. Really, he was exploiting her nature. He knew that she was a woman who collected waifs and strays, and that she was also endowed with a very human characteristic: curiosity. Who wouldn't want to know what he had to say? And there was also the matter of her vanity – something she kept well hidden, but I believe he had spotted it. The possibility of being begged for forgiveness tickled it more than she could ever admit.

For the next couple of hours, Helen debated whether or not to go to the strand. She had made up her mind against it: the weather outside was grim, cold was snapping in the air and there was a hint of rain on the wind. All morning, she thought of Donovan out there, hunched in his jacket on a bench, no scarf, gloves or hat, waiting for her, hope wilting as the hours ticked by. The only sensible thing to do, she told herself, was to stay away. But then, as Iris packed herself into her coat to run across to the Spar for sandwiches, Helen heard herself telling her not to get her anything, that she was going to pop out for lunch before three.

When I have pressed her on this point, she has always made some remark about the force of her upbringing coming through, as though her reason for meeting him was to guard against rudeness – that it would have been impolite to stand him up. I am hard pressed to believe her, preferring to think it was that shiver of curiosity, the 'what if' that propelled her into the elements that January afternoon.

The strand was almost deserted, the tide having receded towards the horizon, leaving the sand wet, cold and rippled. Apart from a few hardened dog walkers, no one was around, and Helen couldn't help feeling relieved about this. The last thing she needed was to be spotted by some officious neighbour or friend of her mother or, worse, her mother-in-law. She found him easily enough. He was sitting on the steps in front of the Martello Tower, looking at the clouds moving across a pewter sky. He glanced up at her as she approached him and nodded a hello, then turned back to gaze mournfully at the beach. She stood there for a moment, clutching her sleeves and banging her hands against her sides, feeling like a school-girl, unsure of what to do. He wasn't budging, so in the end she gathered her coat about her and took a seat next to him.

"Thank you," he began in a solemn tone. "I wasn't sure if you'd come or not. I was hoping you would, but I was afraid you'd decide not to."

"I needed some fresh air," she offered casually, knowing he would see right through her flimsy excuse. "What did you want to speak to me about?" she asked briskly, adopting a businesslike manner, needing to assert her authority.

He squirmed a bit in his jacket, kicking at a stone with the toe of his runner, and he seemed younger than she had remembered, lost and defenceless, inadequately dressed for the cold.

"What happened between us," he began hesitantly, the colour shooting up through his neck and face, "I haven't been able to stop thinking about it."

"Well, you should," she said, surprising herself with a teacherly voice. "I know I have."

"I wish I'd never done it," he said with a vehemence that disappointed her. "It was stupid of me. Stupid of *us*. I don't know what got into us. Christmas, huh? All that fuckin' mistletoe!" He groaned and rolled his eyes, trying to turn it into a joke. "All that guff I said – about you being the most beautiful thing in the shop." He grinned, shaking his head, but she could tell he felt awkward.

"They were just words," she offered. "I didn't take them seriously."

"But what about the other thing?" he continued in a rush. "What we did together. I mean, Jesus, imagine someone had come along. Imagine if someone had caught us – seen us doing that to each other. Ha!"

Until that point she had only seen the harm – the inappropriateness – of what they had done. It had not occurred to her that it had been ridiculous. The difference in their ages was suddenly apparent to her, and the difference in their situations – the great gulf between them. Throwing the gob on the boss. Feeling her up in some alleyway. A married woman at that. That was how his friends would have put it. And, no doubt, he had told them. No doubt they'd had a good laugh about it down the pub. She was overwhelmed by shame and embarrassment. "Well, if that's all . . ." she said, making to get up, but he put out a hand to restrain her and nerves danced in her knee where he laid it.

"No. What I meant to say is that I'm sorry I embarrassed you like that. I'm sorry for putting you in that situation. After all you'd done for me. I should have remembered all of that, instead of letting my – you know – feelings get in the way."

His words came stumbling, limping out, as though saying it hurt. He squirmed as he spoke, and his gaucheness was touching. Redeeming – clarifying. It was not that he hadn't wanted to kiss her, to touch her, it was that he shouldn't have acted upon his desire. This, despite her better judgement, encouraged her enormously.

"Well, it's all right," she said.

He looked at her for a long moment. "It won't happen again."

She bridled. "Of course it won't happen again," she told him. "Now, if there's nothing more . . ."

"I want to come back and work for you," he blurted out, the words coming in a gust.

"That's impossible."

"Please, Helen."

"No."

"Just consider it."

"But there isn't enough work," she said desperately, "and you already have a job."

"Washing dishes? I can't stand it. I'm miserable there. All I do for hours on end is hose down pots, scouring away the crap that's crusting on the inside. I stand in a grubby corner with a sink full of dishes, not a lick of natural light anywhere, the clatter going through my brain non-stop, day in, day out. And don't even get me started on the pricks I have to put up with in that kitchen, the egos that waltz around as if they're fucking king pin and I'm nothing. I get home in the evening and I reek of disinfectant. I can smell it on myself. And my hands stink from the rubber gloves. And when I close my eyes, all I can see is the greasy water in that sink, bits of food floating in it."

Something in his voice made her think he was about to cry. He gazed at her unhappily, eyes watery and red, and she paused, uncertain what to say. She was assailed by a sense of impending doom – and mistook it for Donovan's rather than her own. She thought about the scars on his wrists – those sinister white marks. Some people fall if they're not helped in time. If they're not helped at all, some people slip into darkness.

"Well . . ." She wavered.

Donovan, master of emotional manipulation that he is, saw her indecision and seized upon it. "It doesn't have to be full-time or anything. Just a couple of days a week, like before, and maybe more during busy periods. And who knows? In a few months, if you think I'm up to scratch, maybe you could take me on full-time. Iris is getting on a bit, after all, and she might be thinking about retirement, and I know the ropes. Anything I don't know, I could learn. You could teach me."

He had it all thought out.

Helen was taken aback. She had an uneasy sense of tipping towards the unknown, yet he had touched something old and remembered within her – nostalgia for her youth, when helping her fellow man had been a vocation. More than that, I think what he really touched on was the latent guilt that lay inside her all the time, like an almost inaudible bass to the comfortable melody of her middle-class life. There was something about Helen that always felt she didn't deserve all she had, you see. Part of her couldn't believe her luck. Her need to give something back had been unexpressed for a while, waiting for some opportunist like Donovan to take advantage of it.

He smiled at her then, a curious smile, curious in its rarity. His eyes seemed to soften, all the wariness that swam in them seeping away, leaving an open, guileless expression. I think that smile got to Helen – its innocence appealed to her maternal side. And so, on that cold January morning, staring out across the sandy plain to the spit of land jutting into the sea, the striped towers coughing clouds into the air, the cranes standing firm against the wind – land flattened beneath a weight of industrial purpose – she felt herself waver.

"And I promise, no more fumbling down dark alleyways," he added jokingly. "No more puffing and panting in the shadows!"

Suddenly she was snatched back into the memory of that night in all its squalid detail. If anything, it seemed to have grown, jumping up to assault her – the roughness of his face against her skin, the heat of his breath on her neck, and those busy fingers, reaching for her, searching her out. She gave an involuntary shudder, as if she was trying to shrug off something dead that clung to her. "No," she said quickly, getting to her feet, then repeating the word over and over. "No, no, no. Absolutely not. It's out of the question."

He hastened to stand up and she noticed then the difference in their heights. He stood only a couple of inches taller than her, but with the wind billowing out his jacket, she had the impression that he was larger than himself. She felt suddenly very small.

"You're making a mistake, Helen," he said gravely, a tone she wouldn't have thought him capable of, a tone he seemed too young for.

"I'm not. I don't want to see you again. Now please, leave me alone."

She couldn't bring herself to look him in the eye as she said that, and turned her back on him, moving briskly against the wind. All the way back along the strand, she felt him watching her. She had to push down the temptation to turn and look, but she knew that if she did, she would see him, hands in his pockets, hair blown about by the wind, watching her all the time, his face inscrutable, as she hurried away from him, breaking into a run.

14

When it happened, it was unexpected. That was what William told me. Despite their planning and trying, their repeated efforts and the thinly veiled despair when nothing resulted, in the dying days of 2005, when Helen discovered she was pregnant, it was as surprising to him as snow in June. And how joyful the news was! It seemed to draw him to her, the little packet of cells spinning through the innermost pleats of her body, his progeny, his child. He found he couldn't bear to be apart from her. But, as is the way of these things, it also happened that, late in 2005, William received a small grant from the university to conduct further research into his book on freshwater pearl fishing. Part of it was comparative and necessitated a trip to Scotland, where the activity was more common than it was in Ireland. He put it off for as long as he could, but eventually, in January, he reluctantly boarded a plane for Glasgow.

During those two weeks of research and interviews, those long hours of poring over books in shadowy corners of libraries, he thought of Helen and the life within her. The night before he had left for his trip, they had lain in their bed and she had held his head to her breast and whispered to him, "If it's a girl, I want her to be called Regina." Her voice was firm, but he felt the emotion she was trying to control. Regina – his daughter. It thrilled him to think of her. He said the name to himself over and over. Never in his life had he imagined a daughter of that name. And naming his child after the grandmother she would never meet spoke to his own sense of history. A lineage there – an inheritance. The proud bonds of the past. A recognition of that German blood.

"And what if it's a boy?" he had asked. She had clasped his head closer and said, "Then you can decide."

For the two weeks he was away, he plagued her with text messages of suggested names, each more ludicrous than the last. "How about Norbert?" he asked. "Or Sigmund? What about Gunther?"

And her replies would come: "I don't mind. I'm happy if you're happy."

She had read aloud one day, from one of the books they had bought in that first flurry of excitement, that the embryo was now the size of a peanut, and he had looked at her belly and addressed it: "Hey there, Peanut!" The name had stuck. In one of his calls to her from the bland and lonely Glaswegian hotel room, he had heard the ring of her laughter as she said, "You know, we're going to end up naming this poor child Peanut!" and he felt the connection that stretched between them through the ether.

They always made the effort to meet each other at the airport, despite the traffic, the distance and the waiting around. It seemed to effect a homecoming more successfully.

And there was a certain excitement in the anticipation, knowing that a reunion was about to take place, a gathering up into a warm embrace, the comfort of renewing the familiarity between them. But on that occasion Helen was unable to make the run to the airport because she was involved in a concert. For some years she had been a soprano in the RTÉ symphony choir – an honour, albeit an unpaid one – and on that night in January, they were performing Beethoven's Ninth Symphony in the National Concert Hall. William agreed to go directly there. The reunion would have to be postponed.

At the Concert Hall, Christmas lingers. It is there in the massive, fully lit tree standing guard outside, and as William steps in out of the cold, still clutching his small suitcase, his laptop bag slung over his shoulder, he feels it in the weight of celebration that seems to hang in the clamouring lobby. The entrance hall is packed and he has to fight his way to the cloakroom. Conversation all around him is at a roar and he has to push through politely but insistently. Helen is on the stairs with her father. He sees her before she catches sight of him, and he pauses a moment to take in the deep velvet of her black dress, the scoop neck that shows off the creamy pallor of her *décolleté*. She has swept her hair off her neck and pinned it into a neat chignon; even at a distance, he can see the pearl pendant dipping towards her breasts. She is creating a little fuss around her father, her face animated, hands fluttering. When she spots William, she abandons her father and skips down the stairs towards him. On reaching him she kisses him and rewards him with a beaming smile, then takes his hand and leads him up the stairs. Her skittishness adds to the celebratory mood and he feels drawn in by it, his fatigue and travel weariness washed away in the warmth of conviviality.

"God, I'm in such a panic," she confesses. "I'm going to have to leave you here with Dad and go backstage. We're supposed to be lining up, ready to march in. People are taking their seats."

"Calm down." He smiles. "You'll be fine."

"And I haven't even had a chance to ask you how your trip was!" she wails.

"I'll tell you about it later."

He touches a hand briefly to her belly and whispers, "How's Peanut?"

She smiles, blushes, and reaches for his hand, giving it an answering squeeze. "Peanut is doing fine."

They prefer to save their talk for when they can look at each other's faces, when they are without the distraction of other people and the roar of conversation around them. She kisses him again, reaches for her father and kisses him too, then disappears into the crowd.

"Did you know, William," Tony begins in the slow, ponderous tone he uses for all his anecdotes, "that Beethoven was almost entirely deaf when he composed the Ode to Joy? And that before its première in 1824 there were only two rehearsals? The choir had difficulty singing the music and begged him to take the high notes down. Even the contralto soloist pleaded with him for changes. But of course he refused, with the famous rebuff, 'What care I when the music possesses me!'"

The bell sounds and they start to move amid a shuffling cluster of others towards the doors. Is William aware yet, I wonder, of a familiar face in the crowd? Helen has told me that it was after the concert they met him, but I wonder, does he catch a glimpse of it as he walks his father-in-law into the auditorium, his hand pressing on Tony's back, guiding him to his seat as his father-in-law explains how at the end of the first performance of his Ninth Symphony, Beethoven was so deaf that the soloist had to turn him so that he could see the audience's reaction? He was unable to hear their applause. Do his eyes graze over that face, barely registering it apart from a switch tripping in his memory, alerting him to something unexpected? Yet he is too tired, too focused on reaching his seat to interpret its meaning.

He watches the choir emerge and take their seats. He knows she can see him, knows that she is not permitted to wave or acknowledge him, but he waves nonetheless and thinks he detects a smile. His father-in-law, whose eyesight is failing, asks him to point out which one his daughter is.

The lights dim and the music begins, and in the darkness, William is lulled by the music and the warmth. The first movement passes quickly and pleasurably. Tony does not want to get out of his seat during the interval, and William is happy to remain there, listening to the older man's rambling talk of Vienna in the nineteenth century, when Beethoven lived there. So it is not until the concert is over, not until the applause has died away and the musicians have left the stage, abandoning their instruments, the choir filing out, that the meeting can take place.

Now William is tired. Weary with travelling and from two weeks of continuous investigation, all he wants is to gather up his wife and his bags and head for home. His father-in-law's monologue is starting to grate on him, and the roar of conversation after the music presses against his temples. A throbbing has started behind his eyes and he wonders if he is catching a cold. They move towards the bar, where the choir are greeting their families and friends. His eyes search her out, and he experiences a little lift in his spirits when he sees her, as he always does, and already he is thinking of the moment when they will be at home in the kitchen, his bags dumped in the hall, and he can take her in his arms to hold her.

But when she steps forwards, Helen looks excited. Her face is busy with animation and she wants to talk. The concert went well, their performance has been praised, and she wants to discuss it, seeking reassurance of their success. William realises she needs to share it with him – her triumph, the culmination of all the rehearsals, her hard work – but he is also aware of the ache in his lower back.

"Come with me," she urges him, grabbing his elbow. "There are people you have to meet."

He smiles and congratulates the women she introduces him to. They wear black, beam happily about their performance, make disparaging remarks about minuscule errors that have escaped the audience's notice. They share anecdotes about the choirmaster and the conductor and he joins in the laughter, when all he wants to do is take her aside and say, "Let's get out of here." But then he remembers that they love each other, and how important this night is to her, and admires for the millionth time the way her face lights up when she is excited. And she *is* excited – she is ecstatic – and when she smiles at him over the heads of her fellow choristers, he feels the privacy of that smile, its exclusivity, a smile that is just for him, and regrets his churlishness. It is Friday evening, and they will have all weekend together to enjoy the rapture of their reunion.

"Oh, Maxine," Helen says, and reaches across to embrace a woman with red hair and heavy-lashed brown eyes, "I want you to meet my husband, William."

As he shakes hands with her and praises the performance, he is vaguely aware of a man hovering at the periphery of his vision, waiting for something – for someone. It is only when Maxine turns and gestures towards him that he realises who it is.

"This is my husband. Eric, come and say hello to Helen and William."

He is a small, grey-haired man, with a tanned complexion that highlights the aqua-blue of his eyes. An unmistakably handsome man, dressed in the carefully casual but expensive clothes of an advertising executive or a web designer – a pink open-necked crisp shirt beneath a navy blazer, with chinos. William's eyes travel down to the tasselled loafers and he draws in his breath.

Eric is kissing Helen's cheek, then shaking hands with her father. He has an easy smile – his face seems predisposed to warmth – and when he shakes William's hand, William feels the firmness of the man's grip, is held hostage by the interrogative blue beam of his eyes.

"William," he says on a rising note of speculation. "Have we met before?"

"No." This emerges tersely, and he attempts to cover it up with a bashful smile. "I don't think so."

"Are you sure? You look very familiar. Did you go to UCD by any chance?"

"Trinity."

"Ah. And what school were you at?"

"Belvedere College."

"That's not it, then."

They stand about for a minute. Then Eric smiles again. "It'll come to me, don't worry."

"Probably in the middle of the night," Maxine adds. "He's always doing this, waking up in the middle of the night, suddenly recalling something that's been lost in the back of his mind that day!"

They laugh, and Eric shrugs helplessly.

"Eric, Helen is the one I was telling you about – the florist," Maxine explains.

"Oh, yes. Fantastic."

"Sorry, Helen," Maxine confides in a manner that is anything but apologetic. "He'll be plaguing you now."

"I'm afraid so," her husband adds with that smile of his. "If you'll let me, I'm going to pick your brains."

"Oh?" Helen's cheeks have pinked. She looks flattered to be called upon for her expertise.

Maxine and Eric explain in the manner of a married couple, with overlapping sentences, filling in for each other's pauses. Eric works for RTÉ. He is a props buyer. Not an advertiser or a web designer after all. His job is to source the props needed for dramas and TV serials. William had never dreamed such a job existed.

". . . and I'm working on something at the moment – a

drama – which has quite a serious degree of botany in it. Now, Maxine will vouch for the fact that when it comes to gardening, I'm clueless."

"Clueless," Maxine echoes.

"So the damn script has me baffled. I need someone who has an idea of the difference between a lupin and a tulip, because I haven't."

William watches the exchange silently. Helen is nodding and laughing, enjoying the attention. And Eric, suave, charming, is drawing her into his web. Even with the grey hair, he hasn't changed. Twenty years have passed, but William would know him anywhere. Some faces you can never forget, no matter how much you want to.

It is almost midnight by the time they arrive home and pour into their kitchen, filling the room with talk, a burst of activity. Outside, the January air is cold, a layer of frost forming on the window panes, but inside it is warm and full of familiarity – the lingering odours of suppers shared, the circle of crumbs round the toaster, the library of cookery books lined up on the counter. They pull high stools up to the breakfast bar and Helen makes tea and toasted sandwiches. He hasn't eaten since lunchtime and devours them with delight. Then they look each other in the eye and talk.

He tells her about his trip, the beauty of the Scottish highlands, the cold. He tells her of the jewellers he met and the dinner party he had been invited to where he met an American geologist whose interest was in diamonds although he was branching out into pearls. She tells him of her decision to get a home help for her father and the gym she has coerced him into joining. She uses humour and comedy to describe the shopping expedition to buy her father's gym gear and William is reminded of when they first met and she captivated him with her easy vivacity. They are elated by their reunion, talking rapidly, anxious not to let any silences creep in. There is a sort of frenzy to this kind of talk, as if they both need to assert their personalities – their roles within the relationship – and restore the equilibrium between them.

And, although neither says it, they are relieved. The little nick of uncertainty that hovered over them in those weeks before Christmas seems to have lifted. His trip away, their reunion, this frenzied talk have chased away that uncertainty. There is magic about this reunion – something untainted and pure in its emotion, their simple need to connect with one another. Perhaps that is why she doesn't tell him about the letter she received that week – the anxiety it brought with it. And perhaps, too, it is why he doesn't tell her that he knows Eric. Or, at least, that he did once, all those years ago. He doesn't want to bring up that time again – not now, when he feels washed clean with pure joy. And not now there is the new thing between them. Helen's news, imparted just before William left. The baby. It has taken him the full two weeks to absorb the idea properly. And now, in the comfort of their home, he sees all that is familiar about her as if it is new, too, as though he is seeing her for the first time, when he started to fall in love with her. He gets up from his seat, goes to stand by her chair, puts his arms round her and protectively kisses the top of her head. With a sigh she presses her face to his shirt and loops her arms round his waist. "I've missed you," she tells him, eyebrows puckering briefly with the earnestness of what she wishes to express.

"I missed you too."

15

Dear Helen,

I had to write. No matter what happens in the future, I couldn't leave things the way we did, not after all you've done for me. I've thought a lot about it. It's been hard to think about anything else, to be honest. I've been sitting here for the last hour mulling it over in my head, and I've reached the conclusion that the best thing to do is to write to you. Let you know that I understand why you made your decision.

That day on the strand, you told me it was impossible for you to take me back on. And I understand why you think that. But Helen, nothing is impossible. I know that now. You said that there wasn't enough work for me, but your eyes were saying something different. Your eyes were telling me the real reason. It's because of what happened between us that night before Christmas. We needn't pretend otherwise. I tried telling you I regretted it, that it wouldn't happen again, but you still looked at me with those eyes. You didn't believe me. I can't blame you for that. Who would trust the word of a thief? But the thing is, Helen,

I thought you did trust me. I believe you did once. Remember how we used to talk and laugh together? In the shop alone, when Iris would go for lunch, remember all those great chats we had? You trusted me then – I know you did. And I trusted you. I abused that trust, I know. I wanted to say that – to hold my hands up and claim that as my responsibility, my mistake. Not yours. I messed up, Helen. You showed your faith in me by giving me a job, and I threw it back in your face. Stupid!

If you only knew, Helen, how much I have agonised over what I did – the nights I spend lying on my bed, staring up at the ceiling, kicking myself for that one act of recklessness. I've relived the moment over and over again, each time playing it out different-ly, wishing I hadn't gone for a drink that night, wishing I hadn't walked you to the DART station, wishing I hadn't pulled you back into the shadows with me, and the rest. But all my imaginings can't turn back time. All I can do is say that I'm sorry. And say, too, that I wouldn't have done it had I not had a few drinks in me. We both of us had way too much to drink. So, when you looked at me in the half-light that night, I thought your eyes were telling me something different. I misread the signs. Well . . . it's hard for me to write this, but I think you know what I mean.

And I never even had a chance to ask you about Christmas! Did you like your present? I spent an hour in Eason's agonising over it, trying to find the right book for you. And I have to admit that, before I wrapped it, I read each poem through, looked at each picture, and imagined what you would think when you were reading it or looking at it. Daft, huh? But I think I got the right one, didn't I? And I don't mind about you not getting me anything. You've already given me so much. And hey, next year you can get me something! We can take it in turns! Did William like his present? And don't worry, by the way, about what you told me in Ryan's – about how you think his work is pointless, about how you think he doesn't see you sometimes. I won't say it to anyone. It can be our secret, Helen.

I want you to know that I'm here for you if you need me – and I don't just mean work. If you need to talk, is what I really mean. I'm a good listener. You were the one who pointed that out to me! And I'm always here to listen to you. In fact, I'm very close. I have a new job now – it's no better than the last one but at least it's nearer to you. I can take comfort from that, anyway. Just knowing I'm not far away from you. Those months with you were the best of my life. I think about them all the time. My mam says I live in my head. Well, that's what happens when you do time, I suppose. But these days the world I live in is full of flowers, full of beauty. In my head I'm back in the shop with you.

There's music on the radio as I write this letter, Sinéad O'Connor singing 'Gloomy Sunday'. But I'm not gloomy, Helen. Not with all this richness in my memory, in my imagination. Somehow I know that this is not the end of things between us. I didn't feel an ending when you left me there on the strand. The way *you walked off that day, pulling your coat round you – not even a smile for me! No kiss on the cheek that day. I know why you did that, Helen, and I want you to know that I understand. You had no idea that you were hurting me, and I forgive you.*

We will see each other soon, and I look forward to that. I'm waiting for that. I'll never stop waiting for that.

Yours,
Keith

16

My sense of failure never quite left me in the years after the critics turned on me and all my plays dried up. At first I blamed Frankie, then Carmela, then the country in which I was living against my will. I lashed out at everything around me, yet refused to look at myself. The savagery of the critics and the early closing of plays brought about a depression within me that was hard to shake off. Restlessness took hold of me, an inability to sit quietly in my study and cut myself off from all but my own inner world. Suddenly that world was porous, and the outside world leaked in. I tried to plug holes with artificial stimulants, but nothing would stop it. And still the reviews kept coming. I must have lived through a decade of bad press. It was vengeful, I felt, and it shattered me. One critic went so far as to announce that my career was over. There were a lot of drinks taken that day, I can tell you.

Everyone needs praise and encouragement. We all need a little ego-stroking, some at our achievements, to prevent us feeling morose. And I think that was why Helen took to

Eric so quickly and so readily. When he spoke of picking her brain, she was flattered, then promptly forgot about it.

So it is with surprise that she looks up from her work the following Tuesday morning and sees him closing the door behind him, fixing her with his easy smile, a long, speculative "Hi," as he approaches the counter in a haze of goodwill.

"Hi," she answers.

"This isn't a bad time, is it?"

"No. Actually it's good – we're pretty quiet, as you can see."

He gazes around him, scratching his head in a bewildered fashion; the gesture is somehow endearing. "Wow. This is some set-up," he says admiringly.

"Thanks."

"All these flowers – Christ, I wouldn't know what most of them are!"

His eyes are alert, lively, intelligent, and his hair – Helen always notices hair – although grey, is exceptionally thick and well maintained. An expensive cut. A man in his late thirties, she imagines.

"What are these?"

"Snapdragons."

He laughs. "They look far too benign for such a fearsome name!"

She smiles in agreement, watching him lean forward to sniff at them, putting out his free hand to steady the bloom in front of him.

"And the scent in here. Gorgeous."

His other hand holds a mobile phone – something chrome and sleek with a lambent blue touchpad.

"I suppose you get used to the scent – inured to it after a time."

"No," she says, coming out from behind the counter and joining him, pushing a strand of hair behind her ear. "It's the first thing that hits me every morning when I walk through the door. Your sense of smell becomes more developed rather than numbed when you work in this business."

"So if I blindfolded you and held a flower to your nose, you could tell me what it was?"

She has a sudden image of him tying her up, taping her mouth and securing her wrists to the bedposts. A shocking image, which she tries to shake by taking a swipe at the errant strand of hair which keeps falling over her face. "I suppose so."

"The Pepsi Challenge?" He laughs, and she joins in.

He is easy company, with a ready charm. His presence in the shop brings a kind of warmth. He is breezy and frank. Physical, too. She notices this about him – a lack of awkwardness that is not grace, but confidence. Not that he swaggers, just that he is comfortable enough in his own skin to walk the length of the shop and back, to pause and examine the blooms, to reach out and touch them, testing them between his fingers. He is also not averse to touching her. She feels his hand on her elbow when he wants to emphasise a point. A leaf is sticking to her sleeve, which he reaches across and picks off without mentioning it. It doesn't bother her. Rather, it puts her at ease.

When he catches sight of Iris appraising him furtively –

she is intimidated by good-looking men, Helen tells me, a sort of girlish shyness comes over her – he strides across to her with his hand outstretched, his face and mouth already working through an introduction. He is a gatherer, someone who envelops people in the warmth of his personality. Iris's face relaxes into pleasure.

"So the thing is, Helen," he says matter-of-factly, "I've been given this script for a TV drama and it's full of flowers. Now, as I said, I'm no expert. Daffs, roses, lilies, tulips – that's about where my knowledge starts and ends. But the thing is full of amaryllis, gerbera and solidago, and I'm completely lost." He raises his palms in a gesture of surrender, still clutching his mobile phone. "Any chance you could help me out?" He tilts his head to one side as he asks, like a child. It is an attitude I imagine he uses regularly – on women and men alike – and I imagine it is, for the most part, successful.

She smiles at him, a closed-lips smile, and looks up at him from beneath lowered lids. A flirtatious exchange. Then she tells him to give her the script, and they begin.

For an hour she walks him through the flowers, pointing them out to him, drawing them out of their buckets so that he can examine them. She advises him on cost and availability and he taps it all into his PDA, nodding continuously. She takes out books from behind the counter and they leaf through them together. He seems genuinely interested and eager to learn. She is impressed by how attentively he listens, hanging on her every word, and by how seductive it is to convey knowledge. It is exciting to have something to impart that is utterly strange to another person. And such a handsome person too. But they are both married – they have met each other's spouse. There is no question of anything untoward happening. He is flirtatious by nature – he made eyes at Iris, for God's sake! All of these things she tells herself calmly. So at the end, when he has finished thanking her for her time and patience, then suggests, as it is nearly lunchtime, that he buys her lunch by way of thanks, well, what harm is there? she reasons.

The restaurant is doing good business and they have to wait for a table to become free. They sit for a few moments silently perusing the menu. When the waitress comes, he orders wine, consulting her merely with a desultory raising of his eyebrows.

"Why not?" she says.

"Good girl. What's the point of being your own boss if you can't have a sneaky drink at lunchtime? That's my philosophy."

Good girl. That riles her a bit, but she soon forgets it.

His mobile has been ringing throughout the morning, each call greeted with jocularity, a stream of jokes and innuendo. She envies him a little – the busy life he has, the crowded social scene. How rewarding it must feel to be so in demand, so needed. At times Helen feels a certain sense of exclusion, as if she is living her life in a different decade from her peers, not privy to the complex and demanding world of twenty-four-hour availability, business lunches, power naps, MBAs, 360-degree assessments, travel-club points. But as he switches off his phone – which flatters her – he says with a sigh of mock weariness, "God, I envy you, working away in your cosy little shop, no one bothering you at the end of a phone. I hear this thing in my sleep!"

"Well, it's not all roses, if you'll excuse the phrase. It's a funny old business – it pitches between boredom and utter panic."

"You can't have it all, I suppose."

He pours the wine and they pause to taste it.

"So," she begins, "what's the most interesting thing you've ever had to source?"

They lean their arms on the table and he chews his lip, thinking. "A dessert, would you believe? For a drama set in the nineteenth century. It consisted of a ball of rice, about the size of a human head, with a cream centre and coated with chocolate." He leans forward and whispers regretfully, "They called it Nigger's Head. Can you fathom that?"

She gasps, and he nods vigorously in agreement. "I know. Shocking, isn't it?"

"And it was a well-known dish?"

"Apparently. And do you know what's even worse?"

She shrugs.

"When I told the story over dinner once, my mother was there, and out of all of us she was unfazed. In fact, she piped up that when she was a girl, her mother used to make something similar, about the size of a snowball, and they called it Nigger's Kiss!"

"Oh, my God."

"Can you imagine my embarrassment? My own mother, God rest her, coming out with this very politically incorrect anecdote, and delivering it in her own inimitable deadpan style. Jesus!"

Over seared scallops, they talk about parents, and she finds herself telling him about her mother, how every morning she had risen at dawn, drunk a cup of instant coffee, then set about cleaning the house. "Straightening the place up, she used to call it. We would be lying in bed while she was shaking out rugs, working her way through the living room and dining room with a duster, then wiping down the kitchen surfaces with a J-cloth and getting breakfast and lunch ready. By the time we were stirring, she had already left the house. And I never realised it," she tells him. "All those years, I took it for granted that I'd come downstairs in the morning to a clean house, my breakfast and lunch all laid out."

It wasn't until her mother had died that all of this had flooded back. It seemed to swamp her, along with an overpowering awareness of her mother's physicality – the compactness of her flesh in smart suits and dresses, neat, sensible shoes. There was something sensuous and powdery about her – sweetness. And her scent. Months after her death, Helen had been shopping in town, browsing through a rail of clothes, when she recognised L'Air du Temps, the scent her mother had worn, on a woman standing near her. Helen had burst into tears. "It was too much. Too familiar," she tells him.

He knows. He understands. His own father had died while he was still in his teens, and he had been tortured by the well-meant platitudes people trot out at such a time: "He's gone to a better place"; "He was too good for this world"; "He'll never be forgotten"; "He's up there now looking out for us all." They had made him want to howl with fury. "You must deal with it a lot in your line of work," he says. "Grief. People buying wreaths for funerals."

"Yes."

As they finish their coffee and he asks for the bill, a group of teenage girls wafts into the restaurant and takes seats by the window. They clamour with noise and barely contained excitement. For a moment, Helen and Eric gaze at them.

"Who are these girls?" he asks, amused. "I see them all over the place these days – a new breed. They gather in packs and hang around coffee shops and restaurants, sipping smoothies and talking loudly, saying 'Oh, my God,' and playing voice-messages on speaker-phone so we all have to hear." There is a kind of jaded exasperation in his tone but she can tell that his sexual interest is piqued by the girls, with their glitter belts, gold lamé handbags and clear skin, the sunglasses perched on their heads.

"They'll be working with you in RTÉ soon," she teases.

"Oh, God." He groans. "When we were at school, there were Goths and Cureheads. There was personality. Not this blandness."

"Or blondeness."

"Exactly. You wouldn't catch these girls shaving the undersides of their heads."

"Did you go to a mixed school?" she asks now.

"No. All boys. Boarding school, actually. Clongowes."

"Oh, William went there," she says before she realises it.

"I thought he went to Belvedere?"

"Yes, he did, but he went to Clongowes for a year and then his father took him away. He thought Belvedere would be better for William."

"Ah. Maybe that's where I know him from." Eric's eyes narrow. "I knew I recognised him."

The bill arrives and he places his credit card on the plate and asks, "So? Can I call you?"

Momentarily, she is confused. Call her? About what? More information? But as his gaze lingers, those blue eyes watchful and intent, it dawns on her that this lunch has had nothing to do with his work. Instantly the colour rises to her face and she is filled with confusion. "Eric, well . . . I'm not sure."

Suddenly she is struck by her complicity in this. The lunch, the conversation, all those glances and shared intimacies. She is not above rebuke for her part in his proposition – they have both been flirtatious. And she thinks again of Keith, the unwelcome memory pounding furiously in her brain. How much had she encouraged him? She leans forward, feeling the colour running to her cheeks. But then a third voice speaks – a reprieve.

"Helen? It *is* you! How are you?"

She is a buxom woman in a denim jacket, her hair swept back off her face and held at the nape of her neck with a slide. Her friend from college, the social worker from the Young Offenders' Rehabilitation Programme. They have not spoken in months.

"Antonia!" Helen introduces her friend to Eric, briefly explaining the connection.

"I sent Helen a young man to help her for a few months," Antonia explains, then fixes the full wattage of her optimistic smile on her friend. "So how did you get on with him?"

"Okay. Yes, good. He finished before Christmas."

"Oh, I see." Despite Antonia's cheeriness, Helen detects disappointment that the employment had not continued.

"There wasn't enough work to keep him on," she explains. "I would have liked to, really, it's just that—"

"Of course. I understand!" Antonia says gaily.

"What did he do?" This from Eric. "What was his offence?"

"Oh! Nothing too serious." Helen smiles. "Breaking and entering."

"That sounds serious enough."

"Well, yes, but it's not like he killed anyone."

Antonia's expression changes, the perfect smoothness of her brow fracturing into a frown. "Well, it was a little more serious than that, Helen. Yes, it was B and E, but there was violence involved."

"What?" Helen feels something cold rising from the pit of her stomach.

"He put a woman in hospital. She caught him in the act and he shoved her against a door frame. She suffered a fractured skull and was badly shaken. She was eighty-two. You don't recover from such a fright at that age."

"No!" she blurts out. "There must be some mistake." Her hands have gone cold. Everything about her is frozen. He put a woman in hospital. A violent crime.

"I thought you knew that," Antonia says, alarmed at Helen's sudden pallor. "Good Lord, Helen, they don't put people in prison these days for robbery. They haven't the space! You need to do something really atrocious to get locked up in the current climate."

He lied to her. That letter he sent . . .

"Whatever did you think?"

Both of them are looking at her expectantly, but Helen is too numb to speak.

After a moment, she recovers her composure, promises to call Antonia soon and they say goodbye. Eric, mercifully, does not pick up on his own request to call her. But as they get up to leave and he helps her with her coat, Helen feels a sensation like a hand trailing over the back of her neck. Nerves bristling. Eyes lingering. Someone watching. She turns but no one is there, only the staff in their starched white shirts, folding napkins and pouring water. Yet still she feels it – someone watching her – but as Eric ushers her out into the afternoon sun, she tells herself she is mistaken.

17

Dear Helen,

I have been awake all night wondering whether I should write to you, wondering what I should write if I did. Such a week it has been for me – more worry and anxiety than I have ever experienced. It reminds me of those first few weeks when I went inside and I would lie in bed at night staring up at the ceiling, feeling the walls coming towards me, closing in on me like a scene in some bad science-fiction movie, listening to all the unfamiliar sounds – the creaking of beds down the hall, coughing, pipes hissing and gurgling – and wondering how I was going to stand it, how I was going to get through it. At least then I had the small comfort that it was all my own doing – I was responsible for my own misery. But this time, Helen, the blame must rest with you. Have you any idea how much you hurt me? How you have tortured me? I have swung from one emotion to another so often these last few days that I feel dizzy – seasick. But now I have reached a point of understanding and, Helen, I feel at peace. I really do. I have gone through my thoughts and examined my feelings, and yours too, your motives, your reasons for doing what you did. I kept thinking: What are you trying to do to me? Hurt me? Drive me away? But now I understand. I know what you were trying to tell me, which is why I'm writing to you now.

I told you before that I would be there for you always, and I meant that. I felt that strongly, a need to be near you, to protect you. Did you know that I got a new job in Sandymount village? Closer than you realised, perhaps, but if I am to look out for you, I need to be near you. I began my job a couple of weeks ago – it's a kitchen job. Not very glamorous! More pot-washing and cleaning up, but I'm learning new things too, and they're nice people. I think they see I have potential. The manageress gave me a talk when I first started about opportunities, proving my ability, climbing the ladder and so on. She went on and on about how it was up to me to work hard and take an interest in the running of the place, decide whether I might like to stay in the kitchen and go the chef route, or work out front behind the bar or as a waiter. For half an hour she went on, painting a career path for me, and I nodded and agreed with her, even spouted some guff about wanting to be the next Jamie Oliver. You should have heard me, Helen! You'd have laughed yourself silly! And she lapped it up, never once guessing that the only reason I was there – the only reason I chose that place at all – was so I could be close to you. I'd have taken a job in Ryan's or Spar or Tesco, but I didn't want to be too obvious, didn't want to make things too awkward for you. This way

I can keep an eye on you, watch over you, from a distance. I know you'd prefer that.

When you came into the restaurant on Tuesday, I was in the kitchen helping the commis-chef. Even though the kitchen is clearly visible from the dining area, you didn't see me because you were with him – talking and laughing over the table. Have you ever felt despair, Helen? Despair like cold water running through you, making every part of you cold? I stood there staring out at you, the commis-chef barking instructions at me, but I couldn't move, couldn't drag myself away from you and him. Who was he? What were you doing with him? He had his back to me, so I couldn't see his face, and my eyes were only for you, anyway. But you just sat there staring straight ahead without even seeing me. That hurt, Helen, and I tried to look away. I tried to concentrate on what I was doing, busy myself with what was being asked of me, but I kept coming back to you. I watched you smiling at him, throwing your head back with laughter. All of it like stab wounds to my heart. Why were you torturing me like that? Why would you taunt me with this strange man? After all we had shared, all we had talked about and confided in each other, Helen? Did you give your affection away that easily? Was it that easy for anyone to come along and claim your love? I had thought I was special to you, that we were special to each other and then you went and did that.

I waited till you left that day before I slipped out the back for my cigarette break. My hands were shaking, Helen. I was in shock. And then I remembered again your coldness towards me, and thought you were punishing me for some reason, and I began to cry. I couldn't help myself. Couldn't stop myself. I just stood there in that back alley, out by the bins and the empty kegs, with that cigarette in my hand, shaking and sobbing out loud.

When I went home that night, I told Mam I'd eaten in work, which was a lie, and went straight upstairs to my room. I was so low I couldn't eat, couldn't sleep. I called in sick the next day, which was not a good thing as I'm not even there a month yet, but I couldn't face it, couldn't risk seeing you again. And I was afraid too that you would pull that stunt again – bring him back there for lunch just to twist the knife in me. Fuck you, I thought (forgive me, please!), you can watch out for yourself, the fuck I care! I think I began to hate you a little, Helen. It pains me to admit this now, but I know I must. We have to be honest with each other. We have to have truth between us, nothing hidden, no dark secrets. I thought, Do you know how lucky you are, Helen, how privileged? Sitting in that expensive restaurant having your organic this and your corn-fed that, wine in a bucket and waiters fussing round you? Do you think you're owed that? That you've done something to deserve it? How could you think that when you were being so cruel to me, making me suffer in this way after I had never shown you anything but love?

But then I remembered something. "Nothing good comes easy." That's what my mother says. Isn't it funny the thoughts that come along to rescue you just when you're about ready to throw yourself off the edge? There I was lying there considering doing something terrible to myself, wanting to hurt myself just to show you, Helen, how much pain I was in – how much you were making me suffer – and then those words of Mam's came floating into my head, pulling me back from the edge of darkness. That's the thing, Helen – you never know who you'll rely on to save you.

Do you know what I noticed most about you that first day we met? Your hands. Your quick, clever hands. I was so nervous that day I don't think I spoke a word. I couldn't even bring myself to look you in the eye. So I kept staring at your hands. The way they moved. So strong and yet so small! I think if you asked me which part of you I love the most, I would answer, "Your hands." Most people would say eyes or hair or tits or legs – something obvious, something any fool with no imagination could say. But I noticed your hands, the way you created beauty with them, the way your fingers trailed so softly over the stems, the tenderness of your touch. Even now, when I close my eyes, I can see your hands clearer than any other part of you. I wonder what about me is clearest in your mind's eye?

And I remembered that evening in the street a week ago when I saw you there with William, walking along side by side, back to your car. I noticed that he didn't hold your hand, didn't put his arm round you, didn't touch you at all. How strange that was! I felt the coldness between you, even from a distance. You're

right, Helen – he doesn't see you. At least, not the way
I do. I thought at the time that if you were my wife, I
could never walk alongside you without holding your
hand, feeling the softness of your palm, those fingers
twisting with mine.

One day we will look back on this and laugh about
it. I know it.

Yours always,
Keith

18

How do we choose? Frankie chose me, even though at the time it appeared that I was doing all the watching, waiting for the right moment to make my move, to swoop in and rescue him. Biding my time, stalking him, waiting for the perfect opportunity to step up and offer him my shoulder to cry on, if that was what he needed. All my life I have watched people, their reactions, their body language, the little semaphores they unconsciously broadcast. And they were beaming out from little Frankie that day. "Save me," they cried. "Come and rescue me." And I was only too happy to oblige.

It was late in the summer of 1991 and I decided to go to Cape Cod to work there during the autumn and winter on a play I had been writing since the spring of that year. I rented a shingled bungalow directly on the water somewhere near Provincetown. I had the occasional visitor, but for the most part I was alone, and happy to be so. Work was going well: I felt excitement bubbling in me about this new play, but with that came the anxiety that I might not be able to pull it off. All distractions had to be set aside so that I could accomplish it.

And yet I sought relief from my greatest affliction: the loneliness that follows me like a shadow. It was my habit that summer to frequent a bar in Provincetown, near the waterfront, a clapboard building with a low veranda and a reputation for cruising. It was a casual, laid-back place, where young men would lounge around, drinking lazily or sunbathing, and I liked to sit in the shade of the lounge and watch them, occasionally sniffing out a conquest to take back to my bungalow for the evening.

That particular day must have been during the week, I think, as there were few people about, only the bar tender locked in conversation with a customer and a couple of young men with backpacks sitting quietly in a corner reading. I went to the bar to order my drink. Immediately I sensed an atmosphere. After a lifetime of people-watching, gleaning scandals and gossip, I can sniff out a drama quickly. The bar tender took my order and set about fixing me a daiquiri. He was a small young fellow with a long face and solemn brown eyes. He was not an American – in fact, I found it hard to place him geographically. His looks were Mediterranean, Grecian even, yet he was so quietly spoken, with so little to say for himself, that his accent never revealed itself. But what I noticed about this encounter was that while he was getting my cocktail, the man with whom he had been locked in conversation before I interrupted watched him closely throughout the brief commercial transaction. An older man, slightly dishevelled, as though the heat had crumpled his clothes, with small, ferocious eyes that gave out an angry stare.

I took my drink to a table in the corner where I could observe them and make up a story about them. Lovers?

No – the angry one seemed too old and not obviously gay. A customer who felt wronged or slighted? Perhaps he had made a move and the boy refused to comply. Still no. His employer? But I couldn't shake the idea that the man appeared lost in there. I saw nervousness in his demeanour – tension across his narrow back. A small man coiled up like a spring, speaking under his breath, hissing at the boy, yet I sensed that at any moment the whisper might morph into a bellow. And all the time the boy was gazing at the counter, listening quietly, taking whatever was being said to him without defiance. The only part he was playing in the conversation was an occasional slow shake of his head. Yet there was something defiant in that – something firm and resolute. A definite refusal.

I watched the older man's hands grip the edge of the counter as if he was trying to restrain himself. I watched the strain of his neck, the tension running right up to his jawbone as he held himself back. He was an elastic band pulled too tight, ready to snap. And then it happened. He lashed out, so quickly I hardly saw it happen. A snapping slap across the face. It made a popping sound. It was so brief and so sudden that the boy just stood there, hand to his cheek, staring in amazement. But the surprise soon died in his eyes, replaced by anguish, some inner torment. He gave one last shake of his head, said something in that low voice which I couldn't make out, and the old man was making for the door, grief all over his face, jowls trembling and tears already flowing, yet holding his back straight, his head high, eyes locked on the exit. And I saw at once what was going on. Father and son. An ultimatum. A regretful yet emphatic refusal. I realised that had been final. Something had been severed that could never be put back together. I was witnessing a great drama in those men's shared lives: the final parting.

He stood there, staring at the swinging door, and none of us moved – not I, not the two backpackers in the corner who had looked up from their books. Then he glanced over and caught my eye. Held it for a long moment. And turned away, reached for a cloth under the counter and began to mop it, as if nothing had happened.

It stayed with me, though, that look. Over the years I added to it a collection of haughty stares, hurt looks, loving gazes and joyful glances – Frankie's entire repertoire. Pacino is his true heir. But the first had a haunting quality. It was the pained look of a man who had turned his back on his father, his family, the roots of his identity. It had held bravery and anguish, resignation and sorrow. Those downturned eyes, the heavy lids. One day I'd tell him, "I wanted to kiss your eyes." And he would tell me the whole story: how his father had made the long journey from Ireland to beg him to come home, to abandon this "lifestyle" as he called it disdainfully and not to break his mother's heart. If he didn't – if he stubbornly refused – he was never to return home. "Don't you ever come near us," his father had warned, his voice resonant with something barely suppressed. "Don't even try to call your mother. No contact. No calls. Nothing. Never. Do you understand? She doesn't have a son any more, and neither do I. Don't you ever show your treacherous face at our house again!"

He blinked. He had seen me looking – how could he not? An older man with a grizzled, roguish face, eyes watchful and compassionate.

They say it can happen in a flash. I used to think that was a myth, some overblown romantic notion, but now I know that that was the moment when I felt the first glow of the flickering love I would feel for him.

And I wonder if it was like that for Donovan. Something that caught his eye – a look, a glance, her hands touching petals. An image snagging on his consciousness, uprooting some sleeping emotion and shaking it to life.

19

In his argument today in court, the barrister made reference to the strain Donovan's harassment had placed on Helen and William's marriage. It had begun subtly enough, but soon grew to an intolerable level when distrust and animosity came between them. While I don't doubt that Donovan must bear responsibility for a large part of it, these things are never quite so simple. Dig a little deeper and you will discover the bones of old resentments, unshared secrets, guilty longings. It is the blend of all these things that leads to disaster.

I have tried to look at it from William's perspective. The first time I met him, I was struck by his elegance and poise – such dignity in that young face, studiously handsome, as if he had wisdom beyond his years. But that type of face is deceptive: I have learned since, and imagined twice over, how addled he was by insecurities, the turmoil of doubts and fears inside him. I try to picture him on the day of their row, which sparked off a catalogue of woes, and imagine what had led to the tension.

I watch him, in my mind's eye, crossing the cobbled quad, his broad shoulders fitting neatly into a blazer, hands behind his back, or with a briefcase in one, not a man who looks at his feet while he walks, but rather, holds up his head to greet the world with steady optimism. And he is an optimist, William, despite all those niggling doubts. He is aware of happiness in his life. He feels blessed. Perhaps as he traverses the pavement with that quick, purposeful step he is marking off in his head the things he has to feel grateful for. He is healthy, fit and solvent. He is married to Helen, whom he loves. Just thinking of the warmth of her body next to his when he woke up that morning brings a sweeping sense of the miraculous to him – that a beautiful woman loves and wants to be loved by a man like him. He can hardly believe his luck. They have been married for five years, and now a baby is on the way. That thought brings a surge of joy and wonder – a clutch of cells is growing and dividing within her. His parents are alive, healthy and self-sufficient. He has a number of good friends. He owns his own house – the house he grew up in, and is glad of the security and sense of continuity this provides. He loves that house, with its high ceilings and cornicing, the warmth of the big old kitchen. It has history and he feels that by keeping it in the family he is knitting his history with that of the house and extending it into future generations.

Then there is his job. When he goes to work in the mornings and sees the drawn faces on the DART, the boredom in the eyes of the young men and women around him, he feels a warm murmur inside – thank God, thank God. Here, in that hallowed seat of learning, he has his own small office. I imagine a little cubicle tucked at the end of a long corridor, snugly fitted between his colleagues' rooms, a window with a view of the alleyway leading to the car park, perhaps, but it is his own space, his sanctuary. I imagine it is dominated by a large desk that extends and merges with a meeting table where he sometimes sits with students to discuss their work. Smooth walls are hung with framed prints and certificates, and one is taken up with a blackboard on which he chalks his equations and findings, all those numbers and symbols like a mystical tongue to which only he is privy. How fortunate he is to work in such a civilised space – a place and job that match his temperament, quiet and studious. The discovery of science, the expansion of learning, the understanding of life in all its forms. Such high-minded ideals!

It was never going to make him rich, but it gave him a sense of purpose, a sense of belonging in the world, which meant more to him than the accumulation of wealth. Perhaps all of these blessings are occurring to William as he walks into his building that bright spring morning, a full day ahead of him, with the luxury of an hour to himself before his first class. I like to think they were apparent to him that morning, that he had a last chance to count them, feel the warmth of true happiness and contentment before everything began to fall apart.

He stops by his cubby-hole and collects his post, flicking through the envelopes as he climbs the stairs. Mostly official-looking envelopes – bills, magazine subscriptions, a couple of invitations and an unstamped envelope in looping script that at first glance he imagines to be from one of his students, an apology for an uncompleted assignment, a doctor's certificate or a plea for an extension on an essay due. He would get to it later. But before he reaches his office he is interrupted by Dr Cummings, head of the department and William's boss. "Got a minute?" he asks peremptorily, then retreats into his office, not waiting for the reply.

William follows and takes a moment to admire, as he always does, the lavish surroundings of Dr Cummings's room. Its size alone is impressive – his own cubicle would fit into it four times. There have been murmurs of discontent through the years from several of his colleagues about the poor design and the waste of space, although it's not something William can get worked up about. The heavy mahogany table is spread with piles of papers weighed down with a variety of rocks, an antique desk lamp spreading a circle of warmth over them. William's eyes sweep over the paperwork in a circumspect search for his recent report on his trip to Scotland. He has yet to hear back from Dr Cummings.

"Listen, William," the man begins, not turning to William, but watering the row of plants he has lined up along the floor in front of the window. Outside, the football pitches are sparkling with melting frost under the spring sun. The light reflects off Dr Cummings's bald head. "I wanted to catch you early to run two things past you."

"Oh?"

"The first is your report on the Scotland trip."

"Great. Well, I've been hoping you'd get back to me on that before I present my findings at the staff meeting this—"

"That's what I wanted to say to you, William. If it's all right with you, I think we might give it a miss today. Time is not on our side, and it might be more pertinent to give the half-hour presentation slot to Brian. His findings from the Alaskan trip are quite astounding and merit discussion."

He doesn't turn away from his plants so avoids the sight of William's falling face, his disappointment.

"No. No, of course not. Perhaps at next week's meeting, I can—"

"Why don't you circulate the report via email? I'd say that's the best bet. If anyone has any comments, they can get back to you directly."

The slight is keenly felt. The relative unimportance of his work. Not for the first time, William feels as if he is invisible.

"The other thing is – and I'm letting everyone know about this – we have a new member of staff joining us shortly."

"Oh?"

"Yes, and we're quite excited about her. She comes highly recommended from the Virginia Institute of Marine Science, where she has been conducting innovative research into molecular genetic variation in Tarpon in the northern Atlantic."

William feels dryness crawling up from his throat to fill his mouth.

"She's one of ours, though, originally, Dr Veronica Post. You may have met her?"

Veronica. Roni. The woman he had dumped for Helen.

"Yes, I think so. We were in the lab together for a while."

"Excellent! You can be her guide, show her what's what. Make her feel welcome."

How did he feel, I wonder, as he left that office? Was a chill sinking through his stomach, or an uncertain queasiness rising? As he went about his day, teaching his classes, conducting seminars, assisting his students in the lab, was it in the back of his mind, this memory of her, the betrayal? Perhaps it didn't come back in a flood but as a slow trickle of information, a piecing together of all the sensory perceptions and remembered facts about her. Standing in front of his second-year students, he is aware in the back of his mind of the angular body, the meanness of flesh on her limbs. In the darkened auditorium, turning to the projector and pointing out with his pen the roundness of the Margaritifera's muscle tissue, he is suddenly reminded of her fleshy breasts, the hard pointy nipples that always appeared to be eyeing him accusingly.

Over lunch he ponders the wisdom of sending her an email to welcome her and perhaps soften the shock of their reunion. Part of him wants to get in first, set the tone for their working relationship, show that there are no hard feelings, that what's done is done, water under the bridge, bygones. He tries to compose something in his head. Tries again when confronted with a blank computer screen, but all he can see are Roni's eyes – dark eyes that were even darker after he had made his admission. The cruelty of it. The unapologetic callousness. Those hard, dark, intelligent eyes fixing him with that metallic stare. Whatever he says in an effort to smooth things over, though, the fact remains that she is returning triumphantly – an eminent marine biologist, published by Cambridge University Press, *Marine Biology* magazine, and even *New Scientist*. And here he is in his broom closet, still struggling with his pearls after all these years, not even getting presentation time with his colleagues.

And somewhere during the course of the day, maybe late in the afternoon, at that sleepy hour when his students slump in their chairs and even he needs to dig deep for enthusiasm to get through the lecture, maybe then the memory of a confession comes back to him. After one long night of sex, warmed by too much red wine, lying in her arms, his head resting against those soft breasts, her nipples for once not digging into him, he tells her about that scene from his childhood. The one burning moment of shame when his whole life had spun out of control. He doesn't know why he shares with her this most private piece of his history. And even as he is telling her, he knows he doesn't love her, yet he blurts it out anyway. And for what? So that she will feel warmer towards him? So that she will feel rewarded in some way that he is allowing her closer to him, allowing her a glimpse of his private misery? Or is he telling her out of deceit, knowing that by sharing something so private and painful, he is letting her know that he trusts her without having to say so? He is avoiding saying "I love you."

But what he fears in that moment is not a strengthening of her embrace; he hears no warm words of support. Instead he feels a stiffening. A cool moment of pause, where nothing is spoken, nothing said, and he can almost hear the whir of her brain processing the image. The armour of her breasts over her beating heart seems suddenly hard against him. And then come the words: "Oh how awful. Oh, you poor thing. How embarrassing. How humiliating." And then her own tale of bullying, a vendetta that involved hair-cutting and glue, which on the face of it is told to make him feel less isolated, yet he can't help but feel that she is trying to trump his story with hers. Always the competition, the hunger to win. It wears him out.

And now she will be back, bringing that knowledge with her. A cool hard stone of doubt lodges somewhere in his belly. He carries it around inside him all day. And it is only after the last class, when he returns to his office to collect his coat and briefcase, that he sees his unopened post still lying where he had thrown it that morning. He pauses now, in that pedantic, neat way of his, and sets about opening it and seeing to it. When he gets to the unstamped handwritten envelope, he opens it quickly, prepared to give it a cursory read-through, but what he finds there is so startling, he has to stop, refocus, read again. An unsigned note in handwriting he doesn't recognise. He leans against his desk and studies it for a long time. A terse few lines, but despite its brevity, it has evidently cost the writer much effort. It is a kind of agonised scrawl – upper and lower case mixed together. The writer has used a ballpoint pen and the pressure on the pen is evident in the Braille-like push through the paper.

Ask your wife who she had lunch with on Tuesday last.
Ask her about the man she was with.
Ask her and you will find out what she's up to.

When he told me about it, many months later, William said he had stared at that note for a long time, perplexed. Who had written it? Whatever was it supposed to mean? It appeared grubby in his hands, he said, and a wave of disgust rose within him. He promptly dropped it into the bin. He had an overwhelming urge to wash his hands and hurried to the gents, where he rinsed them under hot water, then splashed his face with cold.

"I just stood there, Reuben, dripping in front of the mirror," he said sadly, "and felt new doubt assail me. The one question I would never have asked myself was now spinning in my brain."

20

And what of Helen and her day? It had started badly when her car broke down en route to a delivery. She had spent forty minutes on the phone to the AA but in the end she had to flag down a taxi, which cost her sixty euro on account of the extra load. When she arrived with the bouquets and buttonholes, she was treated to a lecture on punctuality from a distressed father of the bride, who refused to listen to the reason why she was late, shouting at her incoherently, accusing her of extortion and laziness. Even when Helen had calmed him down, he still regarded her resentfully.

When she arrived back at the shop, Iris was not pleased to have been abandoned all morning. Helen had to withstand her ill temper while she hurried through the rest of the orders. Just before lunch, Iris informed her of her decision to cut back on her working hours – a decision born of tiredness, she said. Time was marching on and she was no spring chicken: it was about time she took things a little easy. Helen would have preferred an out-and-out retirement, but it was an arrangement Iris had made with her mother and she felt there was little she could do about it. She was unable to consider what this meant financially, let alone the difficulties of training someone new, especially now when she should be considering maternity leave. It had always been clear to her that when the baby came she would leave the running of the business to Iris in the first few weeks and employ some relief staff to help her, but that looked unfeasible now and she had no idea of an alternative.

Sometime during the afternoon, while she was on the phone, jotting customer details in the diary, Helen became aware of a prickling sensation at the back of her neck – a shiver of nerves. Looking up, she saw Donovan sitting in his usual spot, eating his lunch on the bench on the green, but there was something different in his demeanour. It took her a few seconds to realise what it was. Usually when he sat there it was with a vague, dreamy expression on his face; he would look about him distractedly as if lost in his own imagination. But today, he sat still, staring straight ahead. At her. It was unnerving. With a lurch, she remembered his letter – poisonous, hidden in her handbag – and considered again whether or not she should confront him. She remembered Antonia's words, "there was violence involved", and the dread within her plunged deeper to meet rising panic. She felt a wave of nausea and told herself it was morning sickness. Yet still she felt the cold press of dread in the pit of her stomach. Perhaps she should march across the green and fling his letters at him, threaten him with the police, her husband or his parole officer – anything. But while she mulled it over, he got up, walked to the bin, dropped in his lunch wrappers and stared at her for a long moment. At last he turned away and went back across the green to his work.

Perhaps it was the unsettled feeling he had provoked in her, or even her own haste, brought on by the morning's delay and the clumsiness it induced, but somehow she tripped on a low bench, kicked over a row of potted plants, cracking their earthenware jars, and landed on her hands and knees. Instinctively, her hand went to her belly. She was possessed of a new protectiveness she had been unaware of until then. Fussing and scolding mildly, Iris sat her down with a cup of tea and, for once, Helen felt truly grateful to her.

A long day, and when she gets home, all she wants is to kick off her shoes and lie on the couch, ordering take-out and a DVD. But when she gets there, she finds her mother-in-law in the kitchen, her head lost in a cupboard, scrabbling at the back.

"What are you doing?" Helen demands, unable to keep the irritation from her voice.

Miriam's face reflects her surprise at being addressed so abruptly, but then she holds up a canister of baking soda. "So sorry, dear. Just rummaging." Helen cannot hear the apology in her voice. "Didn't mean to be a nuisance, but we've got Bill and Edwina coming for supper and I wanted to make that pear and blueberry tart but, alas and alack, no baking soda! I thought you might have some so I let myself in to look. I'll get out of your hair now." She gives a little laugh to lighten the atmosphere.

"Anyhow, I left you something for your supper," she says in a conciliatory manner, nodding at the fridge. "Veal steaks – I picked up a couple extra when I was shopping for us. Nice and fresh, lovely with salad. Expensive, too, so be sure to use them or I'll be very cross!"

Helen's dreams of Domino's pizza are spirited away in the unwanted generosity of her mother-in-law. Pain runs down her legs from the bruised knees and at the thought of standing over the stove, cooking the politically incorrect meat.

And all the time, even after Miriam has made her escape and Helen is alone in the cavernous quiet of her house, it's with her – the sensation that is never far away these days, not since the letters started coming. Disquiet, a physical sensation she cannot identify. A sense of things running out of her control. The memory of his dark gaze, the unsettled calm with which he has carried out his insidious campaign. She has tried to keep it from her mind, but now it is breaking out all over her body, a prickling down her back and across her shoulders, an unresolved queasiness in her gut. It might be the pregnancy, she thinks, but she knows it is not.

When she hears William's key fit into the lock and turn, she experiences a trill of relief. She wants to go to him so that he can put his arms round her and hold her to his chest. But when he enters the hall and places his briefcase on the floor by the coat stand, she sees something weary and restrained in his movements, a tightness about the muscles in his face that holds her back. He perks up a little when he spots her and advances towards her, but his brief kiss seems half-hearted, almost dismissive. She feels a sigh rising inside her.

"God, I'm starving," he says, moving past her into the kitchen. She follows his eyes, which roam over the counters. "What's for dinner?"

"Your mother dropped up some veal."

She goes to the fridge to get it out and – perhaps because she is tired, perhaps because she feels a sudden disappointment at his lack of affection, his inability to see the need etched in her face – she adds, a little pointedly, "She let herself in again when I wasn't here. You'll have to say something, William. I'm sick to death of coming into my own home and finding her sniffing around in the cupboards."

This is unfair of her: she has made it sound as though Miriam is always there. But she has said it now and won't take it back.

"Fine."

"I mean it. We have to have some boundaries."

"I said fine." He adds, almost under his breath, "It was just a bit of veal. It's not like she was going through your underwear."

She stares at him. "Are you all right?"

"Yes, yes." Irritation in the repetition. "Just a long day." And then, as an afterthought, "How about you?"

"Long day too. You don't want to know."

She wants to tell him about it, wants to pour out her woes, but something holds her back. The tension in the muscles of his neck. His failure to look at her directly since he came into the house. She wants to cry out to him, ask him to enfold her in a loving embrace, but instead she sets about preparing the veal and putting together a salad, all the time aware of him sitting at the breakfast bar, fiddling with the corkscrew.

Something about him tells her there might be an argument. She loves her husband, loves his quiet, thoughtful manner, marvels at his capacity for silence. But there is an unusual quality to this silence. She knows, too, that he is the type of man for whom certain things become irksome and difficult. He can be petty and over-serious. When he sees those car bumper stickers of a cartoon football fan urinating on the jersey of a rival football club, his brow wrinkles with distaste. Tossed aside cigarette butts cause him endless frustration. Untidiness is a source of irritation. Yet it is not within him to mount a challenge to the things that bother him. He lacks the aggression, perhaps even the courage, for confrontation. Shying away from arguments, from openly addressing those things that bother him, he internalises them, mulling things over in his head.

The silence is making her uneasy. She is in no mood to tease out whatever is bothering William, so instead she tells him about her day. To hell with it, she thinks, and lets him have it all – the car breaking down, the row with the wedding party, Iris, the fall, everything. Except Donovan. That she keeps to herself. But instead of the sympathy she is seeking, his response is churlish and hostile.

"That car has been due a service for months now," he reminds her. "It was bound to conk out sooner or later. You have to look after these things, Helen, if you expect to rely on them."

And Iris?

"You've known since your mother died that Iris would go part-time within a few years. Did you not have some kind of contingency plan?"

There is no note of compassion in his voice. The tone is raised and there is harshness, reproach, skirting the edges. Even his response to her fall lacks softness. He tells her pedantically that she needs to slow down and be less clumsy. Instantly she resents the implication that her role now is as receptacle for his heir. Already she feels she is losing worth in his eyes. She wants him to place his hands on her belly and whisper his wishes for her and their child as he has done almost every night since they learned of her pregnancy. She wants to show him the romper suit she bought today in a flurry of sudden excitement – their baby's first clothes – to have him feel the softness of the cotton and smile at the bright red apples printed on it. But William is not in that place. She fears a lecture on the bad luck that buying clothes for an unborn child may bring. So she lets it go. Her aim now is to get through dinner, then crawl into bed where she can settle into the darkness, turn her back on him and the whole wretched day, lose herself in sleep.

"How was work?" she asks, turning the veal steaks in the pan. "Did you give your presentation?"

"No. Cummings bumped me for Brian's sodding anemones."

He stops fiddling with the corkscrew to deliver this piece of news, and she sees the disappointment on his face, naked and uninhibited. It is the face of a child whose treat has been swiped from him.

"Never mind, sweetheart," she says, sounding cheery but sympathetic, trying to bolster him.

But the look that comes over his face tells her she has taken the wrong tack. He seems wounded. Then his eyes narrow and examine her with a strange intensity. "Never mind?" he repeats. "This isn't my school homework we're discussing, Helen. It's my research – my *career*. Don't you see? Can't you understand that in bumping me like that

Cummings is telling me he doesn't give a damn about my project? And that's the message he's sending out to the rest of the staff."

"You'll get your chance."

"My chance? Christ, Helen, it's not a playground. It's not a question of waiting for my go on the slide. He's dismissed my research! He thinks it's insubstantial. Inconsequential. Pointless."

Helen, who has privately thought on occasion that his work is a little frivolous, can't think what to say.

He sees her hesitation and pounces. "You agree with him, don't you?"

"William, I—"

"You do. You think I'm wasting my time."

"No, it's just that . . ."

"Just that what?"

She doesn't know why she said it. The "just" came from nowhere. Despite herself she has been drawn into arguing with him. She is unsure how to proceed. He is waiting for her to frame an answer, preparing to rip the accusations from it. Somewhere during this exchange he has got to his feet and is standing there now, hands on his hips, steadying himself for the perceived insult of her response.

"You're taking this too seriously," she says quietly.

"On the contrary, you aren't taking it seriously enough."

This is a new voice from him, thick with unspoken accusation, and she wonders whether something else is troubling him. It slips behind his eyes like a fish she can't grasp – some hidden recrimination, some undisclosed wound. The air darkens round them.

She is better at argument than he is. She's had more practice. And William, for all his intelligence, is bound by politeness, caught up in the web of his upbringing. He has never honed the skill of argument with brothers and sisters, shied away from conflict at school to lose himself in his dream world. As an adult, he has always preferred considered debate to the dangerous freedom of passionate rows. He is easily wounded and sensitive to the capacity for hurt in others. To a degree it frightens him. Helen knows all this, knows that if it comes to it, she can turn this round, deliver a stinging defeat and elicit an apology from him. But victory can be hollow when it demands so much from you. Answering his questions makes her suddenly tired, so she turns away and lifts the pan off the heat.

"You're right," she says. "I'm sorry. I'm tired, William. It's been a shitty day."

He doesn't respond, just continues to watch her, not ready yet to let go of his injurious mood.

"Shall we eat in here or take our plates through and plonk ourselves in front of the telly?"

Her voice is light and hits the wall of his silence. He seems to be considering something.

"Who did you have lunch with last Tuesday?"

This throws her. "Who did I have lunch with?"

He nods, reaffirming the position of his feet. She studies him, alerted by the warning chill in his voice, the straightening of his back, the distrust in his eyes – and it is this that frightens her. It angers her too. Steeling herself, she looks at him coolly. "What's this about, William?"

"It's a simple question."

"Is it? You've never asked me before."

"Well, I'm asking you now. Who did you have lunch with last Tuesday?" His voice quavers with uncertainty.

"I had lunch with Eric," she replies calmly, but can't help adding waspishly, "not that it's any of your concern."

"Eric." He pauses, trying to locate a face to put with the name. Then his eyes widen. "Eric? From the concert hall? What were you doing having lunch with *him*?" There is venom in the last word. She deflects his question with one of her own. "Why are you so concerned?" He is shaking his head now, pacing, then stopping to put one hand on the counter, the other drawing down over his face. She reads exasperation in his gesture and moves to alleviate it. "He called into the shop and asked my advice on that drama he's doing. Remember? The one he told us about. So I helped him, and then, to say thank you, he took me out for lunch. Does that answer your question?"

He continues to shake his head, agitated. "Eric," he repeats. "And what were you talking about over lunch?"

She drops the pan onto the counter with a thump, taken by anger. "For God's sake, William, what is this? An interrogation?"

"Keep your voice down, will you?" He gestures to the basement below, which further incenses her.

"To hell with your parents! I don't care if they do hear me! What gives you the right to ask me what I talk to other people about? Do I ask you what you discuss over lunch with your colleagues?"

"No."

"Damn right I don't. And not only because it would bore me stupid but because I respect your privacy, William, something I would have thought you could reciprocate."

"I don't like him," he says, his face sullen.

"You don't even know him!"

"I knew him well enough once, and I can't think he's changed so radically."

This is out before he can stop it, and already he is moving from the counter, opening the fridge and taking out a beer, as if attempting to disown the remark. But she is latching on to it. "When did you know him?"

"At school."

"But I thought you said—"

"It's nothing," he says, "and I didn't even know him very well, had few dealings with him. I just didn't like him much."

"Oh, for God's sake, William."

She sees this as another example of his fastidiousness, his agonisingly painful way of categorising people. She sometimes suspects him of snobbery, an ugly characteristic in anyone, and is faintly repelled by it.

"What?" he says, coming at her again. "Can't a man take an interest in whom his wife sees? And I have to say, Helen, lately you've been behaving so oddly – so secretively – that you can't blame me for being suspicious."

She is so astonished that she can only stare at him and while she is struggling to frame her thoughts, he is back with another complaint. "All these fucking people coming out of the woodwork. And now Roni's coming back to the department. A triumphant return! Cummings told me today. I think he took some kind of delight in telling me, acting coy and pretending not to know that we were once together."

All she hears is the self-pity in his voice, the paranoid perception that those around him are ganging up on him –

first her, now Cummings. Her need for affection, to be soothed out of her troubled day, has been extinguished by his accusations, spoken and unspoken, his grim pessimism and ardent deliberations. And all the time she is aware of something else running alongside the argument. He is off now, bleating on about Roni and her accusing stares, her intellectual prowess and his imminent humiliation at having to bow and scrape to her. But she doesn't hear any of it. She has found it now, caught hold of it. A nasty suspicion.

"Who told you?" She keeps her voice level, her gaze on him.

"Told me what?" But his voice tells her that he knows what – he is being disingenuous, evasive.

"Told you that I had lunch with a man. Who was it?"

"What does it matter?" he says in an attempt to shrug off the question.

"It matters to me," she answers coolly. "I'd like to know who's spying on me."

"They weren't spying, for God's sake. There's no need to be dramatic."

"Then tell me who it was."

He becomes flustered, refusing to look her in the eye, picking up the corkscrew and fiddling with it again. "It doesn't matter! Jesus, can't we drop it? I'm sorry I brought it up."

"No. You're going to tell me who it was, William. I told you, after all – told you it was Eric – now you can have the decency to tell me which of your beady-eyed colleagues was reporting back to you on my eating habits."

"Okay, fine," he says, throwing up his hands in a gesture

of mock surrender. "It was Cummings, all right? His wife saw you. Happy now?"

As though he is aware that his reply might collapse under scrutiny, he gets the oil and vinegar for the salad out of the cupboard, but he is too late. She knows him too well, can read when he is being deceptive, which is rare. She deciphers it now in his unwillingness to meet her eyes, the tone of his voice – sharp, staccato, almost shrill – and the speed with which he moves to the cupboard, anxious to have the conversation behind him. She knows how much he hates lying – to her of all people.

But Helen has had enough. The betrayal makes her feel sick – this blatant lack of trust. Unwilling to let it go but too tired and heartsore to fight it out, she goes for the dramatic gesture. She pushes past him, finds her shoes, slots her tired feet into them, then snatches her coat from the back of the chair and swings it over her shoulders.

"Helen," he calls after her, but she doesn't stop. "For Christ's sake, Helen, where are you going?"

She opens the door and takes one last look at him. "Fuck you," she says coldly, then slams it with all the strength she can muster.

She gathers her coat about her and hurries down the steps to her car. It is only when she is inside it, with the key in the ignition, that she sees Donovan leaning against the fence on the other side of the road, watching her intently.

Fuck you too, she thinks. As she drives past she raises her hand and gives him the finger, watching him in the rear-view mirror. He is staring at her with an expression she cannot read before she turns the corner and is gone.

21

We are gathered in this room to determine one thing: a man's guilt. It seems to hover in the air about us, a question mark beside it, flashing. Guilt. It's a funny word: it seems to have physicality, like a weight dropping through the air. Or the sudden upsurge of something bitter and indigestible. Guilt. It has a metallic taste. And which of us has not tasted it in one form or another?

I remember standing in my kitchen, the telephone pressed to my ear, the taste of guilt flooding my mouth, as if I had bitten a thermometer. It was Frankie's good friend, Ed Keane, who rang to tell me. He had been sitting with Frankie and a couple of other friends at an outdoor café in Dalkey when Frankie had leaned forward, coughing, and blood had poured from his mouth. He'd gone straight to the hospital, X-rays had been taken and the dark lung area discovered. Cancer, a cloud of it, too close to the heart to be operable, and too advanced for surgery anyway.

As I stood there, remorse took hold of me, freezing my limbs. All those months I had watched his decline, the weight dropping off him, the lethargy that never lifted, the persistent coughing fits at night, and I had turned away from them, choosing not to grasp the seriousness of his deterioration. His ill health had become a nuisance to me, and I had cast him out of my life. The single most treacherous and shameful act of my life.

And it stays with you, that type of remorse. It has drastic side effects. It clings like a shadow and you think that all the world must see this taint, this persistent dark twin. Even now, sitting in the courtroom, two years after it happened, I still feel it hovering at my ankles.

For me it was a sudden, shocking thing – a punch in the stomach – but for William was it more of a slow dawning, a creeping realisation?

I think of him listening to the reverberation of the slammed door echoing around the house. Perhaps he just stands in the hallway, in the silence, mindful of listening ears downstairs, their music turned down, the conversation stopped, the hush that has fallen as they exchange a glance, and suck in their lips, disapproving? He stands there for maybe three or four minutes before his anger makes itself felt – its cold glow propelling him back to the kitchen, where he sets about eating the veal, to spite her, for he has lost his appetite, but the petty voice inside him is insisting that he feeds himself, that he carries on as normal despite the starkness of her storming out, the argument still hanging in the air around him.

He eats at the breakfast bar, pours himself a glass of wine, eyes the rain hitting the window panes and tries not to think about her out in that weather, focusing instead on the dullness of his anger, his isolation. It is childish, this emotion – nobody understands me – and although he is aware of this, he is reluctant to shake it off. Methodically, he cleans the kitchen, pours another glass of wine and repairs to the living room. He switches on the TV and flicks through the channels. He watches the news, then flicks to *Newsnight* and surrenders to Jeremy Paxman's speculative tone. Does it start then? I wonder. Distantly, in his head, his voice repeats the lie. Cummings's wife. Whatever had possessed him? What was this new instinct that lay within him, cowering among an arsenal of deceits?

By midnight, he is agitated. The rain is lashing against the glass now. He walks from room to room, trying not to ring her mobile. Then the thought comes to him. The shop, the little rooms above it where she once lived, now used for storage. He takes his car keys, struggles into his coat and dashes out into the rain.

He drives quickly through quiet streets, the wipers working to clear his view, the noise of the rain obliterating the clamour that crowds his mind. His anger has all but dissipated. It lingers now as a dull beat, drumming beneath his thoughts. But guilt is settling in, spreading its tentacles. He reaches the shop and sees her car parked outside, the little window upstairs lit. She is there. He stops the car but doesn't turn off the engine, listening to it turn over as he decides what to do. I imagine it as a struggle within him – the knowledge that he shouldn't have lied to her, with the guilt fighting alongside his simmering anger at her dismissal of his woes, her lack of compassion and understanding. They fight it out within him as he contemplates getting out of the car and going up to the flat. Reconciliation is within his grasp: he can go up and confess his mistake, his error of judgement. He can take her in his arms and feel the warmth of her body against his, listen to her as she murmurs a litany of soothing words into his chest. All of that is still possible. But instead, he turns away. She is the one who walked out, he remembers. She can come crawling back. Anger wins over guilt.

He sleeps alone, a restless sleep, and when he wakes to hear the telephone, he is briefly confused by her absence, then feels the lingering sorrow he always experiences after a row. He struggles out of the sheets, pads across the hall, barefoot, then downstairs where he lifts the receiver.

It is Helen. Her voice sounds distant and small. Something tightens in his chest when he hears it. "William?" she says. "I'm at the hospital. You need to come right away."

And that's when it happens. His anger pours away in a dwindling stream, and the guilt hits him — loud and huge — to snatch victory.

And maybe she feels it too. Maybe she feels it in the car as she drives away, tears of rage coursing down her cheeks. Maybe it doesn't occur to her until she is alone and pacing about the chilly rooms above the shop, the bald lightbulb swinging from a flex above her head, casting a cold light on the harshness of her surroundings, the lack of comfort. She begins to regret her petulance, to remember her own deceits and disavowals. Or maybe it is later, deep in the night, when she is woken by a throbbing pain and dampness between her legs. Certainly, she must feel it when she is in the hospital, with the antiseptic smell in her nostrils, lying on the bed watching anxiously, trying to control her panic as the ultrasound slides back and forth over her belly.

"No, there's nothing," she is told, and she watches the face of the doctor – a rabbitty woman with limp hair and a pale, drawn face fixed on the monitor. "There's nothing alive in there."

The cruelty of those words! And then they are taking away the equipment and covering over her belly, and the doctor is peering down at her, telling Helen she's sorry, these things happen sometimes in the first three months, nobody knows why. Words meant as comfort but they're just stirring her grief – fresh, raw, not yet fully formed.

"We can admit you straight away and take care of it," the doctor informs her. "A fairly simple procedure – a D and C – to scrape out the retained tissue from the womb."

She winces but feels lost, confused, and agrees. And it is then, when the doctor leaves the room and she is alone, that she thinks of Donovan, the look he gave her, full of reproach. Was it only the previous day that she had seen him watching her from across the park and felt that shiver pass through her? How deeply had it touched her? She imagines the fear travelling deep inside her, settling in the lining of her womb – a cold cradle for the embryo. And then she gets it – the metallic taste, like bile at the back of her throat. Guilt is in the room with her. She is alone with it – and her dead baby.

I wonder is she thinking of it now. She is sitting next to me, her back ramrod straight, her stark white face trained on the prosecution counsel's back, giving nothing away. Donovan is not on trial for the baby's death. That piece of evidence is inadmissible.

PART THREE

22

Sometimes guilt brings something else with it: a cleansing. Such an unexpected thing.

He showed amazing stoicism, my little Frankie, taking the diagnosis on the chin. I persuaded him to move back into the house with me. Not as lovers, we were well past that, but as old comrades – war buddies. For all the damage you inflict on another person's heart, you may yet end up able to sit quietly with them, enjoying a sunset and a bottle of chardonnay. They gave him six months, and the six months passed, and still he endured. He went past that time, weakening steadily but giving not an inch of his fierce pride. There were few visitors, at Frankie's insistence: he didn't want witnesses to his decline. Except me.

"I'm used to you," he said once by way of explanation, then turned away and closed his eyes.

I believe that was the closest he ever came to a declaration of love.

And, for a time, my guilt was silent.

Perhaps William and Helen experienced a similar cleansing. There is something about grief that unites people.

She cried in the hospital, and all the way home in the

car. When they got inside their front door, she turned to him and he took her in his arms. "I've never seen such debilitating grief, Reuben," he told me. "It frightened me a little. I was upset about the baby too – of course I was – but not to that extent. I thought perhaps it was because I was at a remove – the baby wasn't in my body – that I wasn't as upset as Helen was."

It transpired that the loss of the baby had brought with it a fresh wave of grief in Helen for her mother, Regina, whose death she had never properly come to terms with. That week, it all came rolling up from the depths of her, shuddering and strange, and the two of them clung to each other, riding out the storm.

"I suggested we go away," he said, "a week in the country, but Helen wouldn't have it. So we stayed at home – and do you know, Reuben? It was the most marvellous two weeks. In some ways now, when I look back on it, I think it might have come close to the happiest time in our marriage. The strangest thing, occurring then, after we'd lost the baby and before – just before – life became so different."

The strangest thing. Those two weeks they spent together. It was March and spring was in the air, still cold but with that breath of freshness – newness – that meant the advance of something, the excitement of a new beginning. They went for long walks together along Bray Head, Dún Laoghaire pier and Howth. They drove to Wicklow and walked in the hills. They spent hours in coffee shops, steam rising from their cups, and talked endlessly. They rediscovered conversation, remembered how they had first connected. They talked about the baby they had lost; they talked about Regina, about Helen's dad, about William's parents. They needed a new project and their focus turned to the house. Plans were made to tear down the old kitchen units and put in something more modern. They traipsed round showrooms, gathering brochures, considering furniture, trying out paint samples. Some things they could do themselves and lost no time in getting to them – days went by of painting and wallpaper stripping, quiet industry, no noise but the radio playing.

"What about the shop?" Helen asked.

"Don't worry about it," he said with a new firmness. "Iris and I have everything under control. You're not permitted to call or get within even a half-mile of the shop until I say so."

This new confidence he had – this strength – had emerged overnight. And Helen was happy to surrender to it. For once, the fight had left her. She wanted decisions taken out of her hands. She wanted him to dominate. I believe that time brought out the best in William.

"That week, I would get up early in the mornings," he told me, "come downstairs and turn on the radio while I cooked breakfast. For some reason, I couldn't listen to the usual current affairs or news programmes that I hear every other morning of my life. Instead, I was tuning in to breakfast DJs with their jokes and anecdotes. It was as if there was no place in my home for gloom or depression. I noticed, that week, that our house seemed suddenly full of light. And Helen would join me, sitting at the breakfast bar while I made pancakes or a fry or smoothies. And I loved having her company. I loved to see her smiling at me, enjoying the fussing I was doing for her."

After a trauma like that, something is rebuilt. And I think, more than anything, that the gain is forgiveness. The fights, the injuries inflicted on each other, the small grievances, the minor shows of selfishness, the petty irritations that build when you live with another person, all are swept away when you are confronted by something so much bigger. When you are threatened by an event that overshadows all else, then you cling to each other for strength.

And so it happened with Helen and William. They emerged from that time triumphant, stronger, more in love than ever, with a new understanding of themselves, of what they wanted, of what they could achieve together. And perhaps there was the shock too – at their failure to notice how it might all have slipped away, that they had begun to drift and had done little to draw back to each other. It caused a little shiver in each of them. A premonition, perhaps, of what was to come.

William never told her what he had said to Iris, whether he had invented some elaborate excuse or merely told her the truth, but it became clear to Helen as soon as she walked through the door that Iris knew what had happened.

"If you'd seen her, Reuben, arms outstretched, smiling, coming to me from behind the counter, this barrel of benevolence – I didn't know what to do with myself."

I can imagine Iris with her pitying looks, her simpering smile, her voice fulsome and warm, marvelling and exclaiming at everything Helen said, proclaiming womanly empathy and understanding.

"And the strange part was that it didn't bother me," Helen told me. "For all the times she'd got up my nose in the past, there was something about her warmth that felt sincere. We were never the best of friends, but then I felt a true fondness for her."

Helen herself had been full of apologies for leaving Iris in the lurch with so much to sort out on her own. "You've been a trouper," she told Iris. "A real star. I can't think what I would have done if you hadn't been here."

"Think nothing of it," Iris said. "Sure, don't I know this place inside out? I could do it in my sleep . . ."

"Well, that's true. But still."

"And I had help."

"Oh – Claudine, was it?"

"No!" Iris said, a twinkle of merriment in her eye. "You're not going to believe what happened. The very morning William rang to tell me about your . . . about the miscarriage," she said, lowering her voice, "I was tearing my hair out, wondering what on earth I would do, how I was going to manage, and who walks in the door?"

She waited expectantly, watching Helen's blank face, then announced, with shrill triumph, "Keith!"

Helen stared at her.

"Can you believe that?"

Stood and stared.

"Talk about a godsend. I have to hold up my hands here and say that yes, in the past, I wasn't his biggest fan, but I take it all back. The effort that young man has shown, the way he just pitched in and rolled up his sleeves, not waiting to be told what to do, and here every day without fail, even Saturdays – he's the real star here, not me."

Helen's mouth was dry. She nodded and smiled, but really she felt slapped in the face. "Where is he now?"

"Just upstairs, getting down some more ribbon for me."

"I see."

"And, Helen, I hope you don't mind, but I, well . . ." She paused, looking sheepish yet pleased with herself, "I've told him about my plans to scale back and how, if he worked hard and proved himself, there was a good chance – and really, Helen, I think you'd be a fool to pass up the opportunity – you'd consider taking him on full time."

Forcing herself to smile and answering Iris's cheeriness with a calm she didn't feel, Helen said, "We'll see about that."

For the next few minutes she listened as Iris filled her in on the comings and goings, the snippets of gossip, the well-wishers, but all the time she was straining to hear noises from upstairs – the creaking of floorboards, the groaning of hinges – aware of a resolve forming inside her that she had to act now, nip this thing in the bud. After a few agonising minutes she excused herself and went upstairs.

As soon as she reached the landing, she saw him. The space in that little apartment over the shop is small, cramped and hemmed in by the low, slanting roof, made smaller still by the scarcity of light from the tiny windows beneath the eaves. And in that shadowy space she could see his nerves, his indecision. He had dropped the spools of ribbon when he saw her, bent now to pick them up, and gave her a cursory glance – his eyes grazed her face – then looked down at his hands.

"For some reason, Reuben, it made me feel relieved. I

saw I had the upper hand, that our situation had returned to what it had been in the beginning, and I held the authority."

It was the first time she had been alone with him since that afternoon in January, but she didn't feel as pushed and anxious as she had imagined. His rounded shoulders, the downturned mouth, made him appear pathetic, not a threat, merely a nuisance. It was hard to believe she had felt such menace from his letters. As he cowered before her, crouched under the eaves, cringing from her gaze, she even felt an ounce of pity for him.

"Well, then," she began, "you're back."

He went to say something, then changed his mind and simply nodded.

"It would appear that you can't stay away," she said wryly.

"I was just helping out," he mumbled.

Her eyes passed over him, taking in the thinness of his bird-like frame, the bony arms extending from T-shirt sleeves. He had always looked malnourished. Every time she saw him, he conjured up pictures of microwave suppers in her imagination. She asked, "What about your other job?"

"I packed it in."

"Well, that wasn't very smart. What're you going to do now?"

He shot her a look, a curious mix of hopefulness and anxiety, but a look that also seemed to say, "You know what I'm going to do."

"You can't stay on here," she told him, her voice low so that Iris wouldn't hear. "I meant what I said that day on the strand. I don't want you hanging around here. And after all that's gone on since – your poisonous correspondence – there's no way in the world I'd have you back."

He shifted his weight from one foot to the other, appearing to her now as a sulky teenager. "You were happy enough for me to cover when you were sick," he said on a whining note.

"I didn't know about it. If I had, I would have stopped it," she hissed. "This is not what I wanted. In fact, I'm furious with Iris for letting you back here."

"It's not her fault. She didn't know."

"Since when did you two get to be so chummy?"

That silenced him.

It was hot up there under the eaves, hot and airless. She went to open a window, and when she turned he was looking unhappy.

He took a deep breath, then said, "I thought you'd be pleased. I thought you'd want me to be here. What have I done to make you treat me like this?"

Noises from the street were coming through the window, sounds of traffic, a dog barking.

"Well, there's those letters you've been sending for a start. You seem to have it in your head, Keith, that there is something between us. Let me disabuse you of that notion." Her tone was icy, her eyes glacial. "We are not friends, we are not anything. I don't want you here. I don't even like you. And, if you must know, you give me the creeps. All this hanging around you do, loitering in the green, staring at me. Oh, yes, I've noticed you. I don't know what you think you're playing at. Is it supposed to flatter me? Is all this attention some weird courtship in your head? Because I am not interested."

He seemed to struggle with that. He couldn't meet her eye. "I just wanted to be near you," he said eventually, forlornly. "You've no idea what this is doing to me."

Helen rolled her eyes. It was getting a little tiresome. The last thing she needed was a morose teenager about the place. "Don't you think you're being a little dramatic?" she asked, turning away from the mute, pleading eyes, the timorous hunch of his shoulders. "And for God's sake, keep your voice down. This is all so unnecessary, Keith, really it is. Now, I'm sorry you gave up your job, but you shouldn't have. No promises were made, despite what Iris might have said to you. There is no job here for you, not any more. I'm afraid you'll have to go, and that's all there is to it."

"Please don't do this, Helen," he said. "Please stop pushing me away. If you only knew—"

He stopped short. He had an irritating habit of leaving his sentences unfinished. She wished he would get out – storm off in a rage if need be.

But Donovan wasn't going anywhere. He watched her, seeming stricken, and when he spoke again, it was in a tremulous, faltering tone. "I know you love me," he said, "so there's really no need to keep up this pretence. It would be easier just to admit it."

"Love!" she gasped. "Where on earth did you get that idea?"

She was trying to be laconic, but her heart was thumping. The rhythm in the room had altered, a subtle shift of mood.

"You don't need to pretend with me. Not after all we've shared. Not after all we've meant to each other."

"You're delusional. This isn't love. This is infatuation, bordering on harassment."

"Not love?" he asked sharply. His eyes were narrowing and his features seemed to sharpen. "You'd let just anyone shove his hand inside your snatch, yeah?"

The vulgarity of his statement shocked her. She was caught by an unexpected, piercingly physical memory of that night in the alleyway, the two of them drunk and panting against each other, his fingers crawling towards intimacy. Revulsion and shame jumped within her and, as if attempting to shake it off, she shuddered. "Don't be so disgusting."

He seemed to draw back, wiping a hand over his face as if disavowing the remark, then came at her in a new way. "I didn't mean that, Helen. All right? It was uncalled for. It's just that I get so worked up when you try to push me away. All I've ever offered you is love, so why do you continue to treat me like I'm your enemy?"

He said this in a reasoned tone, looking at her for confirmation, but Helen was thinking, What do I have to do with this boy? How do I make him understand? It was exhausting trying to reason with him, pushing against his emotions, the tangle of troubled thoughts he was nursing. In that moment, she felt tired, and sick of the whole thing.

"Look, Keith, we're not going to discuss this any further. I don't want to see you again – not here, not anywhere. There is no job, there is no us. We are nothing to each other. Do you understand that? Is that clear enough for you?"

At this point, to her horror, Donovan put his hands over his face and started to cry. Noiseless, shuddering sobs. Through them he was trying to speak, gasping and spluttering. "I just wanted . . ." he was saying, struggling for breath, ". . . I just wanted you to love me. I thought you did. Why are you doing this to me?"

All at once everything about him saddened her – the tears, the hunched shoulders, the ill-fitting clothes, his troubled past and uncertain future. But at the same time she was aware of a dangerous edge to him, an unpredictability that caused her to harden herself to his distress. She could hear shuffling at the bottom of the stairs, then Iris's voice calling up in a tremulous query: "Is everything all right up there?"

"Fine, thank you, Iris," she yelled back, wondering how much Iris had heard.

"Look," she said to him, trying to sound reasonable but firm, "I have to go. I'm sorry you're so upset, but there's nothing I can do for you. You'll get paid till the end of the week, but I want you out of here today. Is that understood?"

He was watching her face with a kind of hunger – despair and confusion, too. "You can't do this," he whimpered. "I'm not going to let you push me aside like that."

For just a moment, she thought he might strike her. There was coolness in his voice behind the tears, and she found herself considering his physical size compared to her own. He had a boyish, gangling frame but he was wiry, with a kind of coiled-up strength, and she didn't like the way he was looking at her with his hands on his hips, placed between her and the stairs. She felt that passing him would be dangerous and began to panic a little.

"Please, Helen," he said again, his eyes clear now. "I'm begging you."

His intensity caused her to pause and think, for a moment, about how strange it was to be held hostage in the mid-afternoon by some sad kid, this earnest, hopeless, crushed-looking boy with his tragedy-mask eyes and his supplicant whine.

"What is it you want from me?" she asked with weary finality.

"I want you to love me," he wailed.

She shook her head, bewildered by his emotion. "That is never going to happen, Keith. Not in a million years."

And with that she moved to go past him. He didn't try to stop her. But as she reached the top step, he said something that caused her to draw breath sharply, mumbled words, but he meant her to hear them, intending the cold slice into her heart that they inspired. "I'll tell your husband."

Those words hung in the air, pulsing with menace.

She looked at him coldly, feeling a surge of hatred that surprised her with its force. "No, you won't," she told him, her voice laden with disgust. It was almost a challenge. "You'll do no such thing."

And with that she pushed past him, holding her head high as she flounced down the staircase, blood roaring in her ears. Never in all her life had she felt such anger. She felt huge with it. She felt lit up from within.

Iris was standing behind the counter and greeted her with an uncertain smile. She was opening her mouth to speak, but Helen cut her short.

"I want you to get rid of him, Iris," she said through her teeth. "I don't care what promises you made to him, I want him gone by the time I get back. He is never to come here again."

And before Iris could protest, before she could even ask

why, Helen headed out into the March sunshine. So bright and full was her fury that she did not look back. She did not glance up at the window to see his face looking down at her. In her haste she forgot about the key still in his possession – which she had given him.

23

This thing becomes harder to write. Ever since Helen moved into my home, I have felt the burden of this book. In France, everything was different. There was distance between us, physical and emotional. I didn't need to worry that she might walk into my study and discover my covert project. Also, we weren't as close as we are now. In the months that have passed, my feeling for her has grown – an oddly paternal emotion. How refreshing it is to discover that even now, in this late stage in my life, I can be surprised by the curious leanings of my heart! But it is being squeezed by my conscience. I watch Helen closely, and I know she is faltering. Lately, I have been troubled by the idea that this affair will break her. But I have sat back and watched it happen – watched, and taken notes.

It is Sunday night, and we have spent a few hours, Helen and I, ploughing our way through the last of my French wine. When I returned from Bonnieux with Helen almost a year ago, we had filled the car with crates of it, yet somehow it has vanished. It has fuelled several late-night discussions, I suppose, so it cannot be said that it was wasted. She has been morose this evening, cradling her glass with both hands, curled up in an armchair with her head to one side, gazing at something in the distance.

She seemed tired out and I might have left her alone on another night, but I was wavering between the need to protect her and the hunger to taste something of the success I had once known. I long for a return to the time when the mere mention of my name would provoke raised eyebrows of recognition. Now it seems as though with every introduction I have to trot out my credentials before there is even a flicker.

But then, this afternoon, I received an email from my agent and all my doubts about the book dispersed. About a week ago, I had emailed her in New York with a few chapters as well as an outline for the rest. Out for my Sunday afternoon stroll today, I had ducked into an internet café in Dalkey village on the off chance that Carmela had replied. Lo and behold, a message from her was waiting for me. And what a message it was! Brief and to the point, like the lady herself: she had read what I'd sent her and would be in touch soon to discuss it.

Oh, delight! I rocked forward in my chair with eagerness, bolstered by a swell of excitement. I was back, I was sure of it! I have known Carmela for many years, far longer than either of us will admit to, and I have experienced the paper-cut sting of her dismissive emails and sardonic criticism. She is not a woman who spares my feelings. "That's not my job, Ruby," she has said to me when I have wailed and ranted about her lack of sensitivity, her callous indifference to the artistic temperament. "I'd be doing you a disservice if I pandered to that shit," she has said in her rasping drawl. So I know that she would have had no hesitation in emailing me a blunt rejection were she unimpressed. This had to be good news.

Buoyed by her missive, I sauntered home, savouring the evening, the bright, crisp sunshine, the voices floating from open pub doors, nodding to fellow walkers – if I had had a cane I would have twirled it, such was my pleasure in the world. Then, turning the corner into my lane, I heard raised voices and saw Ingrid's Volkswagen Golf parked on the kerb.

As I approached, I heard snippets of conversation carried on the wind. Helen's voice travelled farther – she was worked up and shrill.

"It's not a charade!" she shrieked. "Don't you think I feel betrayed and let down too?"

Ingrid's response, in her low, mannish tone, was muffled.

"To hell with your reputation!" cried Helen. "I'm sick to bloody death of hearing how half of your firm are looking at you funny and how I'm somehow the cause of it."

Coming up the drive, I could see them on the steps, Helen swamped in a baggy sweater, face tight with rage, Ingrid's long, lank hair hanging down over her bulk.

"Hello! Hello!" I called cheerily. "What's all this, then?"

Ingrid turned to glance at me.

"Hello, Ingrid," I said with a degree of warmth. I place equal emphasis on each syllable of her name – *Ingrid* – to annoy her. We do not get on, she and I. She treats me with barely concealed hostility, and I enjoy getting up her nose.

"You're back, then, are you?" she said.

"Demonstrably!" I chirruped.

Ingrid is a short, bulky wedge of a woman, and although there is only five years between them, you would swear Helen was at least a decade younger. Prematurely ageing, Ingrid tries to compensate for her collapsing figure with the stringy hair that should have been cropped years ago. It looks as though it has been washed in cold tea and is held back off the lunar plains of her face with an Alice band. Where Helen is fey, Ingrid is solid, earth to her sister's fire. We had taken an instant dislike to each other, but it was not until William kicked Helen out of the house and she declined Ingrid's offer of shelter in favour of mine that we began seriously not to get on. It has never descended into an open exchange of fire, but there is time yet for that.

Helen has tried on several occasions to convince me of the goodness that exists within her sister, buried deep though it may be under the layers of spite and resentment she has heaped on top. For Helen, all of the bile that her sister came out with was a result of her unhappiness.

"She's depressed, you see. And she begrudges anyone who leads a life that's full and happy. She's a workaholic, if the truth be known, constantly striving to achieve at the expense of the other aspects of her life. She has few friends, and no husband or boyfriend. Not even a cat, because she's never there to feed one, always at work. If you only knew how lonely she is, you'd forgive her – you'd be nicer to her. If you understood how afraid she is of failure . . . There's such a deep-rooted fear in Ingrid, you wouldn't believe it."

I *don't* believe it. Ingrid is like a bull terrier. She has thighs that look capable of snapping a spine in two and her Medusa stare could stop the blood in your veins.

Of course, all this was said before Ingrid found out the lurid details of the case, back in the time preceding this blow-up with her sister and the subsequent bullying campaign she has been waging to get Helen to stop this nonsense and go back to her husband, spare them all the humiliation and ridicule. As if it was ever going to be that simple. Now they are barely on speaking terms.

"Well, this is nice," I said, joining them on the step. "What are we discussing?"

"*We* were discussing something private," Ingrid said rudely.

"On the doorstep where the whole world can hear? Why not come inside and talk over a nice civilised glass of wine instead of shouting your heads off like fishwives?"

I directed this last comment at Ingrid. With her ruddy cheeks and flared nostrils, she could be in no doubt who I meant was the fishwife.

"I don't think so," she snapped. "It wouldn't be very private there."

"Well, my dear, I'd leave you two alone, of course," I said suavely.

"Yes, but the walls are rather thin, aren't they?"

"I can assure you, my dear" – my dear again? Why not! – "I have no interest in eavesdropping on your vapid conversation."

"This is preposterous. And what is wrong with that dog?" Ingrid asked irritably. Pacino had greeted my arrival with a savage display of barking.

"It doesn't matter anyway," Helen said. "I've nothing further to say to you, and you can't possibly have any more to say to me."

But she was wrong about that. Ingrid had lots more to say. She stood on the step, her barrel body shaking with indignation, her voice low and venomous. "I don't know how you can do it to us, Helen. The shame! You think it's just William who's affected, but you didn't give a thought to me and Dad. I'm only glad Mother isn't alive to witness it. To have to live through the disgrace of your lasciviousness!"

"Now that's enough!" I weighed in. "This is my front porch and I will not have you causing a scene and the neighbours talking. I have my reputation to think of."

"Pah!" Ingrid said with a yelp of disbelieving laughter. Fatuous bint! "Fine. Suit yourself. Helen, come with me."

She marched back down the path towards her car. Helen sighed and walked after her. I had a fleeting image of Ingrid with her hair plaited and pinned to the sides of her head, her body rigged out in Nazi-commandant get-up, goose-stepping away.

But once they were in the car, their anger was locked fast and all I could hear were the cracked high notes of hysteria and shouting. Such a caterwauling! They were like mother and teenage daughter, the one stern and disapproving, the other passion and indignation.

A door slammed, brakes screeched, and Helen came back into the house. Her face was like murder: eyes tense, lips sucked in, tear stains on her T-shirt.

"Don't say a thing, Reuben. Don't say a bloody word."

She flounced up to her room and flung herself on the bed.

Honestly! These gusts of emotion! The open hostility I have to endure from these people! Sometimes I ask myself whether or not it is all worth it.

Pretty soon she came down looking sheepish, her face red with crying. She sloped into the kitchen and seemed to hover at my elbow as I put together a light supper and fished in the fridge for a crisp sauvignon blanc.

"God, what a scene, eh?"

"What indeed?" This avuncular tone – I can't shake it off!

We sat in silence, the only sounds the crunch of salad leaves and chewing. Inside I was bursting to tell her about Carmela's email, but that would mean letting her know about the book, and how could I do that?

"How strange life is, Reuben," she said eventually, "with its dips and unexpected turns. Two years ago I could never have imagined being estranged from my husband or my father or having an ugly scene like that with my sister. Even in the immediate aftermath of the accident, I couldn't imagine Ingrid turning on me like this."

She was curled up in the armchair in an S-shape, cradling a glass of wine and staring out at the green darkness of the garden. Something in the curve of her body, the graceful lean of her neck, the sideways gaze, made me think of a painting by Modigliani. I have always admired beauty and grace in a woman, and have understood – where others of my kind haven't – why so many artists have worshipped the female form.

"Did you know that Ingrid stayed at the hospital the whole time I was in the operating theatre?" she asked me. "Then she kept vigil for two days, eating and sleeping in the hospital, not even going home to change her clothes. When I came round and saw her – her and William – she was in the same clothes she'd worn to the dinner party that night. It threw me a little. It was hard to accept that

I'd been unconscious for two days – seeing Ingrid made it feel like a few hours."

I tried to imagine Ingrid dressed for a party, but I couldn't get past the drab sequence of brown or navy-blue trouser suits she wears with creamy blouses and fussy brooches. The image I settle on is a sensible black skirt with black pumps and the obligatory Alice band, set off by a red jacket – carnival red – a flare of colour, with a gaudy gold pin attached to the lapel. Why is it that Ingrid's wardrobe seems to comprise of uniforms?

"She stood there, holding my hand, while William explained what had happened to me. When I looked at Ingrid, tears had cut through her make-up, and the way she was looking at me . . . At first I couldn't work out her expression. Sadness, maybe? Or pity? In fact, I think it was remorse – that, or regret."

Guilt, more like. After what she had done – the part she had played in the débâcle, with her drunken revelation. She had dropped her bombshell with smug satisfaction. Then came the overwhelming shock at what happened next. The slow seep of guilt as she learned the extent of her sister's injuries, the what ifs creeping in to torment her. Oh, Ingrid was guilty all right. And for months she carried around the burden of that guilt until she learned the truth of her sister's less-than-pure involvement with Donovan. Then the guilt had turned into anger, a cold, hard stone of it. Anger at Helen for allowing her to hang on to the guilt for so long, for failing to disabuse her of her culpability. She thought it had been her actions, her words, that had driven Helen out of her home that night, but it was something else. And in the end the anger was compounded by the shame of discovery: a colleague at

Ernst & Young had pointed out an article to her in one of the tabloids as he asked: "Hey, isn't that your sister?"

She took a long swallow of wine. Evening had closed in around us. The air was still.

"What was it like," I asked gently, "your heart stopping?"

She looked at me blankly.

I said, "You hear all sorts of stories of people having near-death experiences on operating tables, feeling their spirit leave their body, looking down from the ceiling to see themselves being worked on."

She gave a bitter laugh and I felt my face tighten. "Well, there was no white light, Rube, if that's what you mean. I didn't see my mother with her arms outstretched."

I looked into my glass, peeved and disappointed. I hadn't expected mockery. And maybe she saw this in my face, for she softened. "I don't have any memory of A and E, or the procedures they carried out. And even after I'd come round and William told me what had happened and what they'd had to do to me, it didn't register."

Another swallow of wine and she gazed out the window again, but continued to talk in a wistful tone. "There was a doctor in the hospital – the consultant who operated on me – an emaciated man who sat on the edge of my bed and explained what had happened. When I was stabbed, an artery was severed, so the blood pumped out of me quickly. By the time the ambulance got to me, I had already lost a large amount, and when I got to hospital, when I was in the OR, my heart stopped. They had already cracked open my sternum, trying to find the source of the bleeding, when I suffered cardiac arrest." Her brow knotted. "The way he explained it to me, there is a covering around the heart called the pericardium and, inside this membrane, a large amount of blood had gathered, pressing on my heart, not allowing it to expand. He told me how he had made an incision in this membrane to drain the blood so that the heart could begin to fill. It all sounded so mechanical. He told me then that he had wrapped his fingers around my heart and gently squeezed it, pumping out the blood, and after a few seconds, it started beating itself. So strange, Reuben! That man held my heart in his hands. I kept looking at his long fingers, with the square pink nails. So well scrubbed."

She glanced across at me then. "Are you all right?" she asked.

"Fine."

"Some people find the details a little hard to take. Their hands fly up to their faces. But you're not squeamish, are you?"

"No. Not any more."

"Nor am I. I flinched a little when they first took the bandage off to clean the wound. I kept thinking of the noise the drill would have made as it went through the bone." She gave her head a brief shake, then seemed to steady herself. There was poise about her – a pause – that made me think that I should take heed. I leaned forward in my chair and looked across at her.

"All this talk about hearts," she said, "when ultimately it's just a muscle. It has a bodily function, that's all. Hearts don't break, they're not light or heavy, empty or full. They can't be warm or cold. All this talk of giving and receiving them. And do you know what, Reuben? When that doctor sat on my bed, explaining it all to me, William sitting alongside him listening, or interrupting with questions, I began to drift away. I saw my heart as something other than flesh and blood. I saw it as something cool and hard, like metal or glass. A cool, hard, living thing with a smooth surface. My glass heart." Her face darkened and she seemed, in that moment, to stare inwardly. "That's how it feels still. In so many ways, I feel I haven't truly been living since then. I feel so removed, so cut off – even from my own emotions. I look at myself and consider how I'm handling this, and I realise how cold I've become, how untouchable I am. My heart is impenetrable now, too cold and hard to be moved."

She drained her glass.

How extraordinary she is in these moments, so bright and refined. So eloquent. I savour her words, store them up. Later, when she goes to bed, I will write feverishly, anxious not to lose a single word. But in that moment, with that image of her heart, crystalline and still, and the sadness in her eyes, I feel the tiniest beat of indecision. Perhaps I shouldn't go through with this.

But then she is on her feet, padding off to bed, and I remember Carmela's email. Pretty soon I'm back at my desk, typing furtively long into the night.

24

And so to that night. I've tried to be meticulous in putting together the facts. For the most part, I've had to rely on Helen and William's individual accounts. I put a few questions to Ingrid, but she glared at me so suspiciously that I gave up. The other guests are more difficult – I don't have access to them, but I don't feel it matters. I'm happy with Helen and William's testimony. Listen to me – testimony! Ha! That's what comes of spending so much time in court: I'm picking up legal pretensions.

There are the news clippings too. They were pretty sketchy at first, but as the background details leaked out, interest grew and some of the less cerebral papers ran a few salubrious articles. On the face of it, the crime is depressingly familiar – a burglary was interrupted and the villain pulled a knife – but when an attack takes place in a choice suburban setting and a relationship was known to exist between the victim and the perpetrator, well, now, that's far more interesting. Relationship, you say? What type? And what was she doing dressed up like that at that hour of the night? An ivory silk dress. One newspaper described it as a négligée. Dressed up to the nines – for a lover? And that lover was . . .? They had a field day with that! It all came down to sex. She walked out of her lovely home and away from her nice husband to a clandestine rendezvous with an ignorant boy who didn't know any better. Who would have thought it? And who was the true victim? The articles reeked of moral outrage.

But the evening hadn't started like that. It had been a celebration of Helen and William's narrow escape. They had recognised, although neither had admitted it, that they had begun to drift and it had taken the loss of their baby to avert disaster. They had been balm to each other's wound and wanted to re-establish the other areas of their lives – work and friendships. What could be more natural than to invite people into their space, where they would present a united front to the world: "Look! See how happy we are! See how we appreciate what we've been given." They felt generous with relief.

A meal. Friends. A new dress. Flowers. Candles. Wine. Food carefully prepared and served. Those last hours ticking away before everything would collapse around them.

It was an ambitious meal, three courses, everything made from scratch. Helen is a good cook, innovative and unflappable in the kitchen. And there was something so important about this night that she felt it needed to be marked with truly outstanding food. It was springtime, with that crisp bite in the air, but she shied away from lamb or anything summery. No, something warm and cosy, mildly wintry, from which they could draw comfort. Onion tart with a bitter salad to start, then roast monkfish with pumpkin purée and mushrooms. For dessert, quinces poached in Muscat with lemon ice cream. An aspirational meal – a performance. *Pretentious?* The newspapers made something of that too, printing with glee the "exotic" (meaning expensive) ingredients, which highlighted the vast plain of difference between Helen and Donovan.

Helen and William prepared the meal together. I imagine them in the kitchen, side by side, chopping, sautéing and kneading, filled with the delicious anticipation of what they were about to achieve. The warmth and conviviality of a kitchen filling with mouth-watering aromas, each engaged in his or her tasks, but calling upon the other to taste, to approve, to praise. Moving about, they touch each other as they pass, a hand trailing across a back on the way to the sink – little touches, the prelude to a grander act of love later that night. In a way, a meal is an act of love. In its preparation there is a sort of healing power.

They have cooked together on many occasions, but this time feels different. This time is notable. William opens the fridge and jumps back at an overpowering smell. She laughs and explains that it's the cheese she bought – Roquefort, Stilton and Gruyére. "You and your smelly cheeses," he says softly, with a smile. There is a connection in that statement; there is fondness and ownership. I know you, it says. *I know all these small details – these pieces of information that together, make up the whole of you.*

They will eat in the dining room, which is undergoing extensive surgery. In the burst of creativity that had been sparked over the past few weeks, they had attacked various rooms with vigour. The dining room walls were deeply scarred, great strips of wallpaper ripped off, leaving a blend of forlorn pattern and raw plaster. But the glory of this room was the table, a great expanse of mahogany that had history in it from generations of meals eaten at it. And Helen had chosen to leave it bare of a tablecloth, adorning it instead with a centrepiece of lilies, gardenias, chrysanthemums and baby's breath, a host of white tea lights scattered round the edges, their wedding silver and crystal glasses, white napkins in shiny rings. Simple and elegant. I imagine something bridal about that table – with all those white flowers, the hostess in ivory silk. Feminine and textured. Sensuous.

And what of that much-maligned gown? I think of Helen slipping upstairs with half an hour to go, touching up her make-up, applying lipstick and scent, brushing her gorgeous long hair, and all the while that dress is lying on their bed, waiting for her. An expensive, luxurious item, bought on a whim. When she put it on the material seemed to slip like water over her skin and clung to her in ripples. A dress like liquid, a fabric that invited touch. Too much for a dinner party, but, as she explained to me, her body had suffered from the loss of the baby. The procedure that had followed – the scraping out of her womb – had been clinical and cold. She felt her body deserved to be honoured. And the dress, well, it was an extravagance, something she would never have thought of buying before, but now she was open to trying new things. She felt she deserved that.

And descending the staircase, her dress shimmering around her, a pearl hanging at her throat, she pauses on the step and feels herself submerged in the warmth of her surroundings: the glow from the lamp at the bottom of the stairs, the delicious smells emanating from the kitchen, her husband humming to himself, the quiet popping of a cork, jazz seeping from the sitting room. She feels as if the house itself is enfolding her in an embrace.

The doorbell sounds and she takes a deep breath to compose herself as she runs down the last few steps and reaches for the latch.

"Ingrid! How lovely to see you." She swoops down to plant a kiss on her sister's cheek.

"My God, what are you wearing?" Ingrid asks, looking worried. She takes in Helen's appearance, then gazes at her own outfit and says accusingly, "You never told me we were dressing up."

"Oh, we're not! I'm just going a bit over the top. I'm the hostess so I'm allowed to be."

She ushers her sister inside and closes the door, but Ingrid is still uneasy. "If I'd known, I'd have put on that dress I wore at Christmas, the black velvet one."

Helen looks at her sister, who is plucking at her skirt and the boxy red jacket, taking furtive glances in the mirror, her brow puckered with self-consciousness. "Don't be silly. You look lovely. Come in and have a drink."

In the living room, Ingrid comments on the emptiness.

"You're the first to arrive."

"Am I early? You said eight. Do you think I'd have time to go home and change?"

"Ingrid!" William arrives and kisses his sister-in-law, then thrusts a gin and tonic into her hand. "Get your chops round that."

"Oh, William, thank you," she says. Relief sweeps over

her face when she sees he isn't wearing a tuxedo, or even a tie, just cords and a lilac shirt.

Ingrid. First to arrive, but last to be invited. As Helen watches her sister, still plucking anxiously at her skirt while she sips her drink, she feels a surge of love for her. So capable in many ways, yet at social events she is cast adrift in a sea of fears, assailed by the unknowns, unsure of what is expected of her. When Helen told me that, I had to bite my lip so I didn't laugh in disbelief.

The doorbell rings again and Helen goes to answer it. She finds Maxine and Eric outside, smiling broadly, clutching champagne and wine.

Now I was surprised to hear this, for I knew about William and Eric. Why had they been asked? How could William bear to have the man in his home? And how could Helen have invited Eric after his thinly veiled advance to her?

"It happened by accident," Helen told me. "It was Maxine. She kept saying we had to organise a night out, just the four of us, and I kept resisting, until finally she invited us to their house on the night that William and I had planned our dinner party. I felt awkward, I suppose – put on the spot. Before I knew it, I'd blurted out an invitation. And I didn't know about William and Eric then. About Eric's involvement. I didn't know that until later."

But when William found out, why didn't he stop it? Why didn't he tell her then?

"By the time I found out, it was too late to do anything about it," he told me. "And at that time, I was buoyed up because I felt a new strength in our relationship. It made me feel as if I could take on anything. And if you'd seen her, Reuben, she was so excited about that dinner – we both were – that when she told me she'd invited them, I didn't have the heart to tell her to uninvite them. I think part of her reason for asking them was to reassure me. She thought I was jealous or suspicious of how she and Eric might feel about one another and that was her way of putting my mind at ease, of telling me I was loved. So I told myself that it had happened a million years ago and it was time to bury it. And I hoped to God that Eric would do the same and he wouldn't breathe a word about it."

The room seems to fill once Maxine and Eric have entered it. They are an overwhelmingly sociable couple, bringing with them a store of anecdotes, ready laughter and the kind of warm, confident, good-natured conviviality that attracts attention. People like them seem to give off a glow to which everyone else in the room is attracted. They include Ingrid in their conversation, drawing information out of her. She is Helen's sister? Older or younger? (How they asked that with straight faces, I don't know.) Where did she work? Ernst & Young? A friend of theirs worked there in Accounts, perhaps she might know him . . .

When the doorbell rings for the third time, Helen already feels a sense of relief as her guests relax around her. She opens the door to a man, two women and a dog.

"Hi," says the man, offering an outstretched hand. "I'm Steve. You must be Helen."

When William had travelled to Scotland to research his book, he had met an eccentric American diamond dealer at a dinner party. This man was fabulously wealthy, he told Helen. A geologist by training, he travelled all over the world, buying diamonds and then having them recut to increase their value. A fascinating man, he told her, with an illustrious career and an interesting past. When William had discovered that Steve would be in Dublin for a few days, he had suggested the dinner party. He had rung Steve to invite him, Steve had accepted and asked if he might bring a lady friend. Helen and William had passed an interesting twenty minutes surmising who that lady friend might be, as Steve had a wife in LA. Now Helen is surprised into silence by the presence of two women.

"These are my friends, Laura and Karla," says Steve in his slow, dry voice.

Both women are Italian, impeccably dressed in trouser suits, the jackets cinched at the waist and showing just the right amount of cleavage. Laura seems the older of the two and has a cluster of onyx and pearls at her throat. Karla clutches the small brown dog to her chest and alternates between kissing the dog and beaming her beautiful smile at Helen.

"You're all very welcome. Won't you come through?"

Ingrid is allergic to dogs. Her reaction to Jinx – the sausage-like creature nestling next to Karla's bosom – is one of horror.

"Oh, I wouldn't worry," Eric says reassuringly, moving to stroke the little creature. "This is hardly a dog at all."

The room breaks up into shimmering laughter.

It is hard to tell what the real source of amusement is, the dog or the curiosity of Steve having two girlfriends – if they are girlfriends. Laura, it transpires, is also in the jewellery trade, and Karla seems to be a friend of hers. Looking about at the other guests, Helen is amused to see that everyone seems to be watching the unusual triumvirate and surmising what the relationship between them might be. She catches William's eye and he smiles across the room conspiratorially.

Drinks, and then they are ushered into the dining room. Sometimes when I am working on this part of the story, I think of it as a play, with all the action taking place on a stage and I am the audience out front. I think of these characters now like an orchestra tuning up, the cacophony of sound, each trying out their own voice. A frieze. I can look at each one in turn, examining them, pausing to get the whole picture. Steve, the mogul, sitting between his two ladies, both beautiful, vivacious and flirtatious, like courtesans, flourishing cleavage with panache. The society couple sit opposite them, transfixed and absorbed by their exoticism. Maxine puffs out her chest, tossing her glorious red mane, competing for Steve's attention, unused to being out of the spotlight and unwilling to go silently into the shadows. And Eric: casual and sanguine, yet clearly intoxicated by the glorious unexpectedness of the threesome, his mind turning cartwheels. He can barely keep a self-satisfied smirk off his face. In all my scenes Ingrid plays the disgruntled shrew, I'm afraid. Now she is peering at them all over the rim of her wine glass. She feels huge and uncomfortable, yet invisible – a dull blob in this sea of beauty. She drinks to console herself. William, cordial and good-natured as ever, talks to her, happy to be sitting at a remove from Eric, and making a warm effort to overcome the edgy anxiety he has felt ever since Eric and Maxine entered his house. But he glances down at his wife, casting her eyes at her guests, seeming serene and at peace.

"A toast," he says, raising his glass. They all turn to him. "To an evening among friends."

"An evening among friends."

"Hear, hear."

A clink of glasses, then bubbles spilling across their tongues.

And outside on the street, rain is starting to fall. A light drizzle that is becoming steadier. From the street, the candlelight, conversation and clinking of glasses reaches him. Standing in front of the railings, staring up at the house, he feels the stone of his heart lying heavily in his chest, and thinks of all the angry words he had written – a stream of invective – penned in a tearful rage, the words blurred. He couldn't stop them: they kept coming, swarming across the page.

Bitch. Fucking tease. Lady Godiva. Swanning around, teasing me, making my life a misery. Who the fuck do you think you are? Pricktease. Whore. Letting me finger you like that, letting me shove my hand in your cunt, then pretending that nothing ever happened. Fucking bitch-whore-cunt. I fucking hate you. You and your fucking husband. Self-satisfied prick. You'll get what's coming to you.

Those words, written and delivered. She would have received them earlier that day. Received and absorbed them. Yet when he had seen her open the door, once, twice, three times that night, and oh, God, the beauty of that dress, every curve in her body swelling and pressing against his consciousness, playing with him, torturing him, he thought of that letter, thought of those words, in his hiding place behind the fence, among the bushes, all the miseries of the last few months crowding down on him as she disappeared behind the heavy, closing door.

25

This story has been circling in my head for almost a year now and it is hard to shake off. I have sat with Helen in Bonnieux, listening to her tell her tale. I have kept William company in the dark hours before dawn as he poured out his own sad version. I have sat in a courtroom among strangers witnessing Donovan's account – his warped testimony. But when I return to that night, the dinner party, the startling revelation, the account I am most interested in, strangely, is Ingrid's. It was she who dropped the bombshell. But she won't discuss that night with me, so I must fall back on the accounts I have been given, along with my imagination. It's what writers are supposed to do, isn't it? Put ourselves in other people's shoes. I know one writer who imagines he is stepping inside a character's skin. He envisages the character standing before him, then mimes climbing into his or her body, feeling his way into their limbs, wiggling fingers and toes, rolling his head on his neck, getting comfortable in the new skin. He performs this pantomime before he sits down to write.

Now, I don't propose to do anything of the sort. I shudder at the thought of crawling inside Ingrid's sturdy body and peering out at the world through her eyes. But I do try to imagine how she felt that night, carrying with her all the weight of her expectations, her history, her insecurities. I attempt to understand what led her to create that terrible scene.

All evening, she had agonised over what to wear. Standing in her flat, she surveyed clothes strewn over her bed and on the backs of chairs, a dress laid out on the sofa like a bodiless corpse, and she in the midst of it in her underwear, panicking and berating herself for being so ill-prepared, for not having taken herself into town and bought something new, expensive and flattering. But Ingrid is intimidated by shops. No, it's not that – she's intimidated by having to confront her body in the mirrors of those changing rooms.

I have seen pictures of Ingrid as a child, and she was a beautiful little girl. White-blonde hair and that shiny apple-cheeked pudginess that looks so healthy and adorable. In her white cotton dress and red sandals, with a smile for the camera, she reminds me of one of the von Trapp children in *The Sound of Music*. It must be hard having known what it is like to be beautiful, then growing up into an unremarkable adult, the childish cuteness fading into plainness. The white-blonde locks darken and dull, the healthy glow fades and the smile becomes hard and suspicious. Suddenly people gasp with incredulity at the child in the photographs, and you stare at the person in the mirror and wonder how it could have turned out like this, how your genes could have turned so treacherous.

Helen was not a pretty child. She was small, pale and dark-haired with enormous bulbous eyes. Frequently she was mistaken for a boy. As a baby, she was colicky and ill tempered, her pale face mottled and florid with constant crying. Ingrid, five years her senior, looked upon her with a detached curiosity. As they grew older, she felt protective towards her little sister – she felt sorry for her, the dark ugly child. But at some point things changed.

Teenagers now, they are walking in the street and Ingrid feels eyes pressing on them, which she has been used to since childhood. But when she looks up to confront the hungry stares, she sees, with a tremor of shock, that the eyes are not on her, but her sister. It is an epiphany. Suddenly she is looking at Helen as if she is a stranger, and is shocked to the core. The unattractive child has become a languid beauty. There is something romantic about the dark hair and the small face, the huge blue eyes and dainty nose. The skinny frame has blossomed into enticing curves.

She feels betrayed in some way, and guilty for the pangs of jealousy she cannot control. Helen's beauty tortures her – and she can do nothing about it, but neither can she stop the relentless march of her own physical destiny. She focuses on her strengths, pouring her energy into her work. She is the career girl, hard-nosed, savvy, driven. There is nothing fey about her: she embraces her Teutonic practicality, her prudence and drive, and tries hard not to think about her unhappiness.

Finally, she settles on a long black skirt with the festive jacket. Red lipstick lasts as far as the front door, where she catches sight of it in the mirror and realises she looks tarty. She wipes it off and replaces it with her usual shade.

Ingrid does not receive many dinner invitations, and

she had worked hard to keep the desperate enthusiasm out of her voice when Helen had invited her to join their party. But all week she has played it over in her head, an evening among friends, dining with cultured, intelligent people who will be impressed by her arguments on the war in Iraq, her progressive views on monetary union and her recent reading list.

But when Helen opens the front door and Ingrid sees that dress, the armour of her preparations falls away from her. The reading, the current affairs, the subtle lipstick — none of it can touch the glory of that dress.

Ingrid has been in this house many times before, but tonight she doesn't feel comfortable in it. These people are unfamiliar to her in every sense — not just that she hasn't met them before, but that she has never been confronted by their type. She can just about tolerate Maxine and Eric, but Steve and his two Italian consorts baffle her. She struggles to work out the relationship between them. Steve wears a wedding ring and has made several references to a wife in LA, yet the flirtation between the three is blindingly obvious. Ingrid feels confused and then annoyed. All her ideas for the evening evaporate. Instead, it is Steve who flourishes his erudition. "A pink diamond," he drawls, "is the hardest to cut. Harder even than a white diamond. You gotta have real skill to take on a pink one." He has a dry gin-and-cigarettes voice to go with his tobacco-coloured eyes and thinning brown hair, which Ingrid suspects he dyes.

"This pink diamond I bought last year, I spent six months travelling round the world, interviewing cutters, looking for the right one to take it on. I wasn't giving that baby up to any old fly-by-night."

"And did you find one?" Maxine asks, elbows on the table, chin propped on her hands.

"Eventually. This little guy in the Bronx, would you believe? A Hassidic Jew – they have a long history of diamond cutting, passed from generation to generation. This guy was young but skilled, and he had imagination – that's the difference youth brings. They can see the angles, the play of light in the stone, and know how to cut it along the original lines, the way their fathers and grandfathers cut it, but with youth comes bravery too – willingness to push the boundaries and create something different. That's what I liked about this guy. He had vision."

"Bravery on your part too," Maxine coos. "That's quite a risk to take."

"Sure. But it paid off."

"And what kind of increase in value would you be looking at?" Eric asks, interested.

Steve considers this for a moment, eyes narrowing. "Let's see now. I bought the diamond for close to one point two million US dollars. After I'd had it cut, it was worth at least three times as much."

Eric sucks in his breath and nods. Maxine stares at Steve with renewed interest. Ingrid is open-mouthed with incredulity.

"Three and a half million dollars for a diamond?" she says, staggered.

"That's about it."

"How many diamonds do you have?" she blurts out rudely.

"Well, a few, but they're not all that valuable." He gives a brief list of the types of stones he collects, old and new, the work that goes into preparing each one for market, and the lengths to which he goes in seeking out customers.

Helen asks where he stores the jewels, and he is off on a diatribe about security systems and sealed vaults. Ingrid signals to William that her glass is empty.

Something has occurred to her in the course of this conversation. Whenever she addresses a question to Steve, he directs his answers to William or Maxine or the flowers in front of him. He is rigorously avoiding her eyes. At one point his own pass over her, then return to Maxine, and it is then that she gets it: he is one of those men who will only look at a woman if she is beautiful. He is uninterested in a woman's mind unless it comes encased in a pretty head. He does not like to look at that which is not aesthetically pleasing. He makes his living peering through magnifying lenses at the sparkling glory of nature's most precious stones. His eyes are precious to him: he doesn't want to risk injury by allowing them to rest on her battered old casing. She begins to dislike him.

"And tell me this, Steve," Eric says over the main course, "how can you tell the difference, from a distance, between a real diamond and a fake? I mean, take me. I have to confess I know nothing about diamonds. Absolutely zilch, zip, *nada*!" Eric is the sort of man who feigns ignorance to put people at their ease, to show himself as benign and unthreatening, then pumps them for information. "From ten feet away, I can't tell if something is a diamond or paste!"

Steve forces a chuckle and they engage in banter, during which Ingrid drains her glass again and tries to avoid rolling her eyes at William as Eric launches into an anecdote about sourcing jewellery for a drama he's been working on.

This interests Karla, who has been feeding her dog with scraps off her plate. She asks Eric what sort of shows he works on.

"I'm doing a period drama at the moment," he tells her. "All very Edith Wharton. Think *The Age of Innocence* – vast ballrooms and dresses, flowers, the subtlety involved in the removal of a glove! Actually, Helen advised me on the flowers for the piece."

"Is that how you two know each other?" Karla asks.

"Maxine and I are in a choir together," Helen explains.

"And we've recently discovered another connection, haven't we, Helen?" Eric says, his eyes twinkling with merriment. "It turns out that William and I were at school together." His gaze swings to the other end of the table. "I knew I recognised you from somewhere, William. Old Clongowes, all those years ago. I never forget a face!"

Ingrid is beginning to feel tipsy. But she is close enough to William to see his smile falter. Until now, he has been discussing the pearl industry in Italy with Laura, who appeared quite knowledgeable about it.

"Indeed," he says, "but that was a long time ago." A warning note in his voice.

But Eric is quite drunk and reluctant to let go of the attention he is enjoying. "Did you know, William," he continues, smiling mischievously, "that they almost kicked me out because of you? Because of that incident in the bicycle shed."

He has everyone's attention now. Even Ingrid, who has

always liked William, and who feels him stiffen now, cannot take her eyes off Eric.

"William was a dreamy kid," he explains, "always mooning about, reciting poetry to the trees. And one of the lads got it into his head one day to play a trick on him."

"Eric," says Maxine, quietly, "I don't think you should tell that story."

"Come on! It all happened years ago! William sees the funny side now, don't you, William?"

For one long, awful moment William says nothing, just stares at his empty plate, eyes fixed on the crossed cutlery before him. When he looks up, the anger has gone, replaced by a kind of controlled bafflement. "I wonder why you would want to tell such a story," he says. Everyone around the table is listening now. The air has become charged. "I wonder why you would wish to tell a tale of bullying, fear and threatened violence – a tale that can only embarrass me, your host, and show you for what you are: a coward, a weak boy who was too frightened to stand up to bullies. Instead, you allowed them to use you as their stooge, their look-out, no matter what the consequences might be. I wonder why you would want to tell a story like that at my table as you eat the food my wife has prepared. I wonder why, of all the stories you could tell, you would wish to tell that one. What purpose could it possibly serve."

There is silence. Helen has been staring at her husband, amazed. She is stunned – not by the quiet dignity of his rhetoric, but by the revealed truth that she has invited the source of his childhood pain into their home. But more than that – *he never told her.*

Eric has been grinning at his plate while squirming in his seat. He cannot bring himself to meet William's gaze. His awkwardness is felt around the table like a held breath, so that when William gets to his feet and begins to clear away the empty plates, Helen rising to assist him, it is like a release. The incident is over.

Once they are out of the room, Eric seeks to regain his position. He chuckles loudly and leans forward, words emerging from the side of his mouth. "Jesus! I really touched upon a nerve there, huh? Who would have thought he'd still be licking that wound? It was fucking years ago!"

"Eric!" Maxine says sharply.

"I guess some wounds never heal," Steve replies sagely.

They've forgotten I'm here, thinks Ingrid. *I'm invisible to them.*

From the kitchen, there is silence – no clatter of crockery or cutlery, no raised voices – and she imagines another whispered conversation taking place. Or perhaps Helen is simply enfolding her husband in the comfort of her embrace.

By the time dessert arrives, Ingrid is drunk, and drunker still when coffee is poured. She strives for conversation with Steve. Something about his dismissal of her has made her angry, which drives her towards confrontation.

They are discussing Steve and his young cutter again, the visionary Jewish youth who had transformed a pink diamond and tripled its worth.

"Well, he's young," Steve is telling Eric, "twenty-four, but it's not like he didn't have the skills. His father'd been training him since he was a kid."

"It wasn't so great a risk," Ingrid says.

"Well, he was still unproven . . ."

"But he had the skills. He had the background, the family calibre."

"Sure, but it's not as if he'd ever taken on a major piece of work like I was giving him."

"And your diamond would have been insured, I'm guessing, thus minimising the risk again."

"Insured against the sum I paid for it, not against the potential worth—"

"Oh, come, Steve," she breaks in. "We all know that any risk you took was very well calculated and—"

At this point, Laura leans across to her companion and whispers in his ear.

"Oh, yeah, baby," Steve chuckles. "Later maybe, if you're lucky." He grins at her, and Ingrid is piqued to have been dismissed by him yet again, her argument cast aside in favour of some lewd suggestion.

"Well, I'm all in favour of giving young people a chance," Eric pipes up, recovered now from his embarrassment and never one to be left out of a conversation. "It's like Helen. She took on this guy for a few months – young fellow from an underprivileged background with a criminal record – and gave him a chance to improve his situation. Some work experience, a reference – that's what these people need, not charity."

"Did you?" William asks, looking up suddenly.

"Yes."

"You never told me."

"I didn't want to worry you."

The look exchanged between them is lost on the others.

They don't see the questioning glance, or hear the inflection in William's voice that tells of his dismay.

"I'm not in favour of giving people money," Steve says, then adds, "but I'm not sure that giving them work like that is the answer."

"What is the answer, then?" Ingrid asks, her tone a bit too loud and brisk, causing Maxine, beside her, to jump.

"I don't know," Steve drawls. "I'm just saying that a leopard doesn't change his spots – not that quickly, anyway."

"A leopard doesn't change his spots?"

"You can't take these people out of their environment for a couple hours a day, show them how to do a few things, pay them a little money, and expect them overnight to shrug off the habits of a lifetime. These things are deeply engrained."

"What things?" Her aggression is rising inside her. She is conscious of the silence that has fallen round the table. Something in the room has changed – an alteration in the rhythm. Everything is suddenly very serious and weighted.

"Criminality, for a start. I'm sorry, I know it's not politically correct to say it, but I believe there is such a thing as a criminal gene. It's biological. Hereditary. Passed on from father to son. You can't beat nature with a couple hours' nurturing here and there. It's much stronger than that."

"A criminal gene?" The blood in Ingrid's head has reached an oceanic roar. She loathes this man.

"Put it this way, the cutter I found, his skill wasn't just learned, it was in his blood. His father had it, and his father's father. It's the same with criminals. A thief begets a thief. I have yet to meet anyone who has been able to break the bonds of criminality."

"What about Helen and me?" she asks quietly.

The question is out before she realises. Now that Steve is looking at her directly, for the first time that evening, his eyes on her, she feels emboldened and unwilling to back down. The whole room is focused on her, their attention fixed on what she will say next.

"What about you and Helen?"

"Would you say that we're criminals?"

Steve looks from one to the other. Helen's face is as pale as her dress, fixed in an expression of dread mixed with perplexity.

"Well? Would you say we're criminals?" Ingrid repeats, her voice rising. She is becoming shrill.

"Ingrid," William says quietly, "I think perhaps you've had a little too much to drink."

She feels his hand at her wrist, but she is too lost in the moment to be stilled by it.

"Well, criminals beget criminals, don't they? That's what you said. 'A thief begets a thief.' How about killers? Hmm? Do killers beget killers?"

"Ingrid, what are you talking about?" Helen whispers.

"If I told you that our father killed someone," Ingrid says to Steve, "if I told you he had done time for killing a man, would that make me a killer too? Would you have to go away and revise your opinion of Helen and me?"

"For God's sake, Ingrid . . ."

But she is too inflamed to hear her sister, too far gone to notice the fear in her voice.

"Our father spent two years in prison after he had

killed someone in a car accident. He was drunk at the time. Now, according to your theory, we should be languishing in a prison too, acting out our genetic destiny, not sitting here dining with you. We seem to be some kind of aberration, wouldn't you say?"

Nobody says a word. The whole room seems to shrink at the knowledge that a family secret has exploded into the room. And from the bewildered expression on Helen's face, it is clear to everyone that she had known nothing about it. Her face seems to crumple in on itself, her eyes casting about the table as if for a simpler explanation, a more vivid truth. But the veracity of Ingrid's words cannot be questioned: they were too wildly dramatic to have been invented.

Eric is the first to react, with a brief gasp of laughter. His wife places a steadying hand on his arm.

But Ingrid is caught up in her sister's reaction. She feels the nudge of panic. The flames of her triumph seem to flicker and fade, chased out by an icy chill. "Oh, come on, Helen," she tries nervously, "you knew about it."

But Helen is too shocked to speak.

"You must have known. For God's sake! Where did you think he was?"

Helen's eyes fill with tears now, yet still she cannot speak.

"Surely you knew! You must have done. Mum told me – I presumed she'd told you too. Helen?" A pleading whine has entered her voice. "Helen, you must have known – I'm sure you did!"

The dread in Ingrid's stomach has become a dull ache, spreading out along her limbs and up her spine into the base of her skull. She knows now she will never be forgiven for her angry revelation. And in the instant that she realises this, two things happen: the dog makes a brief choking sound, then throws up on the table, and the telephone rings in the hall. William gets to his feet, but Helen, finding her voice, says to him, "No. I'll go."

As she sweeps towards the door, she glances back at her sister. It is a look Ingrid will never forget, a look of quiet loathing; a long, accusing stare.

26

For a moment, Helen can't speak. The voice at the other end of the line has to repeat the question, then asks, "Are you there?"

"No, that's fine," she says, keeping her voice level, trying to forget the mad swirl of thoughts that are clouding her judgement. "I'll check it out. I'm sure it's nothing."

She hangs up and for a moment she stands there, listening. From the dining room come sounds of conversation, muted now. But something important has happened – something has been shattered – and the talk has faded to a respectful level. She is reminded of people outside a church after a funeral, careful to avoid a peal of laughter, their tones solemn and hushed.

She stands in the hall, leaning over the telephone, for a long time. Around her she is aware of the house, the ticking of the great clock beside the kitchen door, her face reflected in the hall mirror, and beyond it the angles and contours of the hall. Is that the same staircase she glided down a few hours previously? Is that the same solid door she opened to let in her guests? Is this the same soft rug underfoot that she had stood on earlier, wrapped in her husband's warm embrace?

Everything seems different now, the things around her no longer familiar. Surfaces seem harder, angles more acute. She is aware of sharp edges and coldness. This house, which had been warm and welcoming, seems vast, cold and daunting.

Her father killed a man.

There is a belt of laughter from the dining room, the scraping of chairs against the floor and the clinking of glasses. The diners are restive. She stares hard at the door, thinks of all the people behind it in that room. They seem like strangers now, even the ones she thought she knew best in the world. Her husband, with the things he keeps to himself, too ashamed to share them with her; her sister, with her dark store of family secrets – how had Helen not known? How had they kept it from her?

She feels herself slipping backwards, yet she is standing still. All those words swarm round her and pummel her body through the silk dress, which now seems to mock her. "*Why didn't you tell me?*" she had said to William when they were alone in the kitchen. His face tense and pale, he had turned away from her and put his hands flat on the countertop. She had gazed at his back, the hollow at the base of his neck, the soft spread of his hair, and thought: Who is this man?

Secrets. The look of triumph on Ingrid's face. The guilty pleasure she had derived from her revelation. Helen is grappling with the shock of her sister's malice as much as the news itself. Now she feels her eyes filling. She is stunned, battered. And it is not disbelief that assaults her:

on the contrary, she believed it at once. She understood. She knew. What she feels is a steady series of betrayals; creeping out of the store of her memories, all those occasions when she had questioned, when she had sought clarification, when she had voiced doubt, niggling uncertainties, and the mendacity of the answers she received from her father, her mother and her sister. They are coming back to her now, and she knows that there will be more over the coming days and weeks, an onslaught of grief and sorrow. She wants to cry, but instead she listens to her breathing, the constant grinding rhythm of the hall clock, the rain falling outside and the far-off sounds of people enjoying themselves. They will all have a good story to tell, she observes wryly to her dry-eyed reflection. Her keys lie in a bowl on the hall table. She scoops them up and, not pausing to get a coat or an umbrella, not popping her head through the door to tell her guests or her husband, she opens the door and steps out into the night.

The sound of the alarm reaches her well before she turns the car on to the green and pulls up alongside the kerb. The rain is heavy now and, through the gloom, the blue light flashes intermittently through the dank air. This has happened before. In fact, there is a weary regularity to it. Without even a hint of apprehension, she rushes to the door and fumbles with the lock. Once inside, she makes her way to the back of the shop and behind the counter to the kitchen area. Sure enough, the little window above the sink is open. She shuts it, punches in the alarm code, then picks up the phone to contact the alarm company.

"No, no," she tells the voice. "It was just a cat. No need to call the police."

She gives her code word, listens to the strained politeness of the voice, apologises again and hangs up.

She is becoming a nuisance. This forgetfulness, this carelessness. Which of them was it this time? Helen or Iris? She cannot keep driving out in the middle of the night to turn off the alarm. She doesn't want another lecture from the local police about wasting their time. She needs to get a grip on herself.

But standing there in the darkness, the scent of flowers filling the air, the sudden stillness after the blaring alarm has been silenced, Helen gives way to tears. Her grief is uncontained. She cries because she is married to a man so closed and remote that he cannot tell her about his fears. She cries because she has filled her home with people who are shallow, pompous, materialistic and rude. She cries because her judgement of people's characters is so inaccurate that she no longer trusts it. She cries for the baby she lost. She cries for her mother. She cries because the pain of this new knowledge about her father is so strong that she fears the blow to their relationship may be fatal. She cries because her sister is so isolated and bitter that she will blurt out poisonous secrets at a dinner party to score a point. She cries because her mother went to her grave without disclosing the truth to her. She cries because she knows that she is the type of person from whom people keep secrets. And finally, she cries because she is guilty of harbouring secrets from William, her own betrayals – remembering that look on his face when Eric had let slip about Keith, and it is her own failure in her marriage that causes her the most grief.

It lasts only a few minutes. Then she pulls herself

together, straightens up and swipes at her hair. The skin on her face feels tight and dry and she cannot imagine how desperate she must look. She feels tired and awkward in the dress. She has not been gone long, but her guests will have noticed her absence. She resolves to return home, to see the night through, and then, tomorrow, in the cold light of day, she will face what must come next.

But first she needs to fix her appearance. There is a bathroom at the top of the stairs, and she has hardly set foot on the lowest step when she sees the spill of light at the top and feels a tightening in her chest. Instinctively, she knows it is him. Despite the warning voice at the back of her mind, she is still shocked by what she sees and gasps as she reaches the top of the stairs. The small room is full of light, every bulb ablaze, and the room has been cleared of clutter, leaving only a small sunken sofa and two dingy chairs. But flowers are strewn everywhere, roses and carnations tossed over the sofa, hyacinths and tiger lilies scattered on the floor, tufts of baby's breath disappearing behind cushions, peonies blooming in a crimson flourish on the armchair, rows of orchids lined up against the wall, their delicate heads trembling on their stalks. How had she walked through the shop and not noticed their absence? She sees the flowers every day, yet gathered here in this small room, in this haphazard, crazy fashion, they resemble a silent explosion. The voice in the back of her head whispers quietly: *This is serious.*

Donovan is in the middle of it all, as she had known he would be. As soon as she had seen the light on the stairwell, she had known. He is standing behind the armchair, holding the back of it with both hands, staring at her with a beaming smile, like a child who has presented a parent with a gift they are especially proud of, a gift they have made themselves.

"I knew you'd come," he says loudly. "I knew you wouldn't let me down."

He looks exalted and insane, childish and oddly ancient. His hair is standing away from his head in a tangle as if he has raked his hands absently through it. His eyes are lit up with a strange glow. And a fresh bruise, angry and vivid, sweeps out across his cheekbone from his eye and the bridge of his nose. A joyous smile spreads across his features. She can see how excited he is, reads the wildness in his restless movements, and realises in that moment how dangerous he may be.

"What do you think?" he asks, glancing around at the room, gesturing wildly with his arms.

She knows she should be frightened – there is something barely controlled about him – but the first true emotion she experiences is anger. "You broke in," she says quietly. "You set off the alarm."

"Ah, yes," he replies sheepishly, yet continues to smile, like a mischievous schoolboy. "Technically it wasn't a break-in, though. I used my key. But then I opened the window to set off the alarm. I had to summon you somehow."

He gives a sudden burst of laughter and she jumps.

"You shouldn't be here," she says. "You shouldn't have done this."

She is surprisingly calm. It is as if she is removed from herself, from this room, as if she is witnessing something that has already happened. Nothing about this night feels real, the flowers, her dress, the bruise on his face.

"Oh," he says then, and anguish blended with ecstasy transforms his face. "Oh, God, Helen, you look so beautiful. That dress. This is . . . everything about this . . . all of it is perfect. I've dreamed of this. But that dress . . . I couldn't have imagined it. You – you're a goddess."

He is staring at her body, eyes devouring the swell of her hips, her breasts, her exposed shoulders, the creamy skin catching the light.

"What happened to your face, Keith?"

"Oh, nothing," he answers quickly, but something seems to shut down behind his features, and he hastens to dispel the question by moving towards her and grasping her arms. She flinches and tries to draw back but his grip is firm and determined.

"Here. You sit here," he instructs in a cheerful tone and places her at one end of the sofa.

She feels the flowers brushing against her thighs and tries to push them away with her hands. He is looking about him, debating whether to sit or stand. He decides to perch on the arm of the chair, beaming across at her. From her diminished height, she feels nips of alarm. The chair blocks the exit to the stairs and she feels hemmed in. She sits with her knees tight together. This is the second time he has cornered her in this room.

"What is it you want from me?"

"Helen!" He laughs. "The way you say that! Like a line from a hostage drama! I just want to talk. You and me. We used to have great talks, remember? My God, the talks we had!" And he is away again, gazing happily into the distance.

"What is it you want, Keith?" she repeats, keeping her voice steady.

"Lord, I'm so rude." He gets up suddenly. "Let me find you something to drink."

His voice is overly loud this evening, his movements large, clumsy and jerky; he is affecting a kind of manic suavity. He hurries to the table in the corner, where he has a bottle of wine, already open, and proceeds to pour it into glasses. She wonders briefly where he got them, and then if he has already been drinking and, if so, how much. "What's with the flowers?" she asks casually, but her voice is small. She doesn't wish to provoke him.

"Do you like it?"

His enthusiasm is hearty, childish, and she finds herself irritated. "Not really. You've ruined half my stock. I hope you're going to pay for it."

He gives a high-pitched chuckle. "Don't you see the romance, Helen? A room full of flowers, wine, candle-light, a beautiful dress . . ." Suddenly, he fishes in the pocket of his jeans, draws out a lighter, sparks a flame and puts it to the two candles on the floor in front of her. Their flickering luminance is lost under the harsh glare of the overhead light. She dreads that he will turn out the lights and she will have to confront the shadows darting across his face.

"When you work with flowers every day, they lose their romance," she comments drily, working hard to control herself. She keeps glancing at the stairs, calculating the risk of getting up and walking out purposefully. But she feels how dangerous he is and sits still.

He offers her a glass brimming with red wine.

"No, thank you."

"Oh, come on, don't be a spoilsport."

"I'd rather not."

"Just try it. It's a good one. I didn't skimp."

"I said I don't want it."

"I insist." The smile has dropped from his face and his voice is leaden, so she accepts the glass, holding it between her hands, which are resting on her knee. She doesn't drink. She decides to reason with him. Something tells her that the menace in the air can be dissipated with talk.

"I really need to be getting home. My husband and I have dinner guests. They're going to wonder what's keeping me. Pretty soon William will come. Is that what you want?"

For a moment, he considers this and there is something mocking in the seriousness of his pose as he stands before her. She surveys his long, emaciated form, the spareness of his shoulders in the thin T-shirt, the massive runners on his feet. He strokes his gaunt face. "Do you know, Helen? Maybe it's just as well. He has to find out sooner or later."

"What are you talking about?" There is a tightening in her throat.

"About us." He looks at her, full in the face, and she sees the light behind the bony façade. His gaze is open and loving and fills her with dread. "When I saw you this evening, opening the door to those people, letting them into your home – and that dress! My heart jumped at the sight of it."

"You were at my house? Spying on me?"

He ignores this. "Let's get comfortable, shall we?"

He lunges towards the sofa and sits down next to her, swinging his arm along the back behind her. She tenses and pushes against the armrest in an effort to get further away from him. She is rooted to the spot, although she longs to get up. So close to him, she can smell his stale clothes, a faint, musty, mannish scent of sweat and alcohol. He has had quite a lot to drink.

He gulps his wine and nods in appreciation, crossing one leg over the other and looking about him proprietorially. "You know, it took me a while to realise what you meant by giving me that key. It wasn't until the second or third night I stayed here over Christmas that it occurred to me. How dim am I? You must forgive me, Helen, for not copping on sooner. All this time we've wasted. It's April already! But men aren't as quick as women when it comes to picking up signs. But eventually I understood. I was sitting here on this very couch, all alone – God, I was so lonely, Helen. I was waiting for morning when it struck me! The simplest thing in the world. We should be together. We're meant to be together. And this was your way of telling me."

"You're mistaken."

"You will leave William, leave that big old empty house of yours, turn your back on all that part of your life. Close the door on it, Helen. The two of us, we could make our home here! How cosy would that be? Our own little space! We can be together always. Working side by side during the day, and when the last customer has gone and the door is bolted, we can retire up here together. We can spend the evenings drinking wine and reading books, cooking, talking and laughing – like we used to – and then when night comes, we can lie in each other's arms. We can make love all night, Helen."

"No!" The word comes out of her mouth like a bullet. The image he has invoked appals her. "This is absurd –

insane! There's no way in the world that will ever happen!"

He smiles at her, as if she is being coquettish. "It's all right, Helen. I've thought it through. I knew there was something between us right from the start. That first day when you were so kind to me, so apologetic for mistaking my identity. You made me so welcome, Helen. You made me feel warm, cared for . . . loved. And I'd never opened up to anyone the way I have with you. All the time, the little messages and signals you were giving me . . . That day when I came into work upset over another row at home, and it was as if you sensed it, the softness you treated me with that day, and the little smile you gave me, as if you were telling me everything was going to be all right. I tried not to read too much into it, tried to tell myself it was all me, but when you started touching me . . . your hand brushing against mine when you reached for the scissors. The first time it happened, I was frozen to the spot. And another time you leaned across to reach for something by the sink, and your breast pressed against my arm! Oh, Jesus!" He rolls his eyes in ecstasy. "I knew it . . . Finally I knew it when you turned to me that day, caught up in your own troubles, and exposed your emotions to me. You chose me to share them with. No one else. I knew then, Helen, that it wasn't just me. I knew you wanted it badly too."

How had she not seen the seeds of madness planted in him? All that time, with every word, look and gesture, she had been nurturing them, building up his hopes, feeding the dark need in him, letting it flower. How had she let it come to this?

An ambulance, with a siren whooping, goes by outside,

and in that moment she decides to reason with him. Heart hammering away in her chest, she works hard to keep her voice steady.

"Look, Keith, whatever ideas you've got into your head about us, whatever hopes you've had about the two of us being together, you have to understand that I don't feel that way about you. I love my husband. End of story. I have no wish to hurt anyone, and I deeply regret leading you on in any way, giving you false hope, but this . . . all of this must end."

He continues to smile at her beatifically. "We're so perfect for each other. I know you feel it too. I just . . . God, I just love you," he says then, so readily and confidently, not in the way of someone trying it out for the first time, fearful of his love not being reciprocated. Instead, he throws it out as if he has uttered those words to her a thousand times before.

"No," she says, trying to strike a note of compassion and ensure he does not feel rebuffed, ridiculed. The situation is reeling out of control, and she feels the need to seize the initiative. But the glimmer of light in his eyes is unsettling. "You don't love me. This was never love. However close we may have seemed, however well we might have connected – it was something else, never love. Never that."

His face seems to darken and contract, and she thinks of the letter she received only that day. It contained such violence that she had to clutch the furniture for support. And here he is, its author, gazing at her serenely, eyes brimming with crazed, hopeful love.

"Why are you saying this?" he asks. "I know you love me. I know it because of how I feel about you."

His voice cracks, his chin is trembling and the muscles in his neck strain so that she knows he is struggling with some demon that is threatening to unleash itself. Something else has caught her eye. On the table there is a large kitchen knife with a black handle and a serrated edge. How had she not seen it until now? The blade gleams under the lights. And in that moment she understands that he has brought her here to harm her.

"Keith," she says slowly, mouth dry. She knows that words are the only thing that can save her now. "I know you're hurting. You've been through a terrible time, and I'm sorry. I truly am. I never meant to upset you. That's the last thing I wanted."

His head is in his hands, fingers digging ridges through his hair. She cannot see his face, but she keeps talking. She cannot risk him making a sudden grab for the knife. He is stronger and quicker than she is.

"You've had so much to deal with in these past few years. Dropping out of university, prison, a broken heart. It's a lot to come to terms with. I understand why you're upset, believe me. It's enough to send anyone over the edge. And I can't help but feel that somewhere in your mind you're just trying to compensate for the loss of Suzy. That somehow you've cast me in her place. But Keith, I'm not her. What you had with your girlfriend was something unique and special that I cannot replace. I can understand that you want to get something of that back, but it cannot happen with me."

A noise bursts from his mouth, a loud disclaiming gasp, and he gives her the briefest look – a cold, hard little grin. It disappears from his face as quickly as it came, but its shadow remains in her memory. And she understands it instantly. There never was a Suzy. No girlfriend. No Spanish diplomat father. No drinks in the embassy. He had conjured it all out of thin air.

"Drink your wine," he instructs coolly, trying to regain control.

But the conclusion she has reached is so startling that she cannot move. Everything he told her comes back in a rush and she understands the extent to which she has been taken in, the extent to which his madness has led him to lie. There was no girlfriend, no Lurch or Steo. She sees it now: he was alone and struck out remorselessly at a defenceless old woman.

"Helen. Drink your wine."

University – the woman tutor. From his own mouth she had heard it. Accusations of harassment, inappropriate behaviour, threats and intimidation. And she had believed him when he protested his innocence. She fell for his story of victimisation. She knows now that he didn't drop out. He was thrown out. That woman tutor had been a prelude to what would come later, a dress rehearsal for the sinister drama in which she is trapped.

"For the last time, drink your wine."

The scar on his face seems dark and raw under the light. She can see the freshness of the bruise, the weeping abrasion, and she has a sudden image of him smashing his face against a wall. She thinks of the white scars along his wrists, and imagines him carving them into his flesh. The thought of him inflicting violence on himself in a warped bid to gain her sympathy strikes her with such force that she is petrified by fear, too caught up in the shocking brutality of it to grasp that his temper is about to explode.

"I said drink it!" He makes a sudden grab at her hand in an effort to force the glass to her lips, but the wine cascades onto the silvery fabric of her dress, a crimson splash over her belly. The stain is dramatic. She draws draw back from him, silent and still. It has the opposite effect on Donovan, who is on his feet, gesticulating wildly. "Now look what you've made me do!" he shouts. "You made me do that!"

His tone is shrill, his movements frantic, as he looks about for something to repair the damage. He rushes past her, behind the couch, and she sees a chink of light, recognises the fleeting opportunity. After a second's hesitation, she reaches across for the knife.

The blow to the back of her head causes her to sit forward, her hair falling over her face and the glass in her hand slipping and breaking on the floor, the rest of the wine spreading in a tentacled splatter across the rug.

Then the room is still. Outside, the rain is rattling on the roof. There is a distant sound of traffic. She remains in that position with her hair masking her face, feeling the terror gather inside her.

In the meantime, Donovan is spiralling through a pattern of remorse. He perches next to her on the couch, his hands making fluttering gestures, yet drawing back, not touching her. She can tell he is afraid now.

"Oh, no," he says. "Oh, God. Oh, Jesus, Helen. I don't know what came over me. Fuck, I'm so sorry. Please, please, look at me."

But she stays where she is, her eyes fixed on her stained

dress. She can see the knife where it fell on the floor.

"Please. Oh, Jesus. Please look at me. Helen. Oh, Christ."

His agitation is increasing, hysteria taking hold in his voice. Still she doesn't move. "I just wanted everything to be perfect!" he wails, rocking back and forth, hugging himself. "But now it's ruined! Everything's ruined!"

She cannot look up. The fear inside her won't allow it. But from behind the curtain of her hair her voice is cool and very frightened. "I know you didn't mean to do that, Keith." She can hear, now, the sound of his weeping. "I need to go downstairs. Please don't be alarmed. I'm not leaving. I want to rinse the stain out of my dress. There is soap downstairs by the sink that will do it. I'll be gone for a minute, that's all. Then, when I come back, we can talk this through together. We can work out where we go from here. Okay?"

His sobs rise up from him piteously, and when she allows herself to look up, he is crouched by the table, shuddering. It occurs to Helen that the seeds of madness in him are blooming into full-blown lunacy. That despite the pathos of his sad attempt at romance and the stunning blow he delivered, she is watching him in the clutches of some kind of fit. He is not operating within society's norms but bent on his own agenda, his own skewed notion of what is good and right.

"I'm going to get up now, Keith," she says, "and then I'm going downstairs to the sink. Please don't be alarmed." She rises cautiously. "I'll only be gone for a minute."

His hands are clapped over his face as he weeps so she cannot see his face, only the redness of his ears and the shuddering of his narrow frame, racked with sobs. For just the briefest moment, she feels that old temptation inside her to reach out and touch him, to comfort and console, but it is snatched away by the darker power of her fear.

Slowly, she moves away from him towards the stairs. Turning her back, she feels panic race down her spine and has to work hard to defy every instinct within her to run. He is quicker than she is, she has to remind herself of that. He doesn't look up as she goes down the stairs, taking each step slowly and deliberately, not wanting to alarm him with any sudden movement, desperate not to trigger a rage. By the time she reaches the final step, she is dizzy with nerves. All the way down, she has been making furious calculations. The front door: did she lock it when she came in? If so, where are the keys? She cannot remember whether she left them on the counter or in the door. Did she even bring them with her when she went to shut the window? They might be balanced on the edge of the sink. She pauses in the middle of the shop, darkness stretching around her, and feels the fear pressing up inside her. Through the shadows, she thinks she sees the keys dangling from the lock in the door. She has to risk it. It takes all her courage to move steadily towards that goal. Everything about this night – the dinner, her dress, Donovan, that crazy offering of flowers – narrows and fades until it becomes pointed on this one clear, crucial goal. She must get to the door. She must turn the key and draw back the handle. And then, she must run. But before she can do any of that, she hears his step on the stairs.

When she described it to me, she said it was like a dream. And, as in a dream, she is aware of the impression of fear, or the knowledge that she should feel afraid, but the feeling doesn't filter into her bones and flesh. For the second time that night, she feels as if she has stepped outside her body and is standing by watchfully, observing herself observing him coming down the stairs, sadness ravaging his features. She cannot move. Something holds her there. She can hear his breathing as he comes closer. His voice is a whisper: "You said you were going to the sink. You said you were going to wash your dress out. You lied to me."

"Please," she says. "Let me go."

She can feel his breath hot on her face.

"I only ever wanted to be close to you, Helen," he says. "That's all."

He talks to her about that day in the shop when he kissed her. There is a wistfulness in his tone as he speaks of the moment when he clasped her to him and how it fuelled weeks of desire.

"Right there," he whispers. "Right there is where it happened."

She notices the knife when he gestures towards the back room, a gleam of metal at the end of his crooked arm.

It isn't like a dream now. She tries to say something to appease him, but her voice catches in her throat. He means to kill her. She knows it from his hoarse breathing, the sweat that beads on his forehead, the way he talks. The darkness around her is heavy with a sense of foreboding, the flowers bowing their heads, looking away, but her fear is thumping and alive and threatening to overpower her.

"Come back upstairs," he whispers.

She knows she must not. Whatever else happens, she must not be drawn back up the stairs. In that moment, she must make a decision. It is her last chance. She turns. She does not run, does not want to panic him and have him lash out with the knife. Instead, she walks purposefully towards the door. There is no sound but the quickening of her own breath, the clip of her shoes on the concrete floor. And, just for an instant, she thinks he is letting her go. He is letting her walk away. The door handle is within arm's reach and she feels a quickening of her heartbeat and then his arm is around her and she feels something hot and searing. A stinging sensation and a ripping noise like tearing paper. There is a run of blood over her belly. Her hands and arms are trembling. She looks down and sees a new stain, darker than the splash of wine. It spreads across her chest, a scalding crimson running swiftly through the fibres of her dress, blood blooming like a peony. She is momentarily transfixed. And then there is pain, like scalding water flooding through her flesh, and she turns to see him shrinking into the shadows.

"What have you done?" she asks him.

A clattering sound echoes around them as the knife falls to the floor, then Helen's legs give way and she lies on the ground, falling, falling . . . Her eyes are closing so she doesn't see him crouching above her, doesn't see him racing towards the door and staggering out into the street, doesn't hear the slap of his trainers on the wet pavement as he runs across to the green and is swallowed by the darkness. She gives way to a new sensation, of weightlessness, of the ground falling away beneath her, and she is endlessly pitching down, into darkness.

27

This book will never be published. I know that now – I have made that decision. But still I find myself writing in the dark – for completion, that's all. What an evening! I have lurched through joy and accomplishment, disbelief and rage, self-doubt, regret and a degree of soul-searching. I feel drained. I feel as if I could sleep for a hundred years, and yet I am compelled to write it all down, to capture it before it evaporates. It's a difficult habit to break. Even now, I'm not sure if I've done the right thing. But still I write and wait for the dawn, thinking back over all that has passed.

It started out so full of promise. I was excited, nearly beside myself with anticipation all day in court watching the clock, eager to get home. Helen had decided she needed to be alone and had set up a temporary sleeping arrangement for herself in the rooms above the shop. "I may as well, Reuben," she said to me in a vague attempt at resolve that failed to hide her despair. "I can't stay in your spare room forever, can I?"

I didn't argue. Part of me understood that as the case draws to a close, something within her needed to withdraw, to be silent and alone, and I respected that. But another part of me wanted her out of the way so that I could get on with my work, which had been hampered by her languid presence in my house. I welcomed the freedom her absence brought – the freedom to spread my pages of notes around my living space, to sit at my battered PC and type steadily, letting it all spill out – the excitement of my glorious endeavour.

I was relishing an evening alone with my manuscript, and finally, after a long day in court and a silent meal with Helen, I pulled into the dark streets of Dalkey and chugged along the narrow laneway I called home. I parked the car and bounded up the front steps, taking them two at a time. It was as I was fitting the key into the lock that I became aware of another presence on the porch. It was William, asleep on the bench, knees drawn up, leaning against the wall, with one hand behind his head, the other hanging down and above Pacino. I stood still and watched him in the darkness. Seeing him like that – alone and strangely disarmed – I felt . . . pity, perhaps, or something more complex and shadowy, like a twinge of love.

He looked so peaceful that I almost felt guilty for laying my hand on his shoulder.

He woke with a jolt, bolting upright and asking, "What?" as if I'd put a question to him as he'd dozed off.

"Hey there," I said. "Relax. You're okay."

He stared about him, then rubbed his face and blinked.

"How long have you been waiting here?"

He shook his head. "Not sure."

And then, as if he had suddenly remembered why he was there, he looked up at me, eyes pleading. "Helen isn't with you."

There was something so plaintive about his disappointment that I wanted to rub his shoulder consolingly. "No. She's staying over the shop for now. I think she wanted a bit of privacy."

"Oh."

"Do you want to come inside?"

For a moment he thought about it, staring at the shadows near his feet. I had caught the whiff of alcohol on his breath and could see it now in his slow, steady nodding. William was drunk.

"Come on," I said. "Let's go inside and get you some strong American coffee."

Snapping on the lights seemed to rouse him fully from his stupor, and he wandered after me into the kitchen. There was a coolness in the house that reminded me of imminent winter. I had a sudden premonition of loneliness and was grateful to William for his unexplained presence. He found a stool at the breakfast bar and watched me fill a jug at the sink, then empty it into the Gaggia. The murmur of the machine offset the silence between us.

"I was hoping she'd be here," he explained unnecessarily. "I thought we might talk, that maybe I could tell her . . ." He broke off. His chin dipped and he mumbled into his collar, "Actually, I don't know what I was going to tell her."

"Maybe that's just as well," I remarked, "given your current state."

"I'm drunk."

"I can see that."

"I'm a bloody mess."

*

He dropped his head down into his arms on the counter top, and briefly I thought he might be crying, but he sat up again and said, "I can't understand it. I've been sitting out there on that porch, racking my brain, trying to figure out how all this happened. We had everything, Helen and I. We were happy. We were perfect together. How did it all go wrong?"

I ground the coffee beans, nodding sympathetically as William continued to talk in the manner of a drunk who thinks he is offering wisdom and logic, but is actually boring his listener into submission. I was aware of the blinking light on my answering machine. It had to be Carmela.

"All the time that's passed, and I've been so busy hating her," he said. "It's such a waste. All that anger makes you lose sight of what's important – what we had together. But once the trust is gone . . ."

"Ah, yes. The trust."

I poured the coffee, then set his mug in front of him and watched him stir in some sugar.

Carmela must have received my email. She would have read the latest excerpt I'd sent her. A bolt of excitement caught me, and I had to concentrate hard on his voice to contain myself.

He was telling me now that he loved her, really, that he had always loved her, but the thought of what she had done, that grubby act, was too much for him to bear. He didn't know what to believe any more. I listened to him, but it was nothing I hadn't heard before. The waste of it, he was saying, the criminal waste of all that time, which had placed an immovable barrier between them.

"What do you think?" he asked me then. I looked into his blue eyes and saw in them all the depleted hope and felt moved to help him.

"Well of course Helen still loves you. You love each other – that's obvious. And this thing . . . who knows? Maybe once the case is over you'll be able to put it behind you and move on." Uncle Reuben. It's becoming a habit.

"The things I said to her . . ." His voice trailed off and he seemed locked in the tortured memory of the poison that had spilled out between them.

"William, we all say terrible things sometimes – especially to those we love most. Believe me, sometimes I lie awake at night, horrified by the things I've said."

His eyes narrowed slightly. "I often wonder," he began, "what you and Helen talk about all the time. I think of all the things I've told you and wonder if maybe you've told Helen – acted as my ambassador or my lawyer, arguing my case to her, explaining, perhaps, so that she'd understand . . . I often wondered if you did that and if, maybe, she'd told you anything in return – something that might help me to understand, give me hope. Would you tell me?"

He fixed me with a stare and held it for a long moment. My heart raced and the words dried up in my mouth.

Eventually I found my voice. "Why don't you take your coffee into the sitting room?" I suggested. "I'll be with you in a minute."

Obfuscation, but I was banking on him being too inebriated to pick up on it. I followed him with my eyes as he shuffled away, the weight of his sorrow evident in the set of his shoulders, then hurried to the answering-

machine. I turned down the volume before I listened to
the message.

Carmela is tiny, barely scraping five feet, but that is the
only small thing about her. Everything else is enormous.
She has a large mouth and a loud voice, a rasping smoker's
cough and a broad New York accent in which she
proclaims her bombastic opinions. But the message she
had left seemed strangely quiet and was punctuated with
anxious sighs that raised questions within me. "Ruby, call
me. We gotta talk about this stuff you sent me. It's quite a
piece of work." And from the way she said it, I knew it
wasn't a compliment.

A year or more ago, shortly before I moved to France,
Carmela and I had a long, difficult telephone conversation.
It was a strange night – I was feeling lonely and a little
drunk and had spent the hours after dinner gazing around
at my house, wondering how I was going to live out my life
in its few rooms. What would become of me? Her call came
at a bad time. Without observing the thinness of my voice,
the despair in the silences I let develop between us, she
pushed me to get back to work, forget my woes and get on
with it.

"I want to write," I told her, "but I feel so tired all the
time."

"Tired, shmired! Who says you have to do any more
than a few hours every day?"

"But I don't even know what to write. I don't know if I
can any more."

"Bullshit!"

"What if there's nothing left? I can't help feeling there's
no gas in the tank."

"Oh, for God's sake! Enough of this goddamned defeat-ism. Just get out a pen and a piece of paper and write some-thing down. Christ!"

This went on for some time. I was baffled and exhausted by it. Finally, I broke down.

"Carmela, things are weird with me these days," I admitted. "I have these dreams . . . these things I can't let go of. I'm . . . floundering."

She was dismissive, but not immediately. Not before she had allowed a pause in our conversation, a little intensifier that told me she had absorbed it. We rang off on good terms, but when I woke the next morning, a flood of regret rinsed through me. I winced at the memory of what I had said. I felt panicked by it. I think that, somewhere in the recesses of my mind, I have been panicked by it ever since and that somehow all of this writing has been born out of my reaction to that moment of weakness. A last desperate attempt to turn back time and erase the cowardice of my admission.

Unsettled, I picked up my coffee and followed William. I felt inexplicably tired. In the moments that I had left him alone, William had been quiet and I half expected to find him sprawled unconscious across my sofa.

Instead, he stood with his elegant back to me, his coffee cooling as he concentrated on the page in his right hand. I froze, watching his eyes passing over the sentences, and my heart contracted into a withered leaf of dread.

"What is this?" he asked, sounding astonished.

It came down to this. All those moments of sneaking guilt, those jolts of conscience, the worrying about how I was going to break it to them, and now we were on the cusp of a confrontation I had hoped to avoid. All around him papers were strewn across the furniture, a sheaf perched on the edge of the sofa, another concertinaed across the floor. For a moment I couldn't answer, only watch as he put down his cup and picked up another page and began to read it.

"Jesus Christ," he said quietly, sifting through a whole clutch of pages now. "You've taken every last thing that's happened."

"William, you're upset. You've had too much to drink. Why don't you sit down and we can talk it through?"

But he didn't sit. And he wasn't drunk – not now. Suddenly he seemed to me to be the one in control as he stood there – tall, noble and quietly enraged – while my knees were failing me. I sank onto the sofa, my heart hammering away in my chest and guilt filling up my lungs. As he looked down at me, I couldn't help but admire him – the straightness of his shoulders, the fine features masked with incomprehension and the soft eyes – as he waited for my response, giving me an opportunity to defend myself.

"What is this?" he asked again and, to my shame, I began to lie.

"Just a few notes," I replied unconvincingly. "A diary. Something I've always done – kept an account of things happening around me. It's just for myself, you understand. A private thing. Lots of writers do it."

He looked at me, then back to the sheet in front of him, and reading off the page, he called out the title emblazoned in bold print across the top of every last one of those blasted pages.

"*My Glass Heart*," he read aloud. "A novel."

I sat there dumbly, my mouth slightly open. The silence didn't last. "I ask you again, Reuben, what is this?" He waved some pages at me. "Are you writing a book about all this? Is that it?"

There was nothing for it. I had to tell him. And so I told him about how I had seen the dark scar on Helen's breastbone and become possessed by a story. I hadn't wanted to write it, but it had sucked me in. I rattled on about guilt and longing, breaches of trust and the critical nature of love. I lectured him on the importance of looking at the big picture, of understanding the context within which the story was placed. I spoke of changing names, preserving anonymity and the universal nature of the story. And all the time he stood there, watching me, his expression changing to one of abhorrence.

"You used us," he said in that quietly shocked way of his. "All this time, I thought you were my friend and you've been using us – stealing from us the trauma we've lived through. How could you, Reuben? How could you take the most painful things that have happened to us and treat them as fiction – as make-believe?"

I was a little dazed by the force of his words, so it took me a while to register the full extent of his shock and disapproval. "It's not like that, William."

"You've captured our pain and loss," he said, "and now you want to publish it. To make money from it."

"William," I began, "it's not like that. I'm writing a book that tells your story."

"You manipulated us," he said, with indignation.

"I did not. I am merely giving my version of the accounts

that have been made known to me. I never forced you to confide in me. You did so willingly. And, God knows, you were happy enough to have a shoulder to cry on. All those nights in Bonnieux when you were confused and upset and needed someone to share your doubts with – I was there for you, William. I was a true friend to you."

He stared at me, aghast, and I felt so small beneath the weight of that stare.

"What kind of a friend listens to you pour your heart out, then as soon as your back is turned, scribbles it down in a nasty little novel? Friend? You don't know the meaning of the word," he said scornfully. "A true friend wouldn't have done that. A true friend would have used his position to intervene in the situation, to act on my behalf. Christ – all that information you've been privy to, all the things that Helen and I have told you when we should have been talking to each other."

He sat down suddenly, his features splintering into regret.

"Why did you do it?" he asked.

"Why should any story be told? As a lesson to others on how fragile love is, how secrets can cause immeasurable damage, how—"

"What about withholding information?" he interrupted. "How about that for causing damage?"

"No one was withholding information."

"Oh, please," he exclaimed with a bitter laugh.

And then he did something unforgivable. He began to read out extracts of my writing.

And I have no doubt that William feels that the stance he has chosen has a valiant and noble appeal – his tortured solitude – when in fact it is cowardice. "For better and for worse," I want to remind him, but bite my tongue. And besides, if he had stuck around, I wouldn't be privy to all the richness of information she has provided – this unexpected story.

He turned cold eyes from the page and pinned me with them.

"Are you trying to tell me that's not manipulation?"

The sound of my own words read back to me depressed me beyond reason. I don't know if it was the way in which they had been read, the mocking scepticism of his tone, or the thought of all the time I had spent on it – all those hours knitted together, all that passing life, the cycle of seasons, births and deaths, stars falling from constellations, the tide going in and out in its endless rhythm – at the end of it, what had I achieved?

"I was doing it for you," I said thinly, just to see how true I could make it sound.

He fixed me with that withering laconic gaze.

"Reuben, give me a break," he said.

For a moment, we were both silent. Then something ruptured within me – anger breaking free of my depression, a last insane attempt at defending my corner. If I was being tested, I was prepared to stand up for myself. I laid into him, angry, indignant and supercilious. He wasn't looking at the whole picture. It was impossible to form an opinion based on the fragments he had skimmed. It was a mistake to have read such an early draft, and he had done so expressly against my wishes. But my words sounded hollow, my voice thin.

He listened to me rant and gave a long, slow shake of his head. "I don't know, Reuben. I don't know how you can do it. I'm at a loss to understand."

I didn't answer, just sat there, eyes reproachful, mouth twisted.

"How does a man take people into his confidence, then betray them? All the time we were pouring out our innermost secrets, you were squirrelling them away for your own distorted purposes."

He looked so profoundly disappointed in me that it was all I could do not to break down. Instead, I gave him a desolate smile. "Well, you know what Graham Greene said, don't you? That every writer must have a sliver of ice in his heart."

"A sliver, yes, but the whole organ doesn't have to be frozen."

"Now, just a second—"

"What happened to you?" he asked, his face softening a little. "How did you become like this? I can't imagine you've always been so corrupt, so mercenary. Surely once, back in your youth, you must have understood loyalty. Yes, I think you must. I've read your plays and seen the beauty in them. You, too, have talked deep into the night, sharing your stories with me, remember? *Quid pro quo*. And I believe that at one time you were a man who wouldn't have used his friends' lives to make a buck. I imagine you with a particular kind of decency – a Southern thing, perhaps – perfect manners, unerring politeness. More than that – true goodness of spirit. How was it corrupted?"

"That was a long time ago," I said, seething.

"Yes, it was. The years passed and you became successful. Everyone told you how wonderful you were. I've listened to your stories, Reuben, of hanging out in bars and clubs with actresses and pretty boys. Of parties and love affairs, your picture on the cover of *Time*, the awards and accolades that rained down on you. But do you know what I think, Reuben? That you became selfish and twisted by your success. Warped. You became a bore."

"You don't know me at all," I said, close to tears.

"I know that we're different," he countered. "We have different views on friendship and love. I've listened to you talking about Frankie, about your one great love, but I don't recognise the love you speak of. The love you claim you had seems to me like a pernicious, corrupting thing. It sounds as if he had some part to play in what you have become. He facilitated it, pandered to it with the shell he created round the pair of you, letting no one in, your talent was stifled. That's what I think. When I listen to you talk about him, he sounds lazy and morose. And you became arrogant, egotistical and remote from the world. That was Frankie's legacy to you."

With this last blow, he laid waste any hope of reconciliation between us. I felt the cold hard fist of anger settle in my stomach. "Don't mention his name to me again," I said in a strangled whisper. "I never want to hear you speak about him. Not to me. Not to anyone. Don't you dare." Inside my head I was screaming. "Get out of my house," I said, but he just sat there, observing me with that controlled blue gaze.

"Fine," I said stubbornly and got to my feet. I stumbled out of the study and out of my house, leaving him among the detritus of my book.

Pacino was on the porch, head resting on his paws. He opened his eyes and seemed to cock an eyebrow at me.

"Not you too," I said to him, then went down the steps and staggered off into the evening mist.

I didn't go far, and for once in my life I didn't take refuge in a pub. I needed to be alone. In my fury, I stormed down to Bullock Harbour, the play of light from the street-lamps on the water looming briefly into focus, then fading again. It was quiet down there and I sat with my hands in my pockets, legs crossed at the ankles, breathing in the smell of salt and rotting fish. Gradually, I calmed down. The smell of fish brought with it a painful longing. This was Frankie's place. I was attracted to Dún Laoghaire pier, Sandymount Strand, the walk up Vico Road and Colliemore Road, anywhere there were people – hordes of them in summer – but Frankie preferred to be alone, to sit smoking his Marlboros and watching the sea, savouring his own company and Pacino's.

We moved to this spot – this old, now fashionable, fishing village – at his behest. I resisted at first – the weather, the tiny social scene, the limited cultural life – but he persuaded me.

Carmela had been unimpressed.

"Why the hell do you want to move there?" she had screeched. "I suppose this is his idea?"

They had never got on, Frankie and Carmela. He found her shrill and overbearing, and she was suspicious of his intentions. His lack of a job troubled her, and she made no secret of it.

"Are you enjoying being a lady of leisure, Frank?" she would ask him. "What is it you do all day exactly?"

And he would address her with that sullen stare of his before answering archly, "Every king must have his consort."

It was true what she said about my Frankie. That he was lazy. That he was a leech. I thought about what William had said and knew that that was true too: Frankie had dragged me down, pandering to my moods and my introspection. He had indeed created a shield round me that the world could not penetrate. Within it I was allowed to indulge my ego without question or probing. He had frightened away many of my friends. I knew in my heart that all of this was true.

But I also knew that I loved him. Under the lights of the harbour, I closed my eyes, listened to the clinking of the boats and thought of the stillness of his face, a cigarette stuck to his lip, as he sat reading a book on the porch with Pacino asleep at his feet. I thought of his glimmering flesh as he emerged from the sea, breathless and happy after an evening swim; of the gap between his teeth when he grinned at me and the suspicion fell away from his handsome face; of the mock French accent he affected while he was cooking, the sheer drama of him wrapped in a white apron, hair tousled, sleeves rolled to the elbows; of the powder softness of his voice when he whispered in my ear; of the trust in his eyes when he looked at me in those last days, telling me that he was used to me now; of the reckless humour and boyish joy he took in playing with the dog he loved so much; of his grand detachment when in company he did not care for; of the dignity of his withdrawal during our final sad dealings with one another. I don't think he ever knew how deeply he affected me, how even after his death he continued to stalk the corridors of my heart. A love like that can frighten a man, and I am a coward. It led me to places I didn't want to go, forced me into situations I did not want to be in, and propelled me to commit acts that were beyond the sphere of my love for him. I took other lovers to spite him – flaunted that boy in front of him. And for what? To prove to him that I was not bound by a slavish love? That I could exist beyond him and the world he had built for us? That I would be no man's spouse? I thought of all these things and hung my head.

Then came a new perception of myself. The emptiness in my life, the dreadful maw of vacuity into which I had slipped. And I thought of Helen and William. I thought of Donovan and Iris, Ingrid and Regina . . . the entire cast of characters I had assembled. The stories I had harvested. And for what? I had built walls with them – my way of putting up screens against the loneliness that nipped away at the edges of my life. But in the process I had allowed myself to slip from my position as impartial observer, independent chronicler, and to be caught up in the web of deceit and embittered argument. Worst of all, I had been privy to information I might have used to bring them back to each other. Those wistful rememberings when one or other had laid bare their soul, whispering tales of a love that had diminished recently but had once burned fiercely. And what was I doing with them? Storing them up to remind myself that I was not the only one heartbroken and alone? And I thought again of what William had said – that my heart had frozen. In that moment, Helen's words came back to me: "I saw my heart as something other than flesh and blood. I saw it as made of something cool and hard, like metal or glass. A cool, hard, living thing with a smooth surface. My glass heart." We were the same, Helen and I. And the knowledge of that sameness, that kinship, made me ashamed for having stood on the sidelines – having failed to rescue her in the most real way I could.

Darkness and quiet are all about me as I turn towards home. From a distance, I can hear Pacino – his low canine song a lament. He keeps it up while I climb the steps and slot my key into the lock. I know what I must do.

William looks up at me from the floor, the scattering of paper neatly bundled in front of him. He looks at me, dry-eyed.

"Take it," I tell him. "It's yours. I don't want it. I should never have done it. I wish to God I never had. I'm so sorry . . . I can't tell you. I'm so deeply ashamed. Take it, William. I never want to set eyes on it again."

When he leaves, the sky is flushed with the dawn and Pacino is quiet on the porch. The dog opens his eyes as William walks down the steps, and then he looks up at me, as if his canine eyes can see into my conscience and recognise my last-ditch attempt to salvage my soul, then gives a brief flick of his tail. That tiny semaphore, a cursory reward for my eleventh-hour attempt at goodness, fills me with such joy that I almost hang my head and weep.

28

It all comes down to this moment in a hot, stuffy court-room and the decision of four women and eight men. The judge asks them if they have reached a verdict, his voice laden with a kind of weariness that comes from a career of passing judgment. It feels to me as if we are all holding our breath.

I almost missed it because I overslept. Somehow I had fallen asleep at my desk, waking to find my face stuck to a sheet of paper, blinded by a beam of morning sunlight, a creaking pain travelling the length of my spine. I had rushed into town, still wearing the clothes of the previous day, feeling the heavy burden of an old body that is knotted and gnarled and insufficiently rested.

Under the bright lights of the courtroom, Helen looks pale, her face unreadable. I am conscious of her hand in mine, hot and clammy. In fact, the whole room feels hot. It seems deadened by a sultriness that makes me woozy and leaves condensation on the windows. I have been holding her hand since I arrived, breathless, and found her. "They're back. They've reached a verdict," she told me, a tremor of sudden nerves in her voice, her face stretched with anxiety.

A crowd has gathered by the doorway – barristers and their clients awaiting the next trial and officious bystanders eager to catch a glimpse of the drama. I crane my neck to see if William is among them, my heart heavy with dread, but he is not, and I cannot decide whether or not I am disappointed. I think of him poring over the manuscript he took away, his hangover compounded by the grief and fury it would whip up. But I had hoped that some part of it would help to explain things and ease his path back to her. I had hoped that giving it to him might offer us all some hope of redemption. Even though I knew that there was always the copy on my computer. I wondered if he had guessed at this, whether it had crossed his mind to insist on witnessing its deletion.

But William is not there. Neither is Ingrid nor her father. Just Helen and I, remote in our isolation among the crowd of strangers.

She squeezes my hand again, and I feel the guilt turn over inside me. When we had taken our seats, the air filled with the electricity of an impending verdict, she had told me that whatever happened, she wanted me to know how grateful she was for my support and steadfast friendship.

"No, Helen," I faltered. "You don't understand. Please. I've done something . . . I shouldn't have. I've betrayed you." And I thought again of William, the dismay on his face, the angry reprimand: "Friend? You don't know the meaning of the word." I hung my head in shame.

But there was no time to tell her, no time to relieve myself of the burden of my guilt. The jury filed in and the judge asked their decision.

One word. Guilty. It rings out like a rebuke. And all the

other words that have been spoken up until now – the language of argument and persuasion, the vehemence, cogency and trickery of words – fall away and scatter like dust.

Helen's hand slackens and I cannot bring myself to look at her. My eyes, like every other pair in that room, are fixed on the defendant. He sits there, staring into space, as though he is absenting himself from the proceedings.

Guilty.

I cannot help but think that the verdict is not for Donovan alone. I feel the weight of that word and know it is meant for me too.

Overhead lights cast a soft shine on his hair and throw shadows over his face. I think of all the things he has done, the lies he has told, the violence he has inflicted and the mania in which he became gripped. None of those things makes sense to me now. Perhaps it is weariness, or the knowledge of my own culpability in the wake of this sordid affair, but I cannot for the life of me see any trace of evil in him, no malice in the stoic tilt of his chin and the set of his mouth. All I can see is fear. It flickers behind his eyes, which cast out now around the courtroom, seeking his parents and reassurance that everything will be all right.

"Reuben," she says. I turn to her and see a single tear roll down her cheek, a finger reaching up to flick it away.

"It's over," I tell her and squeeze her hand. "It's over."

And yet it doesn't feel over. I find myself wishing that William would make a sudden dramatic entrance – a fanciful hope – sweep her into his arms and beg forgiveness. But that is not about to happen – even I, with my romantic heart, would never write such a scene. And it is not over yet: she has still to learn of my treachery. But for the moment, I cannot bring myself to tell her.

The jury files out, the barristers shuffle up their paperwork and others come forward to take their places.

There are no guards swooping in to handcuff Donovan and drag him away, protesting his innocence. Instead, he speaks to his barrister as his parents approach him. We are too far away to hear what they say to him. All I can see is his head nodding, his hand gripping his mother's upper arm in an awkward display of reassurance. I notice that he does not look at Helen.

The barrister for the prosecution advances towards us and cannot seem to keep the smug satisfaction from his face.

"That's it until the sentencing," he announces. "Justice has been done."

"How long?" I ask.

"It's hard to say. We'll need to put together a victim impact report and the defence will prepare their own reports. Six weeks, maybe? A couple of months?"

"How long do you think he'll get?"

"A few years, I imagine. However, with the question mark hanging over his mental state, it's fairly likely the governor of Mountjoy will decide to send him to the Central Mental Hospital."

"Can he do that?" I ask.

"Yes. But let's not dwell on it." He leans towards Helen and places a hand on her arm. "He's been found guilty. You must be pleased?"

But Helen doesn't appear celebratory, and I remember the trauma she has been through, how her character has been impugned, all her grubby secrets paraded in public, and I wonder how he can ask the question.

"It seems wrong, somehow," she says, looking across at Donovan as he says goodbye to his parents. "He looks so meek and vulnerable."

"I know, my dear," I say.

"And he's not."

"No. He's not."

All this time, Donovan has avoided looking at her. But now, disengaging from his parents to be led away, he sees her. He catches her looking at him and holds her with the icy beam of his eyes. Then, slowly, a smile spreads across his face. A smile of longing and hope – of crazy desire. It is at once victorious and sinister. It chills me to the core. He holds her for a long moment, and then he is gone, but a shadow of that grin lingers. I know, somehow, that it will haunt me.

"Come," I say to her, shivering. "Let's get out of here."

But before we have a chance to make our exit, we are face to face with Mr and Mrs Donovan. Abandoned now, they seem forlorn. For once, he seems to be leading her and she clutches his elbow, her face a pierrot mask of misery, tears threading with mascara. It is as if, now that it is all over, the façade of her stoicism has melted. She looks sunken in on herself. Pausing for a second at my elbow, she fixes Helen with a stare, but it isn't accusing. Rather, it is an empty gaze – two blank holes of nothing. "Liar," she hisses. "You lying little . . ."

"Enough, Lizzie," her husband says wearily. "Everyone . . . We've all had enough." And with those words, he leads her away.

I watch Helen gazing after them.

"She's his mother," I explain. "She's bound to be upset."

"I suppose." Her eyes remain on them, yet I can't read her reaction.

I glance behind me, but they are gone and all I can see are a couple of barristers, the retreating tails of two black gowns billowing imperiously before they disappear.

"That was the best possible outcome," I tell her. "It's all over. He can't harm you any more."

I meant what I said, but somehow my words sounded flimsy.

I wait for her to agree with me, but she isn't ready to leave her private reverie. We stand alone in the corridor and I feel as if I am back at school and have been sent outside the class as punishment.

"Are you all right?" I ask at last, desperate.

She looks up at the ceiling, closes her eyes and releases her breath in a silent sigh. It is a nameless gesture, at once eloquent, contained.

Then she opens her eyes and, for the first time during the exchange between us, looks me squarely in the face. I can see her exhaustion and relief. "I wish things had been different. I wish William was here." And then, she adds reflectively, "I'm glad it's over. I suppose I feel relieved."

In that instant, I see the briefest shimmer of happiness cross her face and feel an expansion within my chest, a surge of hope emerging from the dark mysterious recesses of my heart.

As I came up the front steps to my house, I found William waiting for me again in the porch. He jumped up quickly as we approached, his hands disappearing into his pockets and that inscrutable blue gaze flicking from me to Helen. My heart was thudding – dreading what his presence might mean – and for a moment, we were silent, each of us experiencing a crushing shyness.

"How are you?" he asked, a small quaver in his voice.

"I'm good," she managed with an answering tremor.

I couldn't bring myself to speak.

"I thought," he began cautiously, "that you might be hungry, so I brought some lunch."

He gestured to some stiff brown paper bags on the bench behind him.

"You brought lunch?" Helen said in a small voice.

"Yes. Italian – mozzarella, ciabatta, olives, anchovies, tomatoes, pancetta . . . And Prosecco. I thought it would be a nice way to celebrate."

"But you didn't know the outcome. You still don't. You don't know if we've anything to celebrate."

He looked at her then, blushing to his collar, and gave me a look. It seemed to me a mixture of uncertainty and wary forgiveness.

"I meant that we could celebrate the end of it. The end of all this. Whatever the outcome." His hands made a vague gesture that was meant to encompass all of what had passed between them – the anger and distrust, the revulsion and animosity, the tearing asunder of what had been a happy, loving union.

"Oh," she said and looked at him for a long moment, her face saying nothing.

*

Lunch passed peaceably enough, despite my trepidation. I had been worried about another confrontation, unable to escape the memory of the last time Helen, William and I had been in a room together. On that occasion a small, sharp, vitriolic woman had been present – William's mother, Miriam – berating her tear-streaked daughter-in-law as she rushed about her house, hastily packing the things she would need, while I tried to counter Miriam's shrill assault. William's head was in his hands. This time, though, there was less rhetoric and more cautious silence. I tried to take command of the situation, but soon slipped into silence. Partly this was due to exhaustion, a creeping fatigue that was compounded by my activities of the previous night. But also, I think, it was nerves. I felt that, despite the rectitude of the conversation, a wrong word or misdirected look could send everything into a diabolic row, and I was not sure if I had the energy to survive such a brouhaha. Particularly when the talk entered the realm of the case.

I needn't have worried. But I still felt the shame of the previous night, when I had returned to find William sitting among my papers. And throughout lunch, despite his constant good manners, I couldn't help feeling that a little hum of hate must be running inside him for me and all that I had withheld from him. I avoided his eye.

Another reason I said little was that if I opened my mouth to speak, I was greeted with a low rumble from under the table: Pacino's sustained campaign to intimidate me with his snarling, growling and general ill humour. When lunch was over and Helen offered to take him for a walk, I did not protest. And it was with hope in my heart that I observed William helping her into her jacket and the two of them setting out smiling shyly at each other.

I stood and watched them go. They walked with space between them, awkwardly, Helen doing battle with Pacino. The late afternoon sun had streaked the sky yellow behind gun-metal grey clouds, and in that moment, I conjured up Frankie's ghost one last time.

"They'll never get anywhere with that old dog," I pronounced wryly.

And as I said it, Helen's step faltered, her treacherous shoes sending her careering up the path, and just as on that first day in Bonnieux, after we had met in the sunny square, William reached out and caught her. It was all in that moment: her vulnerability, his steadying hand. The great distance we have travelled, the cycle of events, and in the end it comes back to that.

I watched them as they righted themselves and moved on, but he didn't let go of her arm, and Pacino, shocked into action by Helen's sudden lunging fall, trotted along behind them, keeping a steady pace. The sight of him – that dumb, irritating animal whom I have fought with and struggled against almost more than any human being I have ever met – at last submitting to the simple pleasure of a brisk walk, struck me as poignant. When Frankie was alive, I would often watch the pair striking off for a long ramble. There was no growling then, no paws digging into the pavement, no curling black lip drawn back over yellow teeth. And I realised that it was only me he disliked, and felt the indescribable shame that comes with earning the disfavour of an animal or a child.

"I'll let them keep the dog," I told Frankie. "He'll be happier with them."

"Do you think there will be a 'them'?" I thought I heard him ask.

"I believe so."

And I did believe it. I knew in my heart that they had not gone beyond all hope, that they could – and would – pull themselves back from the brink.

"Well, he's your dog."

"No. He was never my dog. He was always yours, Frankie. I just got to have him for a little while."

And then I did something that surprised me, even more than my idea to give Pacino away. I took a last look at the sky, then covered my face with my hands and started to cry. I kept gulping in air and shuddering noiselessly, crying for the dog Frankie had loved so much and how my attempt to care for him had slipped into loathing; crying for the last year of my life, which I had wasted on something I had known all along would never come to fruition; for the friendships I had abused and the people I had allowed to slip out of my life; for the loneliness that had consumed me and the emptiness I had felt; and for the feeling that I could have fallen into that emptiness and kept on falling.

"I have to let you go," I said solemnly. And I wasn't referring to the dog.

It's one of the strange things about the business I'm in. You spend hours, days, weeks agonising over words, the construction of sentences, but every now and again you come across a scrap of work you have no recollection of having written. I am always struck by the wonder of it –

the time and effort I invested, yet how easily it slips out of my recall. So when I was clearing up that night, after they had disappeared to their home and their bed, I came across a piece of paper covered with my laboured scrawl. I didn't recognise the words, but of course, they were Helen's, not mine. I had merely transcribed them. I stood there, empty glasses in one hand, the sheet of paper held up to the light in the other, and read:

The first night, after I had woken in intensive care, after I had listened to all the facts and been left to absorb them, I felt that pressure on my chest, and the pressure in my head of the new knowledge I possessed. That for a few minutes I had died. It had taken a man's hand clamped round my heart to bring me back to life. I felt the weight of that knowledge bearing down on me, and it was a physical thing, like something sitting on my chest, a great burden I couldn't move under, pinning me to the spot. It was frightening. I think that that was the most frightening moment – more than the knife, more than lying in the darkness waiting for someone to help me: when I was alone in my hospital bed, tubes everywhere, with that knowledge lying on top of me.

But then I realised I was not alone. William was there, his head on the mattress by my hand, waking now as if aware that I was awake. He straightened in his chair and looked at me, eyes full of sleep. I couldn't speak – and it hurt to cough and move – and he said nothing. Just stroked my hair and held my hand. Suddenly I had the feeling that everything would be all right, that everything was as it should be, that it was natural for me to feel fear and for him to dispel it. The heaviness seemed to lift and I think I felt true happiness. Contentment, perhaps. Relief. I had survived. He was beside me, wordlessly looking out for me, and as I closed my eyes again, I had the feeling that the best of everything in my life was in that room with me. All that I could ever need was sitting in the darkness holding my hand. Something powerful and incorruptible, something real and pure, something I had come so dangerously close to losing. And I knew in that moment what it was . . . Love.

Acknowledgements

Sincere thanks to Bridget Maher and Ronan O'Brien for sharing their respective medical and legal knowledge with me; any inaccuracies or mistakes are mine and not theirs.

Thanks also to Paula Gleeson for kindly and patiently answering all my questions about flowers and floristry.

What I know about pearls and pearl fishing I learned from reading John Lucey's book *The Irish Pearl*.

I am yet again indebted to The Tyrone Guthrie Centre in Annaghmakerrig for a fruitful residency. Likewise, thanks to Ann Sugrue for providing me with a place where I can escape to write.

My particular thanks go to the early readers of this book whose contributions were significant: Conor Sweeney for his illuminating suggestions; Faith O'Grady for her indispensable advice; Ciara Considine for her sage editorial counsel; and Hazel Orme for her fine copy-editing skills.

Finally, I wish to express my gratitude to everyone at Hodder Headline Ireland and to my family and friends for their enduring support.